Praise for

THE AWKWARD BLACK MAN

"The title of Mosley's latest story collection, *The Awkward Black Man*, is both a spot-on descriptor and yet one that only hints at the broad range of people we find in the book's pages . . . **Reading these stories, you feel as if you're sitting with a gifted storyteller while he spins yarns about the strange people living in his mind.** The prolific Mosley delights in the wonderfully bizarre." —*New York Times*

"Despite the trailblazing work of writers such as Toni Morrison and more recently Edward P. Jones, James McBride, and Colson Whitehead, correcting the canon is an ongoing effort. In the **brilliant and bracing** *The Awkward Black Man*, Mosley has given us food for the journey." —*Alta*

"Mr. Mosley is a famous crime writer, but this collection is nearer to the recent work of Julian Barnes and Roddy Doyle . . . In **practiced, plainspoken prose,** [Mosley] presents a gallery of old men facing divorce, illness or perhaps some more unnamable crisis of existence . . . **The humble stories befit their soft-spoken antiheroes.**" —*Wall Street Journal*

"The tough-minded and tenderly observant Mosley style remains constant throughout these stories even as they display varied approaches from the gothic to the surreal. **The range and virtuosity of these stories make this Mosley's most adventurous and, maybe, best book.**" —*Kirkus Reviews* (starred review)

"**These stories tap into the vulnerability and indignity of the human condition, but also its remarkable, even irrational, commitment to hope.**" —*BuzzFeed*

"The cool Black guy stereotype is shattered in this collective of stories about Black men saddled with as much humanity as the rest of us. Follow nerds, weirdos, dorks and oddballs as they take the stage as heroes of their own stories." —*Essence*

Praise for *The Awkward Black Man*

"Mosley delivers a vibrant collection of 17 luminous stories, many with a focus on downtrodden and troubled protagonists . . . Each entry is a testament to Mosley's enduring literary power."

—*Publishers Weekly*

"*The Awkward Black Man* is a treasury of unsung lives, vignettes of the loves of unloved, praise of people who are out of place and time but not out of mind or mortality . . . True to his mystery tradition, these stories are tiny murders of the soul, things that are seldom told from this point of view, showing the insight and talent of Walter Mosley."

—*Newcity Lit*

"Walter Mosley is the kind of storyteller that makes his characters' worst days into something you can recognize and relate to . . . Fans of Mosley don't need to be told twice to go find this book. Just go. If you're new to Mosley but you love short stories, though, *The Awkward Black Man* might be the best book for your life right now."

—*North Dallas Gazette*

"The Mosley voices cover the spectrum from dumb despair to sublime wisdom, from sexual intimacy to orgasms on the Staten Island Ferry. The cities are old, and the jobs are ordinary, but he discovers ways to find some truths and show how all life can play out."

—*Bookreporter*

"These 17 old and more recent stories . . . feature distinctive characters, plus Mosley's jazzy prose and extraordinary insights. It's a tender, sad and gripping collection."

—*AARP*

"Since Walter Mosley published his first book, *Devil in a Blue Dress*, in 1990, he's been exposing, dismantling and subverting stereotypes. Race, ethnicity, gender, class—he's brought a fresh and discerning eye to all of them, in the midst of writing beautifully crafted fiction and thoughtful nonfiction . . . He does all that again in his new short story collection, *The Awkward Black Man*." —*Tampa Bay Times*

"This autumn, Mosley will be awarded the National Book Foundation's Medal for Distinguished Contribution to American Letters, which follows the PEN America Lifetime Achievement Award and the Harold Washington Literary Prize for the author of more than 50 books, including his bestselling Easy Rawlins mystery series. As if to underscore the range of his incredible talent, he is publishing an excellent collection of short stories—17 first-person narratives that wrestle in distinctive ways with the experiences of Black men." —*National Book Review*

"Fifty-plus books into his career, Mosley hasn't run out of inspired plots, and his interest in social issues remains acute, although he editorializes with the lightest of touches; *The Awkward Black Man* teems with sharp, quippy dialogue and not a sentence suffers the indignity of a frill . . . This primo story collection by an author best known for his crime fiction reaffirms his place in the literary pantheon." —*Shelf Awareness*

"Master storyteller Mosley has created a beautiful collection about Black men who are, indeed, awkward in their poignant humanity . . . Mosley's is an essential American voice and his portraits of Black men will have profound resonance." —*Booklist* (starred review)

THE AWKWARD BLACK MAN

ALSO BY WALTER MOSLEY

Easy Rawlins Mysteries

Leonid McGill Mysteries

Other Fiction

Original E-books

Nonfiction

Plays

THE AWKWARD BLACK MAN

STORIES

WALTER MOSLEY

Grove Press
New York

Published simultaneously in Canada
Printed in the United States of America

First Grove Atlantic hardcover edition: September 2020
First Grove Atlantic paperback edition: September 2021

Text design by Norman E. Tuttle at Alpha Design & Composition
This book was set in 13 pt. Spectrum MT with Gentium
by Alpha Design & Composition of Pittsfield, NH.

Library of Congress Cataloging-in-Publication data is available for this title.

ISBN 978-0-8021-5685-3
eISBN 978-0-8021-5686-0

Grove Press
an imprint of Grove Atlantic
154 West 14th Street
New York, NY 10011

Distributed by Publishers Group West

groveatlantic.com

21 22 23 24   10 9 8 7 6 5 4 3 2 1

This book is dedicated to Toni Morrison, who raised the dialogue of blackness to the international platform that Malcolm X strove for.

CONTENTS

THE GOOD NEWS IS

The good news was that after a lifetime of carrying an extra thirty pounds or more, I was finally losing weight. Through middle and high school, into college, and then as a data interpreter for Spanish Bank, I was always bulging at the hip and waist, chest and thigh. Too big for stores that sold regular clothes and not quite fat enough for BGE, the Big Guy Emporium. I wore clothes that were either overly snug or so loose that I needed a belt larger than my waist size that could be altered, as needed, with an awl.

My entire life I avoided looking in mirrors, and felt sure that women who showed any interest in me were the ones who had given up, deciding that they'd never get the kind of man they really wanted.

I married a woman, Blythe Lighnter, because I didn't think things could get any better. I divorced her over a Frenchman named, predictably, François. He was teaching her how to play cello al fresco in a village outside of Paris while I stayed at home in

1

Greenwich Village watching Terra Heart porn videos and imagining that my penis could one day be as large as Brad Bonaboner Backman's—Triple-B.

I could afford the alimony and relieve the loneliness because I made four thousand dollars a week freelancing for Fortune 2000 companies that needed their employee-generated software explained to anyone from their CEOs to users, new personnel, and the federal government at tax time.

I lived in Manhattan in a five-thousand-dollar-a-month studio apartment and so did my ex, with François, who was going to get a job as soon as his papers came through.

I had a girlfriend named Lana who told me she loved me but said that her impression of life was that people should live alone, answerable to no one. This, she said, made love a true choice and not a duty that inevitably transmogrified into spite.

At least Lana didn't play cello, and we would turn out the light before going to bed the one or two nights a week we got together, and so I was emotionally placated . . . if not truly happy.

I didn't complain because I liked being alone most nights and days and weekends or when it was raining or snowing or over those fake holidays when New Yorkers were off celebrating Columbus or the presidents or some religious ceremony that most of them couldn't quite explain.

I wasn't above seeing prostitutes, but I stopped when I realized that I had to take both Viagra and Ecstasy in order to have sex with a woman I was paying to satisfy my needs. I was the fat guy, and she was the svelte woman who wouldn't talk to me if we were standing on line, one behind the other, at the Gourmet Garage with our tiny lamb chops and fresh herbs.

But all that began to change when I started to lose weight.

At first I thought it was because of the high-protein/low-carb regimen that I had been so close to perfecting for years. The problem was that it took three days, sometimes even four, to clear the body of carbs in order for the diet to take control, and I'd buy a pint of Ben & Jerry's Cherry Garcia, like clockwork, every other fourth day. That meant that I'd be chemically dieting only for 3.4 days a week, and that wasn't enough to counteract the glut of calories in my system from the ice cream binges.

But that changed, as I've already said. I pinpointed the moment of my transition to when I was at a 7-Eleven near midnight of an alternate fourth day, and I came to find that they were out of Cherry Garcia except for the yogurt version. My favorite flavor not available, I decided to go without. The following Tuesday I took a sideways glance at myself in the mirror and saw that I was—just maybe—a little slimmer. I dared a full-frontal gaze and saw it was true. The high-protein/low-carb diet was making me a candidate, possibly destined for regular-man clothes stores.

That was the best news I'd had in decades.

Blythe getting married to François was second to that. Her marriage gave him papers and also freed me from the alimony treadmill. But really what was important was that after only six weeks sans ice cream I could fit into trousers with a thirty-four-inch waist and shop at any clothes store I wanted.

Lana and I were invited to Blythe and François's impromptu wedding, held without reservation near the Central Park lake. It was a quasi-Buddhist ceremony conducted by Brother Franklin, an ex-convict Zen monk from upstate.

"Buddhism does not encourage nor does it oppose the institution of marriage," Franklin informed us. "That way the choice of the union is because of love and not duty."

3

Lana nudged me when he said this, but I had already moved on from that relationship. I had been e-mailing with a woman named Rachael Daws. I'd known her for some years, but when we ran into each other at a data-interpretation convention in Boston, she'd commented on how good I looked and said that we should stay in touch.

"You're looking good, Sammy," Blythe said, when I walked up to congratulate her after the wedding. "Have you lost weight?"

"Finally figured out that other fourth day."

"Anyway," she said. "Thanks for coming . . . and don't be a stranger."

She was probably just being nice, but I liked to think that the new, slimmer me was just so damn attractive that maybe she regretted the cello lessons that she'd taken a month off work for—a month away from me that she promised *would make our bond stronger*.

For the ceremony I wore a buttermilk-colored single-button two-piece suit with a cobalt shirt and a yellow, red, and black silk tie, the material of which was culled from an antique kimono. I bought those clothes to celebrate myself.

The face in the mirror every morning and night was smiling at me.

I was looking better and feeling more confident, but that wasn't all of it. My knees, which had bothered me since my first year at Brown, no longer hurt. I still couldn't jog very well, because I didn't have the wind, but I took a couple of laps around the block two afternoons a week and was planning on adding a third day.

The only problem was that I was sleeping a lot more. Lana would complain that the days I came over I didn't want to have sex.

"You fall asleep right after dinner," she accused.

I didn't tell her that she had stopped being frisky with me long before, just after the first few months of our relationship. I wanted to say that it was only because I was looking better that she complained, but I didn't.

"Maybe the diet isn't giving you enough vitamins," she suggested.

"Maybe not," I admitted. "I've been sleeping a lot, and I don't eat sugar anymore. Maybe my body is transitioning."

"My doctor is a nutritionist. I'm sure I could get you an appointment."

I didn't really want to accept her help, because I was feeling mildly guilty. Rachael and I had made electronic plans to go to Miami the following month. I'd told Lana it was another convention.

"OK," I said. "If you can ask I'd appreciate it."

"The bad news," Dr. Lola Bridesmith said, two weeks later, "is that it's malignant."

I had gone the next day to see the MD/nutritionist, and she took X-rays because I hadn't had any in over ten years. These revealed a growth in my abdomen, and so an appointment was made with an oncologist cut-man for the next week.

I called off the tryst with Rachael, because sex and infatuation took a back seat to cancer and possible death.

"The good news is," Dr. Bridesmith said, "that it doesn't look like it has spread. After a full-body MRI you'll have a simple operation, followed by three to five weeks of radiation treatments and then a two-stage regimen of chemotherapy. That approach might very well clear it up completely."

"I have to have all that?"

"To be sure."

*   *   *

Lana left me because, while trying to help around the apartment, she came upon the e-mails between Rachael and me. There were a few questionable pictures involved.

Rachael stopped responding after the mention of cancer, and Blythe somehow got it in her head that I had shorted her on the alimony payments and was taking me to court.

The good news was that my various employers had no problem keeping me busy. As long as I could keep awake and focused, they had work for me to do. Brian Jurgens, of de Palma Distributers, did suggest that I wear a wig when I addressed the senior officers of the company.

"You wouldn't want to make them uncomfortable," he said. "They might talk about replacing you if you remind them of their own mortality."

Brian had been a philosophy major at Princeton, and so he gave highly sophisticated explanations for every pedestrian suggestion he made.

I was sleeping thirteen hours a day and working ten; seven days a week, seven days a week.

The MRI had revealed other growths, and so I had to have a few more biopsies. The good news was that the new polyps were, so far, benign. The operation cut out the malign growth. The radiation did nothing against the missing cancer, but a woman on the subway told me how healthy my fake hair looked. The good news was that there were no other malignancies—that they could see.

I lost most of my clients because I was making too many mistakes.

The forensic accountant that the New York State court forced me to hire found that I had shorted Blythe by exactly $549.27. The good news was that I didn't have to pay it. The bad news was that because the suit had merit, however slim, I was ordered to pay Blythe's $12,347.92 legal fees.

I'd saved enough money to live as I had been living for maybe three years; that was something.

The only thing good about chemotherapy was Maura O'Reilly. She was beautiful, I think; it's hard to tell, because my memory was impacted by the disease and, to a greater degree, the cure. Maura was part of the MVNP, the Metro Visiting Nurse Program, and came every Tuesday and Friday to make up for the days that were lost to me in between. She had a lilt to her voice that came with her from Ireland, and there was something about the way she bathed me that made me feel as if I were just starting out—if I didn't die first.

"What I love about you, Samson Diehl," Maura said to me one Friday, "is your name and how you're always trying to see the best in what's going on."

"Maura, I love you, but I'm about the most cynical person you've ever met."

"Not at all."

"How do you figure?"

"Didn't you tell me that you hated Trump, but he was still the best among the Republicans, even if he wasn't one himself?"

That made me laugh. I spent Wednesday and Thursday, Saturday, Sunday, and Monday waiting for Maura and vomiting. I was waiting for laughter, and she never failed, not once, to deliver.

The poisons I took, the doctors assured me, were wreaking more havoc on the possible cancer than they were on the rest of me. If there was any cancer left, it would be absent by the time I was dead and buried.

I weighed less than I had when I was thirteen.

The last month of the regimen had me bedridden. Maura would drop by most mornings just to see if I had expired in the night. Sometimes I'd come awake and see her folding my clothes and putting them into drawers.

"The good news is that you're cancer-free," oncology coordinator Myron Eddlesworth told me on a beautiful spring day. "We'll have to monitor you for five years, but I'm very optimistic. Going through what you had to endure is like a Dark Ages peasant surviving famine or a war—even the bubonic plague. And here you are, with a full head of hair and a healthy physique."

Yes, the other good news was that I was still thin. I had been eating Cherry Garcia like it was going out of production, but the cancer had been more ravenous than I.

I walked home from the doctor's office on Thirty-Fourth Street and took the five flights of stairs to my room. I don't know what made me think about it, but I searched out my collection of solid-gold coins from ancient Greece. I had purchased them over a twenty-seven-month period when I made triple salary working for a Persian billionaire who sold oil in the East, what people used to call the Orient.

I found the black-velvet box, but it was empty. All seventeen coins—with faces of Athena, Alexander, and even Socrates—were gone. Their value at that time was over two hundred thousand dollars. I was hoping to extend my convalescence with their sale, if that became necessary.

"Hello?" a young woman's sweet voice said over the phone.

"Hi. My name is Sammy Diehl, and I'm calling to speak to Maura O'Reilly."

"I'm so sorry, Mr. Diehl. Maura moved out."

"Oh. Did she leave a forwarding number or address?"

"She went back to Ireland."

"When?"

"Two weeks ago."

I had a padded maroon chair sitting by the hallway door. There were always books and papers in the seat and clothes draped along the back. The only time I had ever sat in it was the day I saw it and bought it at the one and only Plantation Furniture outlet store.

I hung up the phone, dumped the clothes, books, and other detritus from the heavy chair, and pulled it over to the window. The wooden legs dragging on the oak floor sounded like an elongated fart. I sat down, thinking that the only good news was that the sun was shining and I could still feel its heat on my skin.

I wasn't broke or homeless, dying at that particular moment, or fat for the time being. I had time to read, even if I didn't use it, and to watch movies that had come and gone while I was subjected to a procedure that future ages would compare to medical blood-letting. My eyesight had worsened, but I could still see. Russia had retreated from Syria, for the moment, and data interpretation was still a profession that one could ply, if one so desired.

"Hello," she said, in that sweet lilt.

"Hey, Maura, it's Sammy."

She was silent on the other end of the line, many thousands of miles from my Manhattan patch of sunlight.

"I know this must be a surprise," I said. "But you're the only person in the world I know well enough to call. If you don't talk to me, I don't know what I'll do."

"How did you get my telephone number?" she asked, attempting an upbeat tone.

I'm sure she figured that I hadn't looked at my coin collection yet, that I was calling for just the reason I'd stated.

"The Internet told me about the O'Reillys in Derry, and I remembered that your mother's name was Daimhin. Not so difficult really."

"Modern marvels." She could do amazing things with her *r*'s.

"Why did you leave so suddenly?" I asked, affecting a tone of innocence.

"Me mother was sick."

"I'm sorry to hear that. How's she doing?"

"Fine, but a better question would be, how are you?"

"Cancer-free and unemployed. I have time on this Earth that I wasn't expecting."

"I'm so happy for you, Samson."

I believed her.

"Thank you," I said. "It was a hard road, but I'm grateful for it."

"Grateful for all that sufferin'?"

"It started out that I just thought I was losing a little weight. You know, I've always been chubby. I blamed everything on that. But the cancer burned away that fat and allowed me to understand what a lucky man I am."

"That's really quite wonderful now, isn't it?" she said.

"Maura . . ."

"Yes, Samson?"

"Would you consider marrying me?"

Her silence was exquisite. I was completely serious about the proposal. She could lie and say that she hadn't stolen the coins. Maybe she had let in a plumber or a window washer and had to run downstairs to clean the sheets that I'd vomited and shat upon.

It didn't matter that she'd robbed me. She had been there with that gorgeous smile that I could almost remember and with that voice that was first cousin to song. I would have died if she hadn't been there; that much I was sure of.

"That is a beautiful thing to say, Samson. You are kind and gracious to ask. But I don't think you know me well enough. If we were to marry you might feel differently than you do right now."

"I know you, Maura, and more than that, I know myself. If you say yes, I will be your husband through all the years, no matter how lean or how fat. I will be your husband, and you will be the mother of our children. And they will have Irish names, and their second tongue will be Gaelic."

Again the rapture of silence. I could feel her hopes and regrets over the fiber-optic lines.

After a very long pause she said, "Can I think on it?"

"Do you want me to give you my number?"

"I already have it, silly. I was going to call you after your last visit to the doctor."

"OK," I said. "I'll wait for you to answer, but remember, I'm completely serious and absolutely nothing would change how I feel."

We said our goodbyes and disconnected.

I didn't leave my apartment for the next two weeks. I ordered in all my meals (even Cherry Garcia) and sat by the window in the displaced chair, next to the phone.

I was waiting for her answer.

I didn't give a damn about those coins.

After eighteen days I called Maura's mother's phone again. The line had been disconnected. There was no forwarding number. There was no Daimhin O'Reilly listed in all Ireland, Wales, or England.

Maura was gone.

Maybe I should have told her not to worry about the money. Maybe I should have said, "You can consider those coins a wedding gift."

The days went by, and my health improved. I gained back all the weight that the cancer and its treatments took. I went to work as a data interpreter again. Blythe called with a long explanation about how my cancer had upset her so much that she just had to sue me. I didn't understand the logic but accepted her apology anyway.

Lana called and asked me why I hadn't told her that I was dissatisfied with our relationship.

For some reason her question brought Maura to mind, Maura and my stolen fortune. I missed that Irish lass the way parents yearn for the days of their children's cute mispronunciations: "I wuv you." The love I felt for the nurse while I was dying meant more to me than anything life had to offer. She was what I was looking for even before I understood why the weight was coming off so fast.

"Well?" Lana asked.

I disconnected the call and went down to the 7-Eleven, hoping that they had the regular Cherry Garcia and still hoping, ever so slightly, that when I got back upstairs, Maura would have left a message and a number, a few rolling r's, and a question that I could answer.

PET FLY

Lana Donelli works at the third-floor reception desk of the Landsend mortgaging department of Carter's Home Insurance Company. Her sister, Mona, is somewhere on five. They're both quite pretty. I guess if one was pretty the other would have to be, seeing that they're identical twins. But they're nothing alike. Mona wears short skirts and giggles a lot. She's not serious at all. When silly Mona comes in in the morning, she says hello and asks how you are, but before you get a chance to answer she's busy talking about what she saw on TV last night or something funny that happened on the ferry that morning.

Lana and Mona live together in a two-bedroom apartment on Staten Island.

Lana is quieter and much more serious. The reason I even noticed her was because I thought she was her sister. I had seen Mona around since my first day in the interoffice mail room. Mona laughing, Mona complaining about her stiff new shoes or the air-conditioning or her most recent boyfriend refusing to take her where she wanted to go. I would see her at the coffee-break room on the fifth floor or in the hallway—never at a desk.

So when I made a rare delivery to Landsend and saw her sitting there, wearing a beaded white sweater buttoned all the way up to her throat, I was surprised. She was so subdued—not sad but peaceful, looking at the wall in front of her and holding a yellow pencil with the eraser against her chin.

"Air-conditioning too high again?" I asked her, just so she'd know I was alive and that I paid attention to the nonsense she babbled about.

She looked at me, and I got a chill because it didn't feel like the same person I saw flitting around the office. She gave me a silent and friendly smile, even though her eyes were wondering what my question meant.

I put down the big brown envelope addressed to Landsend and left without saying anything else.

Down in the basement I asked Ernie what was wrong with Mona today.

"Nothing," he said. "I think she busted up with some guy or something. No, no, I'm a liar. She went out with her boyfriend's best friend without telling him. Now she doesn't get why he's mad. That's what she said. Bitch. What she think?"

Ernie *didn't suffer fools*, as my mother would say. He was an older black man who had moved to New York from Georgia thirty-three years before and had come to work for Carter's Home three days after he'd arrived. "I would have been here on day one," he often said, "but my bus only got in on Friday afternoon."

I'd been at Carter's Home for only two months. After graduating from Hunter College I didn't know what to do. Even though I had a BA in poli-sci, I really didn't have any skills. Couldn't type or work a computer. I wrote all my papers in longhand and used a typing service. I didn't really know what I wanted to do, but I had to pay the rent. When I applied to Carter's Home for a professional trainee position they'd advertised at Hunter, the personnel officer, Reena Worth, said that there was nothing available, but maybe if I took the mail-room position something might open up.

"They hired two white PTs the day after you came," Ernie told me at the end of the first week. I decided to ignore that though. Maybe they had applied beforehand, or maybe they had skills with computers or something.

I didn't mind the job. It was easy and I was always on my feet. Junior Rodriguez, Big Linda Washington, and Little Linda Brown worked with me. The Lindas had earphones and listened to music while they wheeled around their canvas mail carts. Big Linda liked rap and Little Linda liked R & B. Junior was cool. He never talked much, but he'd give me a welcoming nod every morning when he came in. He dressed in gray and brown silk shirts that were unbuttoned to his chest. He had a gold chain around his neck and one gold canine. The Lindas didn't like me, and Junior was in his own world. Everyone working in the interoffice mailroom was one shade or other of brown.

My only friend at work was Ernie. He and I would sit down in the basement and talk for hours sometimes. He told me all about Georgia, where he went on vacation every summer. "Atlanta's cool," he'd say. "But you better watch it in the sticks."

Ernie was proud of his years at Carter's Home. He liked the job and the company but had no patience for most of the bosses.

"Workin' for white people is always the same thing," Ernie would say.

"But Mr. Drew's black," I said the first time I heard his perennial complaint. Drew was the supervisor for all postal and interoffice communication.

"Used to be," Ernie said. "Used to be. But ever since he got promoted he forgot all about that. Now he's so scared I'm gonna pull him down that he won't even sit for a minute. Used to be he'd come down here and we'd talk like you 'n' me doin'. But now he just stands at the door and grin and nod."

"I don't get it. How can you like the job and the company if you don't like the people you work for?" I once asked Ernie.

"It's a talent," he replied.

"Why 'ont you tuck in your shirt?" Big Linda Washington said to me on the afternoon that I'd unknowingly met Lana Donelli. The sneer on the young woman's face spoke of a hatred that I couldn't understand. "You look like some kinda fool hangin' all out all over the place."

Big Linda was taller than I, broader too—and I'm pretty big. Her hair was straightened and frosted with gold at the tips. She wore one-piece dresses of primary colors as a rule. Her skin was mahogany. Her face, unless it was contorted, appraising me, was pretty.

We were in the service elevator going up to the fifth floor. I tucked the white shirt tails into my black jeans.

"At least you could make it even, so the buttons go straight down," she remarked.

I would have had to open up my pants to do it right, and I didn't want to get Linda any more upset than she already was.

"Hm!" she grunted and then sucked a tooth.

The elevator came open then, and she rolled her cart out. We had parallel routes, but I went in the opposite direction, deciding to take mail from the bottom of the stack rather than listen to her criticisms of me.

The first person I ran into was Mona. She was wearing a deep red one-piece dress held up by spaghetti straps. Her breasts were free under the thin fabric, and her legs were bare. Mona (Lana too, of course) was short, with thick black hair and green eyes. Her skin had a hint of olive in it but not so deep as Sicilian skin.

"I can see why you were wearing that sweater at your desk," I said.

"What?" she replied, in an unfriendly tone.

"That white sweater you were wearing," I said.

"What's wrong with you? I don't even own a white sweater."

She turned abruptly and clicked away on her red high heels. I wondered what had happened. Somehow I kept thinking that it was because of my twisted-up shirt. Maybe that's what made people treat me badly, maybe it was my appearance.

I continued my route, pulling jackets from the bottom and placing them in the right in-boxes. Everyone had a different in-box system. Some had their in- and out-boxes stacked, while others had them side by side. Rose McMormant had no box at all, just white and black labels set at opposite ends of her desk. White for in and black for out.

"If the boxes ain't side by side, just drop it anywhere and pick up whatever you want to," Ernie told me on my first day. "That's what I do. Mr. Averill put down the rules thirteen years ago, just before they kicked him upstairs."

Ernie was the interoffice mail-room director. He didn't make deliveries anymore, so it was easy for him to make pronouncements.

When I'd finished the route I went through the EXIT door at the far end of the hall to get a drink of water from the refrigerated fountain. I planned to wait in the exit chamber long enough for Big Linda to have gone back down. While I waited, a fly buzzed by my head. It caught my attention because there weren't many flies that made it into the air-conditioned buildings around the Wall Street area, even in summer.

The fly landed on my hand, then on the cold aluminum bowl of the water fountain. He didn't have enough time to drink before zooming up to the ceiling. From there he went to a white spot on the door, to the baby fingernail of my left hand, and then to a crumb in the corner. He landed and settled again and again but took no more than a second to enjoy each perch.

"You sure jumpy, Mr. Fly," I said, as I might have when I was a child. "But you could be a Miss Fly, huh?"

The idea that the neurotic fly could have been a female brought Mona to mind. I hustled my cart toward the elevator, passing Big Linda on the way. She was standing in the hall with another young black woman, talking. The funny thing about them was that they were both holding their hands as if they were smoking, but of course they weren't, as smoking was forbidden in any office building in New York.

"I got to wait for a special delivery from, um, investigations," Big Linda explained.

"I got to go see a friend on three," I replied.

"Oh." Linda seemed relieved.

I realized that she was afraid I'd tell Ernie that she was idling with her friends. Somehow that stung more than her sneers and insults.

She was still wearing the beaded sweater, but instead of the eraser she had a tiny Wite-Out brush in her hand, held half an inch from a sheet of paper on her violet blotter.

"I bet that blotter used to be blue, huh?"

"What?" She frowned at me.

"That blotter, it looks violet, purple, but that's because it was once blue but the sun shined on it, from the window."

Lana turned her upper torso to see the window that I meant. I could see the soft contours of her small breasts against the white fabric.

"Oh," she said, turning back to me. "I guess."

"Yeah," I said. "I notice things like that. My mother says that it's why I never finish anything. She says that I get distracted all the time and don't keep my eye on the job."

"Do you have more mail for me?" Lana Donelli asked.

"No, uh-uh, I was just thinking."

Lana looked at the drying Wite-Out brush and jammed it back into the small bottle that was in her other hand.

"I was thinking about when I saw you this morning," I continued. "About when I saw you and asked about the air-conditioning and your sweater and you looked at me like I was crazy."

"Yes," she said, "why did you ask that?"

"Because I thought you were Mona Donelli," I said triumphantly.

"Oh," she sounded disappointed. "Most people figure out that I'm not Mona because my nameplate says 'Lana Donelli.'"

"Oh," I said, completely crushed. I could notice a blotter turning violet but I couldn't read.

The look on my face brought a smile out of the mortgage receptionist.

"Don't look so sad," she said. "I mean, even when they see the name, a lotta people still call me Mona."

"They do?"

"Yeah. They see the name and think that Mona's a nickname or something. Isn't that dumb?"

"I saw your sister on the fifth floor in a red dress, and then I saw a fly who couldn't sit still, and then I knew that you had to be somebody else," I said.

"You're funny," Lana said, crinkling up her nose as if she were trying to identify a scent. "What's your name?"

"Rufus Coombs."

"Hi, Rufus," she said, holding out a hand.

"Hey," I said.

My apartment is on 158th Street in Washington Heights. It's pretty much a Spanish-speaking neighborhood. I don't know many people, but the rent is all I can afford. My apartment—living room with a kitchen cove, small bedroom, and toilet with a shower—is on the eighth floor and looks out over the Hudson. The $458 a month includes heat and gas, but I pay my own electric. I took it because of the view. There was a three-hundred-dollar unit on the second floor, but it had windows that looked out onto a brick wall.

I don't own much. I have a single mattress on the floor, an old oak chair that I found on the street, and kitchen shelving that I bought from a liquidator for bookshelves, propped up in the corner. I have a rice pot, a frying pan, and a kettle, and enough cutlery and plates for two, twice as much as I need most days.

I have Rachel, an ex-girlfriend living in the East Village, who will call me back at work if I don't call her too often. I have two other friends, Eric Chen and Willy Jones. They both live in Brooklyn and still go to school.

That evening I climbed the seven flights up to my apartment because the elevator had stopped working in December. I sat in my chair and looked at the river. It was peaceful, and I relaxed. A fly was buzzing up against the glass, trying to push his way through to the world outside.

I got up to kill him. That's what I always did when there was a fly in the house, I killed it. But up close I hesitated and watched the frantic insect. His coloring was unusual, a metallic green. The dull red eyes seemed too large for the body, like he was an intelligent mutant fly from some far-flung future on late-night television.

He buzzed up and down against the pane, trying to get away from me. When I returned to my chair, he settled. The red sun was hovering above the cliffs of New Jersey. The green fly watched. I thought of the fly I'd seen at work. That one was black and fairly small, by fly standards. Then I thought about Mona and then Lana. The smallest nudge of an erection stirred. I thought of calling Rachel but didn't have the heart to walk the three blocks to a phone booth. So I watched the sunset gleaming around the fly, who was now just a black spot on the window.

I guess I fell asleep.

At three A.M. I woke up and made macaroni and cheese from a mix. The fly came into the cooking cove where I stood eating my meal. He lit on the big spoon I used to stir the macaroni and joined me for my late-night supper.

Ernie told me that Landsend mortgaging got most of their mail from the real-mail mail room, that they didn't get most of the interoffice junk mail.

"Why not?" I asked.

"There's just a few people up there. Most of their employees are off-site."

"Well, could you put them on the junk list?"

"She a white girl?"

"So?"

"Nuthin'. But I want you tell me what it's like if you get some." I didn't answer him.

*   *   *

For the next week I took invitations to office parties, sales-force newsletters, and "Insurance Tips," penned by Mr. Averill, up to Lana Donelli's desk. We made small talk for thirty seconds or so, and then she'd pick up the phone to make a call. I always looked back as I rounded the corner to make sure she really had a call to make; she always did.

At the end of the week I bought her a paperweight with the image of a smiling Buddha's face in it. When I got to her desk, she wasn't there. I waited around for a while, but she didn't return, so I wrote her a note, saying "From Rufus to Lana," and put the heavy glass weight on it.

I went away excited and half-scared. What if she didn't see my note? What if she did and thought it was stupid? I was so nervous that I didn't go back to her desk that day.

"I really shouldn't have sent it, Andy," I said that night to the green fly. He was perched peacefully at the edge of the center rim of a small saucer. I had filled the inner depression with a honey and water solution. I was eating a triple cheeseburger with bacon from Wendy's, that and some fries. My pet fly seemed happy with his honey water and only buzzed my sandwich a few times before settling down to drink.

"Maybe she doesn't like me," I said. "Maybe it's just that she's been nice to me because she feels sorry for me. But how will I know if I don't try and see if she likes me, right?"

Andrew's long tubular tongue was too busy drinking to reply.

"Hi," I said to Lana the next morning.

She was wearing a jean jacket over a white T-shirt. She smiled and nodded. I handed her Mr. Averill's "Insurance Tips" newsletter.

"Did you see the paperweight?"

"Oh, yeah," she said, without looking me in the eye. "Thanks." Then she picked up her phone and began pressing buttons. "Hi, Tristan? Lana. I wanted to know if——" She put her hand over the receiver and looked at me. "Can I do something else for you?"

"Oh," I said. "No. No," and I wheeled away in a kind of euphoria.

It's only now when I look back on it that I remember the averted eyes, the quick call, and the rude dismissal. All I heard then was "Thanks." I even remember a smile. Maybe she did smile for a brief moment, maybe not.

Monday, Tuesday, and Wednesday of the next week I deposited little presents on her desk. I left them while she was out to lunch. I got her a small box of four Godiva chocolates, a silk rose, and a jar of fancy rose-petal jelly. I didn't leave any more notes. I was sure that she'd know who it was. During that time I stopped delivering to her desk. I saved up all the junk mail for Friday morning, when I'd deliver it and ask her to go out with me.

Wednesday evening I went to a nursery on the East Side just south of Harlem proper. There I bought a bonsai, a real apple tree, for $347.52. I figured that I'd leave it during her Thursday lunch, and then on Friday, Lana would be so happy that she'd have to have lunch with me no matter what.

I should have suspected that something was wrong when Andrew went missing. I put out his honey water, but he didn't show up, even when I started eating a beef burrito from Taco Bell. I looked around the apartment, but he wasn't anywhere to be seen. There was a spiderweb in the upper corner of the shower, but there was no little bundle up there. I would have killed the spider right then, but he never came out when I was around.

That night I wondered if I could talk to Lana about Andrew. I wondered if she would understand my connection to a fly.

*   *   *

"What's that?" Ernie asked me the next morning when I came in with the bonsai.

"It's a tree."

"Tree for what?"

"My friend Willy wanted me to pick it up for him. He wants it for his new apartment, and the only place where he could get it is up near me. I'm gonna meet him at lunch and give it to him."

"Uh-huh," Ernie said.

"You got my cart loaded?" I asked him.

Just then the Lindas came down in the elevator. Big Linda looked at me and shook her head, managing to look both contemptuous and pitying at the same time.

"There's your carts," Ernie said to them.

They attached their earphones and rolled back to the service elevator. Little Linda was looking me in the eye as the slatted doors closed. She was still looking at me as the lift brought her up.

"What about me and Junior?"

"Junior's already gone. That's all I got right now. Why don't you sit here with me?"

"OK." I sat down expecting Ernie to bring up one of his regular topics, either something about Georgia, white bosses, or the horse races, which he followed but never wagered on. But instead of saying anything he just started reading the *Post*.

After a few minutes I was going to say something, but the swinging door opened. Mr. Drew leaned in. He smiled at Ernie and then pointed at me.

"Rufus Coombs?"

"Yeah?"

"Come with me."

I followed Leonard Drew through the messy service hall outside the couriers' room to the passenger elevator that we rarely took.

It was a two-man elevator, so Drew and I had to stand very close to one another. He wore too much cologne, but otherwise he was ideal for his supervisory job, wearing a light gray suit with a shirt that only hinted at yellow. The rust tie was perfect, and there was not a wrinkle on the man's clothes or his face. I knew that he must have been up in his forties, but he might have passed as a graduate student at my school. He was light-skinned and had what my mother called *good hair*. There were freckles around his eyes.

I could see all of that because Mr. Drew averted his gaze. He wouldn't engage me in any way, and so I got a small sense of revenge by studying him.

We got out on the second floor and went to his office, which was at the far end of the mail-sorting room. Outside of his office there was a desk for his secretary, Teja Monroe. Her desk sat out in the hall as if it had been an afterthought to give Drew an assistant.

I looked around the room as Drew was entering his office. I saw Mona looking at me from the crevice of a doorway. I knew it was Mona because she was wearing a skimpy dress that could have been worn on a hot date.

I only got a glimpse of her before she ducked away.

"Come on in, Coombs," Drew said.

The office was tiny. Drew had to actually stand on the tips of his toes to get between the wall and the desk to his chair. There was a stool in front of the desk, not a chair.

By the time he said "sit down," I had lost my nervousness. I gauged the power of Mr. Leonard Drew by the size of his office.

"You're in trouble, Rufus," he said, looking as somber as he could.

"I am?"

He lifted a pink sheet of paper and shook it at me.

"Do you recognize this?" he asked.

"No."

"This is a sexual harassment complaint form."

"Yeah?"

"It names you as the offender."

"I don't get it."

"Lana Donelli . . ." He went on to explain all the things that
I had done and felt for the last week as if they were crimes. Going
to Lana's desk, talking to her, leaving gifts. Even remarking on her
clothes had sexual innuendo attached. By the time he was finished
I was worried about them calling the police.

"Lana says that she's afraid to come in to work," Mr. Drew said,
his freckles disappearing into angry lines around his eyes.

I wanted to say that I didn't mean it, but I could see that my
intentions didn't matter, that a small woman like Lana would be
afraid of a big sloppy mail clerk hovering over her and leaving notes
and presents.

"I'm sorry," I said.

"Sorry doesn't mean much when it's gotten to this point. If
it was up to me I'd send you home right now, today. But first Mr.
Averill says that he wants to talk to you."

"OK," I said.

I sat there looking at him.

"Well?" he asked after a few moments.

"What?"

"Go back to the mail room and stay down there. Tell Ernie that
I don't want you in the halls. You're supposed to meet Mr. Averill
at one forty-five in his office. I've given him my recommendation
to let you go. After something like this, there's really no place for
you. But he can still refer the matter to the police. Lana might want
a restraining order."

I wanted to say something. I wanted to tell him that a restraining order was ridiculous. Then I wanted to go to Lana and tell her the same thing. I wanted to tell her that I bought her roses because she wore rose toilet water, that I bought her the tree because the sun on her blotter could support a plant. I really liked her. But even while I was imagining what I could say, I knew that it didn't matter what I saw or what I felt.

"Well?" Drew said. "Go."

Ernie made busywork for us that morning. He told me that he was upset about what had happened, that he'd told Drew to go easy.

"But he just said that I better look after myself," Ernie said. "Man forget he's black 'fore you could say Jackie Robinson."

"Hey, bro'," Junior said to me at lunchtime. "Come on with me."

Junior rarely talked to me, much less offered his company. This was an act of rare generosity, and so I took him up on it. The Lindas had ignored me completely. It was obvious that they knew about my troubles before I did but hadn't seen fit to warn me.

"Where we goin'?" I asked Junior out on Broadway. It was a very crowded street at lunchtime.

"Coupla blocks."

I got the feeling he was taking me somewhere special. I would have been excited, or at least asked him where we were going, but my mind kept going back to Lana. I wanted to explain to her, to tell her why I wasn't harassing her.

"There it is," Junior said.

We had reached the end of Broadway. There was a small concrete island with park benches in the middle of the street. There were lots of young people hanging out and talking there. On one bench, the one Junior was pointing at, sat a muscular ebony-colored man with a bald head wearing a dark blue, thin-strapped tank top. He was just leaning over to kiss a small woman, a white woman— Lana Donelli. I brought my hand to my mouth and made a sound. He pushed his tongue brutally into her mouth, and she brought her fingers to his head as if she were guiding the attack.

I turned away.

"Sorry, bro," Junior said.

I felt his hand on my shoulder. I nodded and said, "I'm going back up." I didn't wait for him to reply; I just started walking.

Lancelot Averill's office was on the forty-eighth floor of the Carter's Home building. His secretary's office was larger by far than Mr. Drew's cubbyhole. The smiling blond secretary led me into Averill's airy room. The wall behind him was a giant window looking out over Battery Park, Ellis Island, and the Statue of Liberty. I would have been impressed if my heart wasn't broken.

Averill was on the phone when I was ushered in.

"Sorry, Nick," he said into the receiver. "My one forty-five is here."

He stood up, tall and thin. The medium-gray suit looked expensive. His white shirt was crisp and bright, but that was nothing compared to the rainbow of his tie. His hair was gray and combed back, and his mustache was sharp enough to cut bread, as my mother was known to say.

"Sit down, Mr. Coombs."

He sat also. In front of him were two sheets of paper. At his left hand was the pink harassment form; at his right was a white form. Behind him the Budweiser blimp hovered next to Lady Liberty.

Averill brought his fingertips to just under his nose and gazed at a spot over my head.

"How's Ernie?" he asked.

"He's good," I said. "He's a great boss."

"He's a good man. He likes you."

I didn't know what to say to that.

Averill looked down at his desk. "This does not compute."

"What?"

He patted the white page. "This says that you're a college graduate, magna cum laude, in political science, that you came here to be a professional trainee." He patted the pink sheet. "This says that you're an interoffice mail courier who harasses secretaries in the mortgage department."

Averill's hand reached into his vest pocket and came out with an open package of cigarettes. He offered me one, but I shook my head. He lit up and took a deep drag, holding the smoke in his lungs a long time before exhaling.

"Why are you in the interoffice mail room?" he asked.

"No PT positions were open when I applied," I said.

"Nonsense. We don't have a limit on PTs."

"But Ms. Worth said—"

"Oh," Averill held up his hand. "Reena. You know Ernie helped me out when I got here eighteen years ago. I was just a little older than you. They didn't have the PT program back then, just a few guys like Ernie. He never even finished high school, but he showed me the ropes."

Averill drummed the fingers of his free hand between the two forms that represented me.

"I know this Lana's sister," he said. "Always wearing those cocktail dresses in to work. Her boss is afraid to say anything, otherwise

29

he might get a pink slip too." He paused to ponder some more. "Twins, huh? They look alike?"

"They don't dress the same," I said, wanting somehow to protect Lana from the insinuations that I barely understood.

"How would you like to be a PT floater?"

"What's that?" I asked.

"Bump you up to a grade seven and let you move around in the different departments until you find a fit."

I was a grade 1B.

"I thought you were going to fire me."

"That's what Drew suggested, but Ernie says that it's just a mix-up, that you aren't perverted or anything. I'll talk to this Donelli girl, and as long as I have your word that you'll leave her alone, I'll forget it. This is personnel's fault in the first place. You're an intelligent boy—young man. Of course you're going to get into trouble if you aren't challenged."

Watching the forbidden smoke curl around his head, I imagined that Averill was some kind of devil. When I thanked him and shook his hand, something inside me wanted to scream.

I found six unused crack vials a block from the subway stop near my apartment. I knew they were unused because they still had the little plastic stoppers in them.

When I got upstairs I spent hours searching my place. I looked under the edges of the mattress and behind the toilet, under the radiator, and even down under the burners on the stove. Finally, after midnight, I decided to open the windows.

Andrew had crawled down in the crack between the window frame and the sill in my bedroom. His green body had dried out, which made his eyes look all the larger. He'd gone down there to die, or maybe he was trying to get out of the life I'd kept him in;

maybe it was me that killed him, that's what I thought. Later I found out that flies live for only a few weeks. He probably died of old age.

I took the small dried-out corpse and put him in one of the crack vials. I stoppered him in the tiny glass coffin and buried him among the roots of the bonsai apple.

"So you finally bought something nice for your house," my mother said, after I told her about the changes in my life. "Maybe next you'll get a real bed."

ALMOST ALYCE

1.

Albert Roundhouse came from a good working-class family in Los Angeles. He did well in public high school and made it through three years of state college before things started falling apart.

There was a young woman named Alyce who came into Albert's life like a typhoon—at least that's what Albert's sister Luellen said.

"Alyce blew in like a storm," Luellen Roundhouse reported to anyone who cared to listen. "She told him that she wasn't the kind of girl that belonged to anyone or who wanted to settle down. And as much as Al tried to understand what she was telling him, he just sank under all that loving like a leaky rowboat in a summer storm."

And it was true, what Luellen said. Sometimes when Albert gazed on Alyce's brown body in his bed at night, he would howl and pounce on her like an animal from some deep forgotten part of the forest. And Alyce loved his hunger for her. She rolled and growled, clawed and bit with him.

And then one day she was gone—out of his bed, out of his apartment, out of the city, with Roald Hopkins, a sailor on furlough.

"He could have been called Jimmy or Johnny," Luellen Round-house said. "He could have been a she for all that Alyce cared. Because she was just hungry for passion from as many lovers as possible. She told Albert that. She warned him."

At about that time, September 1979, Albert and Luellen's father, Thyme Roundhouse, met Betty Pann. He fell for Betty just as his son had fallen for Alyce. But Betty didn't run away—not at all. It was Thyme who ran out. He left Georgia, his wife, the kids' mother, and moved with Miss Pann to Seattle, where they lived in a house that looked over the Puget Sound. Thyme became a fisherman and Betty a nurse. "Blood and Fishes," they had printed on their own personal stationery.

Georgia Roundhouse changed her surname back to Gordon but still refused to give Thyme a divorce. She didn't quit her job as senior office manager for the city of Los Angeles, but after seventeen weeks of absence she was fired.

By then Albert was failing his classes, pining for Alyce. She had sent the lovesick student a postcard telling him that she'd left Roald for another lover, name of Christian Lovell. Her words and tone were so friendly that Albert cried for three days. Luellen convinced her brother to drop out of school and move in with their mother, each to serve as a life preserver for the other.

For a while it went as well as heartbreak would allow. Albert got a job for Logan Construction and came up with the small monthly mortgage payment. The rest of their money came from Georgia's private savings and what little Luellen could provide from her various part-time jobs.

Albert had never done hard labor before. He manned a wheel-barrow most days, moving rock from one pile to another. He lifted and strained and grew callouses. Al was grateful for the exhaustion because it meant he would sleep rather than brood about Alyce at night in his childhood bed.

Georgia cooked dinner every day and ate with her moping son.

The mother loved Albert, but for most of his life they'd had little in common and less to say. But with Thyme gone, Georgia would find herself telling Albert about her family history. She told these stories because Albert rarely had anything to say except that he loved Alyce more and more each day.

Georgia talked about her mother and father and Great-Grandfather Henry, who had been born a slave but became a spice trader, getting his own ship and working from the port of Havana. Henry's wife, Lorraine, had been a woman of the streets.

"Great-Granddaddy Henry married a prostitute?"

"He had got himself stabbed by a Spaniard that wanted to take over his business, but Lorraine found him bleeding in an alley and took him in. She nursed him back to health, and Henry went out and killed that Spaniard. When he came back he told Lorraine that he would marry her and build her a big house in America, where she would never have to work unless that was what she wanted."

"He must have been the most colorful ancestor we got," Albert said, forgetting for the moment his sorrow.

"Oh, no," Georgia said. "Big Jim Gordon, your great-uncle on my father's side, was the wildest, most exciting relative. Big Jim declared war on the town of Hickton, Mississippi, and fought that war for twelve long years."

"War?"

"Oh, yes," Georgia said with surety. "Full-fledged war, with guns and traps, dead men and blood. He lived in the woods around that town and took retribution on those that had harmed him and others of our people."

"When was this?"

"Just after World War One and up to the Great Depression."

"But the Gordons aren't from Mississippi."

Georgia smiled. It was a look of mild cheer, but Albert thought he could see how deep the pain ran.

"You only get so much a night, Al," she said. "Tomorrow I'll tell you how the white men in that town of Hickton hurt Jim and then paid the price."

With these words Georgia Gordon got up and went to her bedroom, leaving Albert to wonder about his great-grandfather the spice merchant and his great-uncle Big Jim, the one-man army.

So taken was the young man with his unknown heritage that he didn't brood over Alyce that evening.

In the morning he got up early, before his mother, and went out to work in Oxnard, where he spent the morning rolling chunks of concrete and granite to a pit that had been excavated by the company bulldozer. He swung a sledgehammer for three hours in the early afternoon and then used an oversize shovel in the gravel pit until his shift was through. He worked harder than usual, imagining a one-man black army declaring war on a white southern town. In this reverie he didn't feel the weight of his labors or the gravity of loss.

When he got home, the house was quiet and dark. Albert couldn't remember the last time he'd entered the house when the television wasn't on.

"Mama," the twenty-one-year-old called.

He expected the "Here" to come from one of the back rooms. But there was no welcome.

Georgia Gordon was dead in her bed, her left hand gripping the edge of the blanket near her chin. Her foot, clad in a gaudy, pink cashmere sock, poked out from the sheets. There was an odor hovering in the room, a smell that Albert couldn't get out of his nose for many weeks.

"Why didn't you call for an ambulance?" Detective Todd Green asked Albert, for the fourth or fifth time.

"I, I could tell she was dead," he said. "Her skin was cold, and she hadn't been out of bed since I left this morning."

"Why didn't you call the ambulance this morning?"

"I didn't know anything was wrong."

"You knew that she hadn't gotten out of bed."

"I left the house at five in the morning. When I got home, all the lights were off and the paper was at the front door. I could tell that Mama had never gotten up. I went in her room after she didn't answer, and there she was."

"Why didn't you call for an ambulance?" the detective asked again.

"I called my sister."

"Your sister? Why?"

"She's her mother too. And Mama was cold, and the room smelled bad. Lu said to call the police, and so that's what I did."

Thyme Roundhouse came down for the funeral with Betty Pann on his arm.

"I'm selling the house, Al," he said at the reception after the service.

"But this is Mama's house."

"Your mother's dead, and I'm still her husband."

The full impact of the death hadn't hit the young man until his father uttered those words. From then on, and through the next few decades, Albert was confused about the sequence of events.

There were some things he was sure of. He began crying upon hearing his father's callous pronouncement. Not loud bawling; it was just that the tears wouldn't stop flowing from his eyes. Luellen and Thyme argued. Men touched him on the shoulder and head. Women kissed him and held him like he was their child.

At some point everyone was gone from the house, and Albert was alone with a fifth of Jack Daniel's that someone had brought for the repast . . .

The first bender lasted for eight or nine weeks. It carried him from the house his father was selling up to Berkeley and Telegraph Avenue. He crashed in the laundry room of a house on Derby Street.

One night he had sex with a woman in the back of a van while her husband watched from the driver's seat.

He moved out of the house and into an empty lot, using a sleeping bag that a man named Hartwynn had given him. He did day labor when the hangovers were tolerable.

The Petals of the Sun commune was located in southern Oregon where a redwood forest met the ocean. There he dried out for some months, though he wasn't sure how many. There was a woman with big hands named Rilette, who had built a one-room cottage and took him in. Rilette had a brother, Marquis. Marquis and Albert went into town one night and bought a bottle of red wine and then another.

When Albert woke up the next morning, Marquis was gone, and Rilette was blaming Albert for stealing her money to buy wine.

He hadn't taken her money, but she sent him away. Albert marked this event as the beginning of his roustabout years.

Finally, after three months incarceration for vagrancy in northern California, he built up enough strength and sobriety to hitchhike across country with a woman named Bergit. She was half Native

American and half Swedish and tall and blue-eyed and completely in love with the world she inhabited. She was leaving her boyfriend in Oregon to visit her husband in Vermont. This husband lived on a commune that raised silkworms and practiced Tibetan Buddhism.

For a year the master of that sect worked with Albert, trying to get him to "get outside of the inebriation."

"You mean you want me to stop drinking, right?" Albert once asked. "I been tryin' to put the bottle down, but every time I turn around I find it there in my hand."

The master had a huge, round, burnt-orange-colored face. He smiled at Albert and shook his great head.

"It is not what I want that matters," the master said. "You must seek your own equilibrium. If drinking brings balance then by all means drink. But if it is only a mask, a beard to cover the real face of your desire, then you must find another way."

Albert would sit in his straw hut at night, wrapped in a down comforter that Bergit's husband gave him. Outside it was below zero, but the round hut stayed warm, and Albert wondered what it meant to achieve balance.

In the spring the master died, and the man who ran the raw-silk production line asked Albert to leave.

"You're just a drunk," Terry Pin said to Albert three days after the cremation rite.

Theodore Bidwell, Bergit's husband, apologized for Terry's rough words.

"Bergit has relatives that work construction in New York," Theodore told Albert. He bought the displaced Californian a ticket for the Peter Pan bus in Saint Albans and gave him forty dollars to hold him over till he contacted the Swedish Indian's cousins.

Bergit had left some months before to return to her boyfriend and his son in the forests of Oregon. Albert thought it was nice of her husband to buy his ticket and give him a recommendation.

On the bus Albert sat by the window concentrating on the idea of balance. He thought about Alyce and his father, his mother, and Luellen. He touched the center of his chest with the middle finger of his left hand. At just that place there was a gap, a space that Alyce had stretched out and then vacated. There was something about this emptiness that kept him from the proper equilibrium. It was like trying to stand up straight atop a gas-filled balloon that always seemed to be shifting away.

Albert rubbed the area that felt hollow, wondering if somehow he could move the emptiness around.

In the window of the bus he peered into his own dark image, thinking about Alyce and Great-Uncle Big Jim. These unknowable quantities, he felt, were what made him stagger through life. Or maybe it was his mother's unexpected death or his father's betrayal.

"My life hasn't really been all that bad," he said to the image of himself.

"What did you say?" asked the woman in the aisle seat next to him.

"Nuthin'."

"It was something," the youngish, round white woman said. "I heard it. I just didn't understand the words."

Her smile was gentle and reminded Al of a time when he wasn't sad.

"I was sayin' that my life hasn't really been all that bad. I mean, I've had some hard times, but every trouble I've had has been at least partly my fault."

"We all make our own beds," she agreed, "but it's God that gives us bedbugs."

Albert laughed deeply. While laughing he tried to remember the last time he felt mirth when sober.

Mary Denise Fulmer was born in Springfield, Massachusetts. She taught middle school there and lived by herself in a small red house near the train tracks. She was unmarried and had never lived anywhere but Springfield.

"Where are you coming from now?" Albert asked.

"My grandmother lived in Montreal," Mary Denise said. "She died last week, and I took a few days off to wrap up her affairs."

Albert told Mary Denise about his mother's death and his on-again, off-again ten-year bender.

"I just can't seem to get straight," he said more than once.

Somewhere outside of Amherst she asked, "Would you like to come stay with me for a while? You could sleep on the couch . . . or in my bed if you want."

Albert hadn't had a drink in thirty-four hours. He felt queasy but clearheaded.

"I really, really want to, Mary D," he said, surprising himself with the clarity. "But I'm on a tight schedule here. I got to get to a place that's mine. Mine."

The plump schoolteacher smiled sadly and put a hand on his forearm. She leaned over and kissed his bristly cheek.

2.

The next twenty-two years passed like overlapping spirals drawn by a tired child on a rainy afternoon. Albert would work for weeks, sometimes for months at a time, and then he'd fall off the wagon.

But even when on a bender, Albert would always find time to beg. This practice he'd learned from his Tibetan master.

"A man with a tin cup allows the more prosperous to pay penance. Without this opportunity, their souls would surely be lost."

Albert could imbibe prodigiously in his younger years, but after he crossed the half-century border his capacity diminished. Where at one time he could drink a fifth and a half of sour-mash whiskey, now half a bottle of cheap red wine was all he could manage before the gut rot set in.

He'd been hospitalized twice by the city and had done three stints in jail, for public lewdness, resisting arrest, and simple assault. The Eagle Heart Construction Company of Queens always took Albert back if he was sober. He'd been working for them as long as most could remember.

Between work and inebriation, jail and hospitalization, Albert lived in a cavity under an abandoned subway tunnel on the Upper East Side. This space was an underground chamber he inherited from a German survivalist named Dieter Krownen, who had returned to Munich when his mother got sick.

Chained together under metal netting in the abandoned tunnel above his subterranean lair, Albert had a collection of shopping carts in which he kept those belongings that didn't fit in his 137-square-foot underground bunker.

Albert hadn't realized he'd passed the half-century mark until he was fifty-three. One day he'd come across his birth certificate in an old alligator wallet in the bottom of one of the carts. The date of his birth was January 12, 1958, the time 4:56 A.M. His race was Negro, sex male, and he came into the world weighing six and three-quarter pounds.

After calculating his age, Albert stopped working for Eagle Heart Construction. Fifty, he thought, should be the mandatory retirement age in order to make space for younger workers. One of his professors at state college had told him that.

So for six months he'd been strolling around Manhattan with his travel cart. He pushed the rickety shopping cart all over the city, whispering words about his father and mother, Luellen, and always, always Alyce. He begged for a few hours each day, thinking about his deceased master and believing that he was doing penance by begging and saving souls.

One sunny afternoon he found himself on Sixth Avenue, two blocks south of Houston Street. There he stood on the corner next to a restaurant with half of its tables out on the sidewalk. He leaned against a lamppost remembering the half-told story about his great-uncle Big Jim who, Albert imagined, had killed a dozen white men in a just war.

Over the years, Albert had fleshed out the tale that his mother had tantalized him with before she died. Albert's Jim was six foot six, with fists like hams, and very proficient with every kind of weapon. He'd fought beside Teddy Roosevelt in the Spanish-American War and had been wounded more than once . . .

While reconstituting the story he'd contrived over the years, Albert became aware of a woman crossing the street.

It was Alyce or, at least, almost Alyce. The woman walking toward him was the same age Alyce had been when Albert knew her; she was taller, with different-color eyes, blond not brunette, white not black. But in spite of all that she had the same style and poise and grace. She had the same wildness in her blue, not brown, eyes. Her gait was brash like Alyce's, and her expression was one of mirth in the face of disaster.

This woman, who every man and woman around was looking at, walked right up to Albert and said, "Hi, I'm Frankie. What's your name?"

"Albert."

"You want to make some money, Albert?"

"OK."

"Well, then," she said, with a wry grin, "let's go."

Stillman's Gourmet Grocer was a chain that had a store in SoHo. Frankie had Albert leave his cart down the block from the entrance and told him to go into the fancy supermarket before she did.

"First, go back to the meat section," she told him, "and then to the fruits and vegetables. Whenever you see me, count to twelve and then go to the next section. Don't act like you know me. Just count to twelve and move on."

She laid out the plan for him to go to five different sections. He committed these destinations to memory, thinking that maybe the Tibetan notion of reincarnation was true and that Alyce had died and been reborn as Frankie.

He went into the store and was shocked by the air-conditioning. The cold made him shiver now and then, even under his coat and sweater. He made his way to the meats and looked into the cold bins with rows of steaks and pork chops, whole chickens and slabs of bacon—all set on rectangular Styrofoam plates wrapped in clear plastic. The food distracted him. He cooked in his subterranean lair but only rice and beans, chicken necks and grits.

After a while Alyce, no, Frankie, yes, Frankie, wandered into the aisle. *One, two* . . . She wore tight-fitting, faded blue jeans and a linen shirt. There was a necklace of blue stones around her neck. Her hair was tied back, and she was so beautiful . . .

. . . *eleven, twelve.*

Albert moved on, looking for the fruits and vegetables.

Store employees followed him openly. There was a guard in a uniform not three steps away.

Albert wasn't worried. He was no thief. His mother hated thieves. At one time his sister wanted to be a cop. Looking at a bin filled with huge pomegranates, Albert wondered whether Luellen still had the same phone number. They hadn't been in touch in nineteen years, maybe twenty.

"Excuse me," the copper-skinned guard, wearing a blue and gray uniform, said.

At just that moment Alyce, no, Frankie, came into the far end of the aisle.

One, two, three . . .

"Excuse me," the guard insisted.

"Yes?" . . . *four, five . . .*

"Can I help you?"

"No, no, I'm just looking." . . . *seven, eight . . .*

"If you're not going to buy anything, I'll have to ask you to leave."

The guard was young and pudgy, with a silly, drooping mustache. His eyes were both insecure and resentful.

When Albert got to twelve he turned and walked away.

The guard followed him.

"Excuse me."

Albert passed the pasta aisle and one with cookies and cakes. Finally there was a row with coffee and teas, chocolates, and wildflower-flavored honeys.

Albert stopped in front of a row of golden jars and stared.

"Excuse me," the guard said.

There were store employees standing at the far end of the aisle.

"Yes?" Albert asked, grateful not to be distracted by having to count.

"I'll have to ask you to leave."

"But I haven't finished looking."

"You have to buy something."

Albert reached into his pocket and took out a five-dollar bill. He showed this to the guard.

"See?" Albert said loudly. "I have money to buy with."

Looking at the guard, he noticed that customers had stopped to watch the argument.

The guard slapped Albert's hand.

"I don't want to see that," the man with the drooping mustache said.

"I got a right just like anybody else to be here, to shop here," Albert said, loud enough that the spectators could hear.

More people were coming into the sweets aisle. Albert glanced around to make sure that Alyce wasn't one of them. No, no—Frankie.

The guard grabbed Albert's left biceps, but when Albert flexed his muscle he let go.

"I'm just lookin' for a candy bar, man. Why you wanna kick me outta here?"

"Chico," a man in a dark blue suit said.

Albert was looking around for Frankie, yes, Frankie, but she was nowhere to be seen. Had he made her up?

"Yes, Mr. Greenwood?" the security guard said.

"What's going on here?"

"Um," Chico the guard said.

"I come in here wanting to buy me a piece a' fancy candy," Albert averred, brandishing his five-dollar bill. "First I looked at the meats and vegetables just to see what you got, and then this man here said that I'm not welcome to shop in your store. I got my money right here in my hand."

Mr. Greenwood was about Albert's age. He was pale-skinned and had amber eyes behind metal-rimmed glasses. He'd made something of himself, that's what Albert thought. He was a man who ran a grocery store, while Albert was just a guy who lived in a hole.

"Excuse me, sir," Greenwood said, forcing a smile. "You are certainly welcome to shop here, just like anybody else."

There were people all around them, but Alyce—no, Frankie—was nowhere to be seen. Albert was becoming light-headed.

"Would you accept a gift of one of our boxes of chocolates?" Greenwood was asking.

"No," Albert said. "I don't want anything from this store if you won't even let me walk around and look. I mean, that's what people do in the store, right? They shop and look and buy if they see somethin' they like. No, I don't want your candy now."

When Albert saw Frankie waiting at his shopping cart, he was overjoyed. He thought that maybe he had actually seen her on that corner but imagined their conversation. Maybe his make-believe had brought him to the store, thinking that she was following him, and he was perpetually moving away.

"You were just perfect, Al," she said, beaming.

She pulled his shoulders and kissed his cheek.

"Let's go to my house," she said. "And I'll make you a Stillman's steak."

There was an office building on Broome Street that had changed hands and was under reconstruction.

"The man who owns it is being indicted for fraud or something," Frankie told Albert. "The trial'll take years. A guy named Childress gets the keys from the construction boss and makes a few spaces available for apartments. I got the one on the sixth floor, and I only pay three hundred a month."

The halls were dusty and dark, but the makeshift apartment was bright and airy, with good furniture, electricity, and a camping stove in the office-supply room that she used as a kitchen. There was even a bathroom with running water at the end of the hall.

"You're not all that dirty," Frankie said, "but you could still wash up while I make us dinner. There's some clothes in a box in the hall that might fit you."

The bathroom had a fiberglass businessman's shower installed in the corner. Albert felt vulnerable being naked in that illegal space, washing with cold water. But he was excited too. Frankie was almost Alyce in his eyes, and for the first time in decades the mantra of love-lost had stopped nagging at him.

With a smile on his face he plunged under the ice-cold spray and experienced exhilaration that spanned his entire life. His father might have been dead by now. Luellen never became a cop. The moon was rounding the curve of the Earth, soon to be aloft in the New York sky. Albert was standing naked in that hidden space, and there was a woman down the hall who wanted to have a meal with him.

Out of the clothes box he took a pair of gray sweatpants and a green T-shirt that was only a little too small.

"You're in pretty good shape for a homeless," Frankie said, as she served him a fried rib-eye steak with white rice and shredded brussels sprouts sautéed in butter with garlic and soy sauce.

"I live in a hole in the ground," he said, savoring the meal. "But I'm not homeless. No more than you are."

"Sorry, I didn't mean to insult you."

"How come you picked me off the street like that?"

"I needed a partner, and the last guy I worked with punked out on me."

"You needed a black man to distract security?"

"Uh-huh. You want some red wine?"

"I don't think so. No, no, I don't."

"You need a job, Albert?"

"I'd like to work for you, Frankie."

"I'm not getting up off of any pussy. My last partner, Joby, didn't understand that."

"These his clothes?" Albert asked. He was thinking about his deceased Tibetan master and the ideal of balance, of the moon arcing through the sky and all the many tons of rock he'd piled over the years.

"Yeah," Frankie said, "but they belonged to a guy named Teddy before that."

"You know a lotta men."

"My father had Huntington's disease," she said, as if in answer. "He'd go into these wild rages, and my mother had me and my sister padlocked in our rooms at night. She gave me a pistol. I still have it."

"Did he ever try to hurt you, your father?"

"Only all the time."

"What's that got to do with all the men you know?" Albert was wondering about the reasoning behind his own question.

"I'm not afraid of anybody," she said.

"I won't steal," Albert said, as if in answer, "but I don't mind walkin' around in a store."

3.

Albert "walked around" while Frankie shoplifted from drugstores mainly, but they also hit hardware stores, art-supply stores, little knickknack places down in SoHo, and some Midtown department stores. Frankie knew the most valuable items to boost (and where to sell them), and all Albert had to do was look at things that interested him.

He was especially interested in portable electronics and colored pens.

He was arrested twice but then released for lack of evidence. He made sure to have twenty dollars in his pocket so that he could always claim to be shopping.

Frankie set up a room for him down the hall from her suite. She padlocked her doors and told him that if he broke in on her, she still had the pistol her mother had given her.

"I've shot men before," she warned.

Early one Thursday morning, Frankie knocked on Albert's door. He was already awake, lying on the futon she'd had the man Childress deliver. She paid an extra hundred dollars a month for Albert. He stayed on Broome Street, even though he had another illegal home uptown.

He heard the knock but didn't answer immediately. He was lying there thinking that he hadn't had a drink since the day he met Frankie.

"Yeah?" he said at the second knock.

"You wanna get breakfast and do some shopping?"

"I have something to do today."

"What's that?" She pushed the door open and walked into the small office.

"I'm going up to Central Park to beg."

"You don't need that. We make more than enough."

"I don't do it for the money," he said.

"Why else would somebody beg on the street?"

"To save souls and redeem karma."

★   ★   ★

They left the building together and walked up Broadway toward Houston Street. Just before crossing Prince, Frankie stopped and turned around, pretending to be looking in the window of a little perfume boutique.

"Stand in front of me, Al," she whispered forcefully. "Stand in front of me. Not there. On the other side."

Albert did as she said and looked around.

Coming toward them were two burly white guys in jeans and white T-shirts. They had crew cuts and tattoos. They were the kind of men that Albert had learned to avoid on streets and back alleys.

One of the men looked at Albert as he passed.

Albert smiled, and the white man sneered.

"Are they gone?" Frankie asked.

"Yeah."

They stopped outside the entrance to the F train near Broadway and Houston.

"Who were those guys?"

"Toad Boy and Westerling," she said.

"They got a problem with you?"

"When the police asked me where they were, I told 'em— because they killed my friend Bobby. I guess the case fell through."

"What'll happen if they see you?"

"You might have to start begging full time."

Nine days later Albert and Frankie were sitting in her makeshift apartment eating a dish she called Yankee stew. It had potatoes and beef and a good amount of beer in it.

"I like you, Al," Frankie said as they ate.

"Me too. I mean, I like you too."

"Is there anything you want from me?"

"You already gimme a job and a place to stay."

"I've played this game with a lotta guys. All of them have tried to get in my pants at least once. I never let 'em. You're the first one didn't want it. Are you gay?"

"No."

"Don't like white girls?"

"I would like one thing from you, Frankie."

"What's that?"

"Could you . . . would you let me . . . let me call you Alyce?"

"Alyce?"

"Yeah. I used to know a girl by that name when I was in college . . ."

"You went to college?"

"I loved her so hard, and when she left my heart broke, and it never got better until I met you."

"You fell in love with me?"

"You took her place, kind of," he said. "You don't look like her, but you have the same spirit. If I could call you Alyce that would mean a whole lot to me."

"You'd rather that than lay up in my bed?"

"Yes."

"Well," she said, bewilderment in her tone. "OK. I guess it could be like our little nickname."

That night Albert reclined on his futon feeling like he'd passed into a new land, a new place. There was a woman like Alyce who didn't mind being called by that name.

He was smiling and sober and hopeful for something he could not quite imagine.

Through his window he could see the crescent moon. Then a loud banging from the hall brought him to his feet.

The footsteps passed his door and continued down toward Alyce's room.

He came out into the hall and saw the backs of two men. They had crew cuts, T-shirts, and tattoos.

"What do you want?" Albert demanded.

The white men turned.

"This ain't your business," either Toad Boy or Westerling said. "We just want the bitch."

Albert surged forward throwing his fists, getting hit twice for every blow he delivered. He pushed and fought and struggled in the narrow passage. The men hit him, and he felt pain, but it was like a far-off experience, like the memory held in an untouched bruise.

He felt something hard strike the side of his head and fell, happy to give in to the pull of gravity. Someone kicked him in the chest, then in the head. They kept up like that for thirty seconds or so.

Albert expected even more punishment, but there was a shot and then another shot.

"Let's get outta here!" one of the men shouted.

After the third shot the same man squealed in pain.

By then Albert was on his back looking up at the ceiling. Alyce ran by and was gone for a minute, maybe two.

Albert closed his eyes for a moment.

"Are you all right?" Frankie, no, Alyce, asked.

Albert opened his eyes, caught a glimpse of his friend, and then passed out.

⋆　⋆　⋆

He woke up in a hospital bed feeling surprisingly healthy. His jaw hurt, as did his side. He turned his head and saw a middle-aged black woman sitting in a chair. She was heavy but not fat, wearing a gray dress and holding a dark blue purse.

"Al?" she said.

"Lu?"

"Baby, I was worried that you were gonna die lyin' right here next to me."

"What happened?"

"Somebody called the police and told them that you was all beat up in this buildin'. They came and found you. You had my name and address in an old alligator wallet. The cops said there was the smell of gunpowder in the air. But you didn't have no gunshot wound."

"It was only me?" Albert Roundhouse asked.

Nodding, Luellen said, "The police wanna question you."

The interrogation lasted an hour or so. The men who broke into Albert's illegal squat were named Toad Boy and Westerling. They kicked the shit out of him, and then there were shots. He didn't know if anyone else lived on that floor. He'd only happened upon the place that day.

The hospital discharged Albert when he told them that he didn't have insurance.

His sister offered to fly him back to Los Angeles.

"I'd like to go back to school, Lu," he said. "I'd like to study history and find out what really happened with Great-Uncle Big Jim and the town of Hickton, Mississippi.

"You can come live with me," she said. "Daddy got sick after Betty Pann died. He bought a house in LA, and I took care of him till he passed."

"I have eighty-three thousand two hundred ninety-seven dollars and forty-two cents," Albert said.

"You do? Where you get that?"

"The money I collected while saving souls. I can give it to you, and then I won't be a charity case."

STARTING OVER

As I do almost every day, I'm starting over again, again. Now that I've passed the sixty-year mark, it seems as if each day is a new passage, a more deeply felt loss, or some unexpected plateau achieved.

When I was younger, life was a self-contained ebb and flow, as predictable as the tides under Luna. Breakfast and a drive, work from nine to five, the children as they became enthralled with one activity and then moved on without warning to new interests. Back then their lives changed daily, while Marguerite and I remained the same for them, even when we were lying, even when we feigned feelings and interest. She loved the children, and they her and me, and I loved the kids and her too. My feelings in the early days did not waver, not even when Marguerite and Gary Knowles ran away together and she was gone for twenty-three days while I was left alone to care for Juan, Alexander, and Trish.

I told the kids that Marguerite had gone back east because her mother was sick. The sanatorium, I said, was in a place where telephones didn't work. I didn't know that Gary had left Marguerite a week into their flight. He just needed somebody to help him out of the jam of his life: his alcoholic wife, their angry children, and the mounds of debt. He didn't know that he was using my wife, and she couldn't see past the euphoria of a world without whining children and a commonplace husband plucked off the rack.

"Jared?" she said, on that first call after she'd left me and he'd left her.

I was surprised, not about her call but because the only emotion I felt was relief.

"Yeah, Marge?"

"I'm so sorry."

"You don't have to be. My mother is staying with us, and the kids think that your mom is sick."

"I miss you," she said.

"I miss you too." It wasn't really a lie. Marguerite's departure left a crease like the misshapen dents in my fatty thigh when I sit too long on a wrinkled sofa. When I was young those crinkles used to smooth out in a few minutes, but as I have gotten older I find that they last, sometimes for hours.

"Can I come home?" she asked.

"It's your home too."

"You should know that we used protection," she said.

This pedestrian vow made me think about insurance. I wondered if I could start a business that would insure a person's life to remain as it was after having been violated by betrayal or, worse, a simple loss of faith.

"Come on home, Marguerite," I told my closest friend. "The children will be so happy that we'll probably have to take them to the zoo or something."

*   *   *

That was a long time ago, before we broke up for good.

The final rupture came years later. Juan and Trish were out of college by then, and Alexander was slogging his way through his sophomore year. He never made it to the halfway point, but I didn't see any problem with that. Alex liked to fish and got a job on a boat up in Alaska for a summer. He was the only black man on that boat or in the little coastal village where he'd met Solla, a Native woman who bore my first grandchild, Senta.

Well before Senta was born, Marguerite and I had decided to end our union.

I remember the evening our dissolution began. I was lighting a cigarette on the back porch, and Marguerite came out to ask me a question.

"Jared?" she called, opening the back door and catching me with the first cigarette that I'd smoked in twenty years.

Holly Martins, the office intern, had given it to me.

That morning Holly had said, for no particular reason that I could tell, "People are so afraid of dying that they don't even live the little bit of life they have."

She was dropping off client files I had asked for. Holly didn't know that it was my fifty-third birthday or that Marguerite and I had been arguing for the past four mornings about her quitting her management position at Rae, Wheeler, Johns, and Picket Financial Advisors. I only wanted her to work for seven more months, so we could take a trip to Rome before tightening our belts.

"I never wanted to go to Italy," Marguerite had said that morning. "And I can't take one more day of those sexist assholes."

"Do you smoke?" I asked Holly later that day, a few hours after her unasked-for existentialist sound bite on the general failure of humankind.

"Yes," she said. "Gitanes. They're French."

"Can I have one?"

She was wearing a flimsy, brown and pink dress that was both too short and too tight for proper office attire, but Mr. Angelo, our supervisor, was afraid to tell her that because it might be construed as sexual harassment.

She ran out of my cubicle, came back in less than a minute, and laid a nearly full pack of the French cigarettes before me. She smiled and stared into my eyes.

Holly was a pretty young woman in her twenties, rounded in ways that made me think of a comfortable sofa in a room full of hard chairs.

I had no idea that her unsolicited pronouncement, the cigarettes, and the faraway architectural vestiges of the Caesars would bring about such deep changes in me and my world.

For months after that day I thought that ideas sometimes worked like viruses, that if you heard even just one word at the right moment, dozens of lives, maybe hundreds, could be deeply impacted by a kind of mental contagion.

"What are you doing?" Marguerite asked that evening when I had just lit my first stubby little Gitane.

"Somebody . . ." I said and paused. I was thinking that if she had come out a minute before, I wouldn't have been caught. "Somebody dared me, and I'm trying to win the bet."

"By killing me?"

Marguerite had been treated for breast cancer six years earlier. They caught the few cells at a very early stage. That particular cancer was the least virulent variety, but it scared us both, and she, ever since then, had been on guard against carcinogens of all types. We no longer ate bacon, used aerosols, or allowed smoking anywhere nearby. Marge started meditating and exercised every morning for at least forty-five minutes. We never ate sweets, red meats, white flour, or starchy vegetables. She wouldn't allow cell-phone use in the house and harried our congresswoman with a barrage of letters urging a ban on the use of microwaves near schools and hospitals and, for that matter, in any neighborhood that didn't want the dangerous radiation pulsing through its inhabitants' flesh.

"That's why I'm doing it outside," I said, taking a drag of the harsh smoke. Even after twenty years I felt that nicotine rush as if I had last savored it only yesterday.

"You won't even put it out when I'm standing right here?"

"I'll blow the smoke out the screen."

"Don't you understand?" she said. "One molecule of that poison could start my cancer all over. That's why so many people who have never smoked die of lung cancer every year."

People are so afraid of dying that they don't even live the little bit of life they have.

I took another drag, and Marguerite hurried back into the house, slamming the door and throwing the bolt.

I was in my boxers and T-shirt on the screened-in porch, smoking that cigarette and loving every poisonous breath.

I rang the doorbell for an hour before breaking the living room window and climbing in that way. Marguerite ran out wild-eyed and indignant.

"What the hell are you trying to do?" she shouted.

"It was cold outside. What were you trying to do locking me out?"

"I was protecting my life," she said as a pronouncement. "How can I trust a man who wants to fill my air with poison?"

"I'll fix the window in the morning," I replied. "Right now I'm going to bed."

"Not my bed."

"No," I said, "mine. If you don't want to get contact cancer from me, you can go sleep on the couch or in some motel that has smoke-free anti-allergen rooms."

When I came downstairs in the morning, Marguerite was sitting at the dinette table drinking tea. Her eyes were both tired and troubled.

"Did you sleep?" I asked, going about the motions of making my French-press coffee.

"This is the end, you know."

"Like existence," I agreed, reminded of a phrase that Mrs. Anthony used in high school physics.

"What the fuck does that mean?" Marguerite had never before cursed in my presence.

"I know that it is," I said, quoting my science teacher, "but I don't know why."

Marguerite stood up so violently that her cedar chair fell on its back. She held her teacup up high by its ear and, with subdued but elegant flair, let it drop. The china shattered under a spray of glittering amber liquid. She stormed out of the dinette. A few seconds later I could hear her footsteps overhead, marching into our bedroom.

When my coffee was finished, I told myself to go up there and apologize for something I didn't quite understand. Child-rearing had taught me that understanding often comes after the apology, but even so I couldn't make that climb.

Instead I made another cup of bitter coffee and remembered a story my father, Bill Thistle, used to tell about himself and his friend Emir Rolf.

"When we lived in Cincinnati," Dad would say, "Rolfie worked the midnight shift at Westerly Fabrications, and I worked for a glove maker in the afternoon. I'd get home at eleven and wake him up. He'd get out of the bed, and I'd jump in."

I loved that story. Something about the burly men and that one bed that did double duty seemed like snugly tied shoes or tucked-in sheets. Their life was balanced and trusting.

"But what if one of you got sick?" I would always ask my dad.

"We never did," he'd say.

Marguerite always made more money than I did. She used her degree to climb the rungs of finance, whereas I worked on the flat plane of insurance claims. It was my assignment to prove that as many claims as possible fell outside the range of my company's, and its shareholders', liability.

That day was the beginning of a new pattern of actions in my life. I didn't buy coffee from the cart downstairs, and though I got in the elevator, I went to the sixth floor instead of the sixteenth.

Melanie Farr of the Belasco Insurance human-resources department greeted me with a smile.

"Yes? Can I help you?"

"My name is Thistle," I said, and she smiled as many do when they hear the lisp folded into my name.

"How can I help you, Mr. Thistle?"

"I've worked here at BI for thirty-one years, Ms. Farr," I said. I was standing before her desk with my hands held together in front of me as if I were being modest. "I started out as a file clerk, but after I graduated from college I was offered a position in claims. I was good at finding little flaws and clauses that helped justify our responses, but I didn't have management qualities and so I've stayed in the same job most of that time."

As I spoke, the smile slowly faded from Ms. Farr's wide, oddly beautiful face. She was in her early forties, I figured, a decade

63

younger than I. She was beginning to worry that I'd be a problem. I supposed that her job was like mine in some ways; people would come to her with issues, and she'd try to resolve them in such a way as to cause the least trouble for BI, its officers, and its shareholders.

"And what is your problem, Mr. Thistle?" She was typing on the keyboard of her computer, as I did whenever a claim crossed my blotter.

"No problem, Ms. Farr. It's just that I need to leave this job."

"You're resigning?"

"Yes."

"As of when?"

"Today. I know people usually give two weeks' notice, but I have an urgent issue that needs to be addressed, and after I'm done with that I wouldn't be coming back anyway."

"Have you told your supervisor?"

"I'd rather you do that. Mr. Mallory doesn't have much patience when people need time off. I'm certain that he'd send me up here if I told him that I'm—"

"You've worked for the company over thirty years," Ms. Farr said, interrupting my explanation. She was reading my personal data off her computer screen.

"Yes. I told you that," I said.

"You have built up quite a large retirement account with us."

"Oh?"

"You don't know?"

"I never really thought about retirement. It just seemed like I'd be at that desk until I died one day. Statistics say that I'd probably die at home or in a hospital, but I suppose I could fall dead of a heart attack anywhere—even at my desk."

The woman's broad face suddenly turned sympathetic.

"You haven't considered early retirement?"

"No," I said.

"At fifty-three," she said, rolling her eyes upward to look at the general figures in her head, "with more than twenty-five years, you could get about thirty-two percent of your current salary."

"OK."

"In order to get that you'll have to go through the early-retirement process. That would take about three months."

"But today is my last day," I said, with a certainty I'd rarely felt.

"That's silly, Mr. Thistle," she lisped. "If you leave today you would only receive the face value of the account."

"What are you doing?" Holly Martins asked as I was putting my belongings into an empty Xerox-paper box that I got from the copy room. The sum total of my work life fit in the space it took to hold eight reams of impossibly white paper.

"Packing," I said to the young philosopher.

She was wearing a red dress and no hose. The flesh of her arms and legs there in that otherwise sexless atmosphere made me happy.

"You moving offices?" she asked.

"Have you ever been to Italy?"

"No," she said, giving the word one and a half syllables.

"When are you having lunch?"

"In twenty-seven minutes."

When I got home, there were still shards of broken china on the kitchen floor. Splinters of shattered teacup were plastered in place by dried honeyed tea. When I went out on the screened-in back porch, the first thing I thought of was smoking.

I had smoked another Gitane on the walk to Samba Sam's Jamaican Delights with Holly. I wanted another one now, but Marguerite was in the backyard, wearing a coral blouse, turquoise pants, and yellow flip-flops. She was watering the hundred or more potted plants with the long-spouted copper watering can. The terra-cotta pots were set on tiered shelving that looked like miniature bleachers at the back wall of the yard.

Seeing my wife at the zenith of her domestic bliss, I realized why she needed to quit working. She had loved her job, whereas I had never really cared about mine. Her advancement had been a source of pride for her before, and after, the desertion with Gary Knowles.

She loved her job, but as the years rolled by that relationship had gone cool. She still hoped for that early passion, but new bosses and different needs pushed her to the side, left her unsatisfied. Now all she had was a backyard that would respond and flower to her touch.

I knew for a fact that Marguerite needed to rest and heal in the safety of that footprint of terra-cotta and green. My empathy, however, was tempered by events earlier in the day. On the way to Samba Sam's, I remembered that I didn't have much cash, and so I went to the ATM machine to find that our joint checking account had a balance of only three dollars. Both savings accounts had been emptied and closed that morning.

Holly had to pay for our lunch.

I'd arrived home at three minutes past three.

Marguerite turned, wiping her brow, and saw me standing there.

"Jare," she mouthed.

I tried to remember anything important that had happened in the last twenty years.

There were the children, of course, but their lives were their own now. There was the house, but I'd soon be moving out of there, with no expectation of nostalgia or feeling of loss.

Marguerite walked up to the bottom stair of the porch and smiled at me. It was a stranger's expectant acknowledgment.

"You're home early," she said.

"You are too."

"I never went in," she replied. "I was too tired, and so I slept until just an hour ago."

"I came home to apologize," I said, matching her lie for lie.

"Are you going to fix the window?" she asked.

"Tomorrow," I said, thinking, *When you clean the fucking kitchen floor.*

"Why don't we sit down?"

Marguerite waved at two fiberglass lawn chairs that I'd bought eleven years before. The skeletal-looking seats had been bright red when they were new, but the years outside had faded them to a pink-tinted gray. While I went to work day after day, their luster had succumbed to sunlight.

"Sure," I said, and we sat at a forty-five-degree angle to each other, the convergence of our stares meeting at the screen door where our marriage had finally failed.

"Are you still smoking?"

"No. That was just a bet."

"Stupid bet."

"Yeah. I guess it was."

"You really scared me breaking the window like that," she said with no real emotion.

"I got a splinter of your china cup in my eye," I replied. Lying to her was becoming . . . second nature. "Had to go down to the company nurse to have her take it out."

"I didn't mean for that to happen," was her apology.

I felt the stirrings of an erection. That and the lying brought about a thrumming in my heart. I turned to look at my wife. She was a new person, a whole Otherness, in the yard that I had never, ever sat in before.

"What?" she asked of my expression.

"My dick is hard," I said in wonder.

"I hope you don't think that I'm going to do anything about that."

"Of course not," I said, in a falsely reassuring tone. "You asked, and I'm telling you that my dick is hard."

"Stop saying that."

I stood up in front of the mother of my children, my pants displaying the outline of the modest erection. Marguerite stared in wonder. I was sure that she'd thought I was lying. Seeing it, a confused look twisted its way across her face.

"I'm going upstairs to jack off," I said.

I rolled against my marital mattress thinking not of sex, not exactly, but of the conversation Holly and I had at lunch.

"You broke the window?" she asked, interrupting the long and somewhat banal tale.

"She wouldn't let me in."

"And that was just because I gave you that cigarette?"

"No," I said again, as I pressed my groin down against the thick wadding of the mattress. "It was because you said that thing about people not living their lives. You said it about everybody else, but I was thinking about me. I am not living my life. I needed that cigarette to live, and Marguerite blew up without even asking why. She thought I was trying to kill her, not save myself."

"No," Holly assured me, or maybe she was trying to convince herself that she wasn't somehow complicit in an attempted murder-by-nicotine.

"She lives in mortal fear of death," I said, knowing the truth as it came out of my mouth. "Dread like that has no room for half measures."

"And what are you going to do now?" the pretty, chubby, and young mocha-brown office gofer asked.

"I'm told that I have a fully matured life policy with BI and a settlement of one hundred and ninety-six thousand dollars for my retirement fund. I want to go to Rome in the next month or so. Would you like to come with me?"

I was thumping down hard on the mattress when remembering the question.

"Like your girlfriend?"

"Like anything you want to be. I just need the company."

"And you'd pay?"

"Of course."

"How long?"

"You tell me that. I don't even know how long I'll be there."

"Sure, I'll go," Holly said. "I might even like you enough to stay."

I groaned in expectation of the orgasm; that groan turned into a shout. I could hear Marge's footfalls on the stairs, but the door was closed and I knew she wouldn't come in. I was sweating and so happy that a young woman would fly with me across the ocean to the site of an ancient empire that once conquered a world.

"Jare!" Marguerite shouted through the closed door.

"Don't come in!"

"What's happening in there?"

"Don't come in, Marguerite," I said again. "I'm just getting used to what's happened."

★ ★ ★

All that was seven years ago. The divorce was civil if not amicable, because I agreed to share all of my money and Marguerite finally consented to buying me out of the house.

I live in a studio apartment in downtown LA and work for myself. I incorporated under the name Big Bad Investments (BBI) and, doing business in that name, bought e-mail lists from BI and a dozen other insurance companies. I then sent out a broad blast to every policyholder saying that I was an expert on the devious ways in which insurance companies refuse to pay. I charge between two and five hundred dollars to review a policy before the claim is made, one thousand dollars plus expenses to dispute any refusal of payment.

I take a long walk every morning. Last week my left knee began to hurt halfway through the constitutional. This pain is new, and I pay close attention, as it catches on every other step.

My children with Marguerite have shunned me, but I still mark their birthdays and call them on Christmas.

Holly got pregnant on the Riviera under a crescent moon. She lives walking distance from my studio, 1,727 little stitches of pain away.

Our daughter is named Roma, and she entered first grade last week.

Holly has a boyfriend named Henry. He doesn't like me, but I think he's a fine young man.

Marguerite had a relapse of the cancer two years after we parted. I stayed with her for three weeks because our children were living too far away and she's the only daughter of parents who were both only children. She blamed that cigarette for her condition. I accepted that. We didn't talk much, and I stayed in Alexander's room. Late at night I could hear her come to our son's door, sniffing the air. She was still searching for a whiff of my infidelity, proof that everything she believed was justified.

LEADING FROM
THE AFFAIR

"**C**ome in," the graying blond woman said, after we made our introductions at the threshold. "Have a seat."

Three padded blue chairs around a low triangular table made up the furnishings of the small office. No desk. No bookcase. The blinds were pulled down over the window. A nonintrusive tan and blue carpet covered the floor from wall to wall. The sounds of traffic could be heard quite clearly, as Dr. Quarterly's room was on the first floor facing onto East Eighty-First Street.

Noting the hiss of tires racing on the wet streets outside, I took the chair set off a little to the right. She remained standing a moment.

Dr. Agnes Quarterly was maybe five eight and slender. In her late forties, she seemed older but not worn or unattractive. There was a gravitas to her bearing, in spite of the smile.

She wore a dark blue dress suit and a white blouse that buttoned up like a man's shirt. Her shoes were dark, dark red with one-inch heels, the leather hard and shiny—almost like plastic.

She sat across from me, her spine erect, not resting against the back of the chair. This caused me to sit up a little straighter.

"So," she began, "Mr. Lassiter, you're looking for a therapist."

"Yeah . . . uh, yes, I am."

Her salt-and-butter hair was combed but only just. It wasn't coiffed or *done*. There was a slight indentation on the bridge of her nose. I wondered where the glasses were and also where was the book or papers that she'd been reading before I'd arrived.

"Have you been in psychotherapy before?"

"No. Never."

"So, what makes you feel you need it now?" She was watching my eyes, looking, I believed, for signs of depravity.

"It's . . ." I said and then hesitated.

"Yes?" Her voice was mild, not commanding or insistent.

"I'm stuck."

Slightest insinuation of a smile appeared on her lips.

"How are you stuck?"

"I . . ." My heart was beating fast, and I could feel my ears getting hot. I hadn't expected this reaction. For a moment I thought I might be experiencing the beginnings of a heart attack.

"Are you all right?"

"Yes. It's just that, I guess I'm a little nervous."

"There's no need. Everything we say in this room is confidential. You are free to speak your mind."

"And can I keep my secrets too?"

"You only need say what you feel comfortable saying," she said. "And what you did say was that you feel stuck. In what way?"

"It's like," I said, falling into an old, familiar groove, "everybody in the world was standing at a line at the start. Millions and millions of people preparing to get on with their lives. A signal was given, and we all began to move forward. Almost everybody was traveling at the rate of ten miles a year. That's like the normal rate."

I realized that I was looking at the floor, so I raised my head. Dr. Quarterly was gazing at me with what I can only call intense passivity.

"Everybody but me," I continued. "Me, I'm racing ahead at fifty miles a year, but at the same time I'm going backward at forty-nine point nine miles. And so at the end of each year, almost everyone around me has traveled ahead ten miles, while I've gone ten times that but am only a tenth of a mile farther from the starting line."

I could see in the therapist's expression that she was impressed with the explanation. She had no idea that I was a fraud.

"What do you do for a living, Mr. Lassiter?"

"I'm a copy editor for about a dozen online magazines run by the Din-Pro Consortium."

"What kind of magazines?"

"Everything from political news reports to sex stories," I said. "Sometimes the magazines morph into different kinds of content. It sounds technological, very twenty-first century, but it's not. I just do what copy editors have been doing for the past two hundred years."

"Do they pay you well?"

"I know your fee," I said. "I can pay."

"I'm not asking that. I'm wondering why you feel that you're not making headway. I mean there must be others around you who would love to have a job like yours. So many people are unemployed nowadays."

"It's not my job," I said. "Somebody else might love doing what I'm doing. That person would be traveling at a normal rate. Another person might have just gotten fired, but he has a wife who tells him that it's OK and maybe a child, so he sees hope for the future.

"I have a job I don't care for and a studio apartment with a TV and a computer, a girlfriend who I think is looking for a better relationship, and no way out."

"You feel lost," she said, and I had to clench my jaw to keep from crying.

"Yes."

We talked about my father, who is dead; and my mother, who no longer recognizes me; my age, which is near sixty; and my girlfriend, whose name is Jool.

"Does Jool live with you?" Quarterly asked.

"No. She owns a condo in downtown Brooklyn. She's very good with money . . ."

I got home at 4:17 by the big digital clock that I have framed and mounted on the wall like a painting. I sat next to the window, with its light-and-dark-gray frame, gazing onto Lexington Avenue. Snow was dancing in the breeze, undecided, it seemed, whether it was falling or maybe just hanging there, twirling.

Night was almost come; the darkness was filtering into my brain.

"Hello?" I said, answering the phone on the first ring.

It was dark outside, and the same flakes still seemed to be spinning, now in lamplight, like some Einsteinian law made manifest through slapdash serendipity.

"I called this afternoon, but you weren't there," Jool said.

"What time is it?"

"Seven forty-five."

"I've been sitting here for hours."

"You didn't call back."

"I wasn't here."

"I left a message."

"I didn't listen to the messages."

"What's wrong, Frank?" Jool asked.

We were lying side by side, not touching, in my queen-size bed. We'd had sex, showered, and then brushed our teeth, side by side.

"I'm stuck," I said.

"You've been telling me that for nine years."

"Then why do you keep asking?"

"Doesn't your therapist help at all?" she asked.

Jool put her dark hand upon my darker chest. Her baby finger tickled my nipple by mistake. I shivered.

"He tries to help me," I said. "One time, a long time ago, he changed my life. Back then I was lost."

"Maybe you need a new therapist," she suggested.

"No. Dr. Aguilera knows me better than anyone."

"Then maybe he could give you some kind of antidepressant or something."

"Did you kiss him?"

"Who?" Jool asked.

"J Silver."

She sat straight up in the bed. At forty-four, Jool still had a youthful figure. Her skin was young, and her eyes always in focus.

"Did you look in my e-mails?"

"Did you suck his dick?"

She shoved back away from me, and for a moment I thought that she was falling out of the bed. But then she stood up and gathered her clothes from the stuffed chair in the corner.

I watched her getting dressed. It was always the same order: panties, bra, blouse, skirt. Then she stepped into her Uggs and picked up her bag.

"It's three in the morning," I said.

She had to put down the shoulder bag to don her gray nylon down coat.

"You never talk to me," she said, once she was ready to go.

"I'm talking now."

"You have no right," she said.

"Let me make us some coffee," I pleaded. "We can at least wait till the sun comes up."

She didn't wait, didn't say another word, just stormed out, taking the last ort of passion from the room along with her.

"She just left you in the middle of the night?" Christian Aguilera asked me three days later. His office was on the far East Side, over-looking the river.

"Yeah," I said. "We were talking in bed, and I asked her about J Silver. It just came out."

"How long ago did you find out about him?"

"Ten months."

"Why didn't you ever mention it in here?"

"I don't know. I thought if I talked about it, I'd get mad and then Jool would leave."

"And is she still seeing him?"

"I don't think so."

"Then why spring it on her in the middle of the night?"

"She . . . she was asking me why I feel so, so disassociated, and then she wondered what good you were doing. She wanted me to take antidepressants."

"And that made you angry?"

"I guess."

"Angrier than her affair with J Silver?"

I couldn't find a way into that question. I'd never met J Silver. I didn't even know what he was—what color or religion. It was hard to be angry at a man without a face or identity.

"I don't know," I said at last.

"Then why didn't you just say to Jool that you didn't want her telling you what drugs to take?"

"Hi, Mr. Lassiter," Kara Gunderson said.

Kara was a counter waitress at the Bebop Diner on West Fifty-Seventh. She always took my order.

"Hi, Kara. How are you?"

"Did you finish editing that nasty article?" she asked.

"Which one?"

"The one about the ad exec having sex with her dog."

"Yeah. She withdrew the piece though."

"Too embarrassed?"

"She sent an e-mail calling me a Nazi censor because I cut out a few of the details that she repeated over and over."

"I guess she just didn't want to be corrected."

"No one does. Do you want my order?"

"Has it changed?"

"No."

Kara's smile was beautiful. The olive-gold skin and lush almond-shaped eyes marked her Asian features with a sculptural quality.

"Which one of your parents is Swedish?" I asked on a whim.

"Neither," she said. "I'm adopted."

At 2:57 A.M. by the framed clock the phone rang.

I was sitting at the window holding the tiny slip of paper that had Kara's phone number on it. From early evening until about eleven I was thinking about making the call, but my mind kept going in circles: She was too young or I was too old. What did younger women want with older men except for security and then marriage? What did I want from her that I didn't already get three afternoons a week at the lunch counter? What would we talk about? How could I touch her?

"Hello?" I said into the phone.

"What do you care what I did or didn't do with Jim?" Jool asked.

"Jim?"

"Jim Silver."

"Um . . . I guess maybe I don't care."

She hung up.

I didn't wonder about the call. We hadn't spoken at all since she'd left. Instead I worried about waiting too long and not calling Kara in time. I worried that if I didn't call her, I wouldn't be able to show my face at the diner again.

The phone rang.

"Hello?"

"How long have you known?"

"I don't know," I lied. "At least nine months."

"And in all that time you didn't say anything?"

The answer was obvious, so I didn't reply.

"You didn't act like you knew," Jool said, now a bit calmer. "If anything you were nicer, more loving."

"I guess."

"I haven't seen Jim in six months. Why ask me now?"

"Because you were telling me to take drugs."

"That doesn't make any sense. I was trying to help you."

For a long while we were both silent.

"Frank."

"Yes."

"Do you want me to come over?"

"No."

"So we're through?"

"It's late."

"Why haven't you called me?"

"You're the one who walked out."

"And so how have you been, Mr. Lassiter?" Dr. Quarterly asked.

I was sitting in the same blue chair. She didn't have that little indentation on the bridge of her nose that day.

Her dress suit was gray.

"I broke up with my girlfriend."

"I'm sorry to hear that. What happened?"

I told her about the late-night talk.

"She thinks that I should prescribe antidepressants for you after just one meeting?"

"What do you think?" I asked.

"You seem to be somewhat unhappy, but I won't know how to proceed until we've had at least a few more meetings."

I sighed, feeling relieved of something I could not have put into words.

"Why did you mention her lover so long after the affair was over?" she asked.

I said something, but afterward I couldn't remember what it was.

"You're very quiet today, Frank," Dr. Aguilera said.

He's a beefy man, much larger than I. Size aside, his dark eyes have always been his most imposing quality.

"Do you think I'm depressed?" I asked.

"What do you think?"

"About what you think?"

Aguilera smiled, then grinned.

"What's wrong, Frank?"

"I realized that I've been coming to see you for thirty-one years next week," I said. "And I don't even know if you're married, have kids, or where you live."

"You've never asked."

"I was living in a shelter when I first came here," I said, as some kind of retort.

"But you didn't tell me about it until you'd found an apartment a year later."

"Back then I changed very fast," I said, performing a ritual. "Because of you, I went to school and became a journalist. I made something out of myself."

"Yes, you did."

"But now I'm stuck again. Jool left me but calls every night. She says that she wants to come over."

"What do you want?"

"I don't know."

"Do you want to see Jool?"

"I don't want anything . . . nothing. All I want is for it all to be over or for it to change into something . . . I don't know, unexpected."

"What does that mean?" Aguilera asked.

"I don't know."

"Maybe we should discuss medication again."

"No," I said. "I don't want to do drugs."

"Hi, Mr. Lassiter," Kara said that afternoon at the Bebop.

"How are you, Kara?"

"I was worried that you wouldn't come back after I gave you my number and you didn't call."

"We should have dinner together."

"When?" Her answer was light and friendly.

"Tonight."

Two nights later I was lying awake thinking about the brief good-night kiss that Kara had given me. We'd had dinner two nights in a row.

"I like talking to you because you don't seem like a New Yorker," she'd said at the end of the second date. We were standing at the subway entrance near Broadway and Houston. "I mean, you seem interested in things outside the city and, and outside you."

That's when she kissed my cheek, a big smile on her luminescent face.

The phone rang.

"Hello?"

"Where were you the last two nights?" Jool asked.

"Where were you?"

After a brief pause she said, "I guess I deserve that. I mean, I'm the one who walked out and, and who cheated."

I was thinking about the double "and" from both Kara and Jool. This united them in my mind, making me feel like there was a blood-knot in my head.

"It's late, Jool," I said.

"We should get together and talk."

"We don't talk so well," I said.

"I'll answer any question you have."

I asked her about Jim and when they'd met and what they'd done. She answered my questions, in great detail, even though I think we both knew I didn't want to hear most of it.

"Then why open yourself up for something that hurts?" Dr. Agnes Quarterly asked.

"At least that way I'm feeling something," I said.

"And is that worth it?"

"It is, just before she starts talking."

"What does that mean?"

"I want to ask," I said, "and I want her to be willing to answer. It's just that once she starts talking, what she says hurts me."

The look on the therapist's face was intent and quizzical, like that of a mathematician staring at a convoluted, inexplicably erroneous equation.

"Maybe we should try you out on an antidepressant. There's a new one called Lessenin-60. We can start you on a low dosage."

"OK."

There were things that Jool had refused to do with Jim Silver. They'd had safe sex, and she'd interrogated him about his health before they had sex the first time.

I filled the prescription for the antidepressant but never took the blue-and-pink capsules.

"I don't think I'll ever get married," twenty-nine-year-old Kara Gunderson told me at a falafel bar in Times Square. "I mean, I don't want kids, and what other reason is there for getting married?"

"I don't know," I said. "You get old and you want company and somebody to share the load."

"Everybody breaks up," she said. "You can't count on them staying with you."

I buzzed Jool's apartment at a little past midnight. Kara and I had made out for a while in a doorway on West Forty-Eighth. She'd disengaged from the embrace, telling me that she didn't want to move too fast.

"Hello?" my ex-girlfriend said through the speaker.

"Hi."

"Frank?"

"Yeah."

It was at least a full minute before she said anything else.

"You, you can't come up now, honey," she said, pitying me.

When I was a few steps away, I heard her say something else but couldn't make out the words.

The next afternoon the phone rang, and I was surprised to hear Bob Brandt on the line.

Bob was the head editor at Din-Pro Consortium. We almost always communicated through e-mails.

"Hi, Frank," he said. "How are you?"

"OK. I mean, I guess I could complain, but nobody listens, right?"

"Yeah. You got that right."

"How come you're calling?" I asked.

"Din-Pro's cutting back, Frank. They've taken a big hit in advertising revenue, and I'm going to have to take half your editing load."

"Oh."

"And they're cutting your rate by ten percent. They wanted to cut it by fifteen, but I talked them out of it."

"Oh. Wow. Thanks, Bob."
Thanks, Bob.

Both Aguilera and Quarterly allowed me to reduce my payments by fifty percent. I kept seeing them—her on Monday mornings and him on Thursday afternoons.

I asked Christian what the effects of Lessenin-60 were and translated that into the experiences that Agnes expected.

Kara got me a part-time dishwashing job at the Bebop. We got more serious, and she stayed over once or twice a week.

A few weeks later, when I was alone, the phone rang a little after midnight.

"Hello?"

"Are you alone?" Jool asked.

"Yeah. Sure."

"Can I come up?"

"Where are you?"

"Across the street."

That was the best sex I'd ever had. Something had been building up ever since we'd separated. I would sit in bed at night thinking of all the things she'd told me, that I'd asked her, about Jim Silver.

"Have you been seeing him again?" I asked, when we were spent, in the early hours of the morning.

"Yes," she whispered.

"Are you in love?"

"It might be that," she said. "But more it's like I have to do something. You're always saying how you're stuck or whatever, and I'm just getting older. Jim wants to move in with me and maybe get more serious. And you wouldn't even let me come over."

"You always said that you liked living alone," I said, "that you had gotten used to your ways."

"That was before you asked me if I had kissed Jim."

"Not when she first met him?" Dr. Quarterly asked.

"No. She'd met him at a design conference and, she says, just kind of fell into a sexual thing. But then when I asked her about it, she started to wonder about why I'd be jealous when our lives were so separate. I guess she realized how lonely she was."

"And how do you feel about that?"

"It hurts when I see her, and it hurts when I don't."

Jool and I saw each other every night for a week, and then it was over. She called and said that she couldn't do it anymore.

"But things have been so strong," I said, almost arguing.

"We're acting like kids," she said. "I'm not sleeping, and sometimes when I'm at your house I'm afraid of the way you look at me."

"It's just that I feel, I don't know, desperate for you."

"That's not what I need from a man."

"Can't we get together and talk about it?"

"No. It's over. I'm not seeing you anymore."

I was sitting on the bed when Jool was breaking up with me for the second time. I felt relieved. Our relationship had run off the road, and that was that.

Sixteen minutes after Jool and I hung up, the phone rang.

I was hoping that it was her calling back and also that she had not changed her mind. I wanted to talk more about getting back together but not to change what had already been decided.

"Hello?"

"Hi, Frank." It was Kara.

"Hey."

"You haven't really been sick have you?"

"No. I've had some, um, some personal problems."

"I don't want to see you anymore, Frank. It's just not working. I mean . . . we're too different. You're too old."

Those last three, or maybe four, words hurt me, not because of my age but because I could tell that Kara was trying to hurt me. Her intention was its own end.

"I've been seeing another therapist," I said to Dr. Aguilera that Thursday at the end of our session.

"What do you mean?"

"For the past two months I've been going to another therapist."

"Why?"

"Because I'm stuck, and everything's falling apart around me."

"I'm surprised that another doctor would see you knowing that you were already in a therapeutic relationship."

"I didn't tell her."

"I don't understand, Frank. It doesn't make sense."

"I can't explain it very well. I've needed to move on, and I didn't know how. Every day is just like the last. I feel like I'm drowning, like I'm asleep and can't wake up."

"We should discuss this at length," he said. "Not at the end of our time."

"Now let me get this straight," Dr. Quarterly said that Friday, at a special time she made available for me. "You have another therapist and have been in treatment with him for the past thirty years."

"Yes," I said, "but I've chosen you."

"You said that you hadn't been in therapy before."

"Because I wanted to start on a clean slate, to be sure that I could make some advancement with you."

"But you lied."

"Those were the secrets I told you about in our first meeting."

"No, Mr. Lassiter. The basic expectation in therapy is that the patient and the doctor maintain as much honesty as they are capable of."

"What are you saying?" I asked.

Both Aguilera and Quarterly ended therapeutic relations with me. Three months later I received an invitation to the after-ceremony wedding reception of Jool Lanscome and James Silver.

Kara moved back to Minnesota to her pseudo-Scandinavian roots.

When Bob Brandt cut my editing down to three online publications, I moved into a rooming house in Staten Island and started an online publication of my own, called *Broken Hearts Monthly*, which has been wildly successful. It started out as a blog telling my own stupid story. But I got so many responses that, with Bob's help, I organized a virtual publication that presents confessionals, artwork, poems, short stories, and also a dating service.

I work so hard at the magazine that I have little time for any kind of social life. But I've been slowly thinking of getting back into therapy. Nowadays I've become so popular that I'm often invited as an expert on love and relationships. The anxiety this notoriety produces is sublime and, at the same time, almost unbearable.

CUT, CUT, CUT

1.

"There's a marked difference between brain functions, knowledge, and mental potentials," Martin Hull said to Marilee Frith-DeGeorgio at Mike's Steaks on Forty-Seventh Street just east of Grand Central Station. The time was 6:46 P.M. on a clear and bright Tuesday in late May.

This was their first meeting—a blind date, inasmuch as they'd met through the online dating service People for People, provided by one of the few surviving alternative lifestyle magazines from California's Bay Area, *The Revolution Will Not Be Televised.*

The questionnaire provided for subscribers to *TRWNBT*'s People for People allowed participants to enter gender identity and preference, intellectual endeavors, personal ambitions, and accomplishments in life. The survey did not ask for race, age, income bracket, religious orientation, or physical proportions. One could *fudge* a few of the banned subjects by surreptitiously including them in the essay-like answers to the questions provided.

Marilee, for instance, had typed in that her most profound political ambition was to one day computerize the voting process in America based on the positive concept of what people wanted and not what they did not want or were afraid of. She added (parenthetically) that she had no patience for people who harbored antidemocratic thoughts.

"In my ideal system," she told Martin that evening, "people would be voting for what they had in common, not what they hated or feared about each other."

Martin considered it his greatest *personal* accomplishment that he had run a half marathon every other week for one year, four years earlier. He did not, could not, mention that he was a dark brown man, descendant of a long line of slaves and sharecroppers from the Mississippi Delta. Marilee was surprised that a *black* man had filled out the People for People form she'd read. But she decided to go through with the date because of the caveat clause in the PFP e-contract.

PFP was the go-between for first dates and electronically queried the participants within a week of the rendezvous. If it was reported that either party had not shown up, or left before the date actually started, a mark was put in the offender's file. If any member of PFP got three such marks, he or she was deleted from the service.

The week before, Marilee had been scheduled to meet a man named Joseph Exeter. Joe was a portly man, and Marilee quite small in comparison. Joe's breathing was loud, and from time to time, a not very pleasant odor wafted from his side of the table at the Midtown sushi bar. When their second drink had not dimmed her olfactory awareness of Exeter, Marilee excused herself to go to the restroom and never returned.

So she would have to sit through this date, because PFP was the best dating service that she'd encountered since her divorce from Paris DeGeorgio, a latent conservative and an outright thief.

Martin Hull was the opposite of both Marilee's last date and first husband. He was two inches shorter and maybe five pounds lighter than Marilee, who was five seven and 135 pounds. She worked out every day for an hour and a half, so her few extra pounds looked good in the step-class mirror.

"But I thought you were a plastic surgeon," she said, in response to his pontificating on the contrasting qualities of the human brain.

"That's my day job," he said with a smile. His grin, Marilee thought, was both goofy and sincere. "But the neurological sciences are my passion."

"Why didn't you become a brain surgeon then?"

"That would be like an abstract artist becoming a house painter."

"Really?" Marilee said. "I thought that that kind of surgery was the very top of the field."

"Not really," Martin said, crinkling his nose and exposing the gap between upper his teeth. "Surgeons all specialize. Cut, cut, cut—that's their whole life. That's the way they get so proficient. They do the same procedures day in and day out—thousands of them; might as well be working on a production line."

"At five million dollars a year," Marilee added.

"Yeah, I guess. But, you know, I'd need a lot more money than that if I had to do the same thing every day for the rest of my life."

"Except for sex, food, and good music," Marilee said. Martin's size and goofy demeanor gave her the courage to say what was on her mind.

He smiled, half-nodded, and looked down, saying, "I meant one's working life."

Marilee felt a twitch in her chest and wondered what kind of sex partner a small, shy man like this might be.

"So you said that you're divorced," Martin prompted.

"Paris DeGeorgio," she replied, nodding out every other syllable.

"Sounds like a good name for a clothes designer."

"That wasn't his birth name. He was born Anastazy Kozubal."

"Polish, huh?"

"You knew that? Everyone else ends up asking me where the name comes from. The first guess is almost always Russia."

"That's because of *Anastazy*," Martin said. "Makes it sound like a tsarina. I like to study those parts of language that make humanity a culture as well as a species. The brain, you know."

"I had a business selling Mexican wheat to various South and Central American nations," Marilee said.

"Mexican wheat?"

"There are some large farms in the southern highlands. I organized them over the Internet and made a two-percent profit. It was going pretty good, until one day I found out that Paris was skimming my profits and donating to this group called the New Redeemers . . ."

"California archconservatives, right?" Martin asked.

"Only," Marilee continued, "he had made a kickback deal with the treasurer and was salting half the money away in a Jamaican bank."

"Wow."

"Are you ready to order?" a tall waiter in a bright green three-piece suit asked.

Martin gestured for Marilee to go first. It was at that moment she decided to take him home.

2.

"That was amazing," she said in her own bed, lying next to Martin Hull, a man she had met only six hours before.

"Yeah," Martin said, unable to suppress his toothful grin.

"I never had a man pay such close attention to my body."

"Well, you know," Martin said shyly, "when you're a little guy with no hidden talents you have to learn to work harder."

"I'm still trying to catch my breath."

"Want me to get you some water?" he asked.

"Is that the doctor talking?"

"You know, I liked your idea about online voting," he said. "The negative side of democracy is that people usually vote either for their pocketbooks or against what they're afraid of."

"I'm sorry I said that stuff about brain surgeons," she said then, feeling that she should be nice to the plain little man with the magic kisses. "I'm sure plastic surgeons do good work too."

"I do a lot of community-service stuff," he agreed. "You know . . . reconstructive work for those that can't afford it."

"Like harelips?"

"Or old scars . . . even regrettable tattoos," he said. "It would be cool if you could vote at home every night. Just turn your smart TV to the political choices channel and make your mark."

"Why do you keep doing that?"

"What?"

"Every time I ask about you, you say one thing and then turn the subject back to me. Is that one of the ways you try harder?"

"I guess it is. I mean, I know that people like talking about themselves, and there's not much I have to say."

"You seem interested in the brain."

"Yeah, but whenever I start talking about it, people always point out that I'm a plastic surgeon."

"I'm sorry about that," Marilee said.

"It's OK. You're right. I should be more, um, revealing."

"You said you were married once?"

"To Sonora Simonson," he said, sitting up with the words.

"That's an odd name."

"Yeah. Her mother named her but never said why she chose it. They'd never been to Mexico, and no one in the entire family spoke Spanish. I asked them all one Christmas."

"Why did you two split?"

"I was conferring with an intestinal-tract expert, Philip Landries. He'd come to our apartment quite often. Sonora made dinner for us whenever he stayed late. One day I came home and found a note from her saying that she was out with a girlfriend at a movie. Philip was supposed to drop by, but he didn't. Sonora didn't come home, and Philip was gone for good. I got a letter from them nineteen months later. He'd gotten a job in Amsterdam and asked her to go with him."

"And they left, just like that?" Marilee asked. "Didn't even say anything?"

"Not to anyone. The police investigated me for over a year. They were sure that Phil and Sonny were having an affair and that I killed them. There was credit-card evidence of them staying in a Midtown hotel."

"Oh my God. Did they arrest you?"

"Not formally, but I was called down to the local station six times. Once they questioned me for over eight hours."

"Did you get a lawyer?"

"No. I knew I hadn't killed them, and so I just continued with my work."

"You don't sound like you were very broken up over their betrayal."

"There was a kind of a, of an unconscious trade-off," Martin said, frowning and allowing his head to tilt to the side.

"A trade-off?"

"Phil was in research," the plastic surgeon explained. "The intestines of all living beings are rife with various kinds of parasites. Many of these creatures, these parasites, are symbiotic. They live in harmony with the systems they inhabit. You gotta love that Darwin."

"What does that have to do with your wife running off with your friend?" Marilee asked.

"Phil wasn't really my friend. I paid him to consult with me about the more exotic intestinal parasites. That's where I learned about the hydra-monotubular-tridacteri."

"The what?"

Martin repeated the name and said, "It's a microscopic parasite that can be bred and altered in a fairly simple controlled environment. You can suppress its reproductive cycles and implant it with differing forms of DNA, which it, in turn, blends into the host system. Those traits make it one of the greatest possible biological and genetic delivery systems."

"And the man that gave this to you was fucking your wife."

"Painful," Martin admitted. "But in the grand scheme of things a minor indiscretion."

"Minor? A woman does that to you and you aren't devastated?"

"No, no," Martin said, though he wasn't really denying her implied accusation. "I mean, I felt bad, but three days before they went off, Phil brought me a rare specimen that I dubbed hydra-monotubular-tridacteri-1."

Unable to think of a response or even a question, Marilee sat up too.

"It's what they call a microsite, almost exactly the same as the original HMT but mutated, with a slightly different DNA count," Martin Hull continued. "I realized that by crossbreeding the species, you could, theoretically, create an HMT hinny."

"A what?"

"It's like a mule. A creature that exists but cannot reproduce, making it a perfect biological delivery system, because after it does its job it dies."

There was now a kind of ecstasy in Martin's smile. Marilee felt moved by a deep passion, even if she didn't understand the ramifications. Years later, after Martin had been sentenced to 117 years in prison, she was still aroused by the memory of his fervor.

She reached out with both hands and pinched his nipples —hard.

Martin bent sideways and tipped over, pretzel-like, in the bed.

"You like that, don't you, Mr. Mad Scientist?" Marilee asked on a heavy breath.

Martin tried to say yes but couldn't manage the word.

Marilee kissed and nipped, rubbed and tickled her new friend, and so their talk about lost wives and barren parasites came to an end.

3.

Through the summer months, Marilee and Martin got together every couple of weeks or so. Martin discontinued his subscription to the dating service; Marilee did not. Twice every other week, Marilee went on PFP-provided dates; every week between, she saw Martin once and went on one PFP date. She didn't feel guilty because Martin was preoccupied with his research and charitable and profit-making surgeries. He was often out of town, in Detroit, Tijuana, or Oakland, doing facial reconstructions, scar and tattoo removals, and more delicate operations. He never asked what Marilee did when they weren't together; neither did he talk about love, long-term commitment, or children.

Marilee was grateful for Martin's detachment. She didn't want to marry him, live with him, or get any deeper into his life. He was extraordinarily knowledgeable and a surprisingly skillful lover. And when they were together, he listened to her every word and remembered everything.

But her other lovers were better-looking, better-heeled, and, well, more normal.

By the first of August, she was thinking that it was time for the relationship with Martin to end. She said to herself that it was because of the mosquito bites she got whenever he stayed over. Martin liked fresh air and was always opening some window. That very morning she decided to send Martin a text saying that she thought they should end it.

Maybe an hour after her decision, Odell Wade came to visit her at Rehnquist, Bartleby, and Rowe.

"Miss Frith-DeGeorgio," the receptionist, Viola Wright, said over the intercom.

"Yes, Viola?"

"A Detective Wade of the NYPD is here to see you."

Marilee gasped involuntarily and felt a sudden chill.

"What does he want?"

"He says he needs to ask you some questions about a friend of yours."

"Tell him that I'll be right down."

She spent the next three minutes trying to think whether there was any reason the police would be after her. She had a small stash of marijuana in her medicine cabinet at home, and she'd declared herself as a private business on her tax forms, using her yearly sale of poorly constructed pottery at a street fair as the proof. When her mother died, she discovered a secret bank account of twenty-six thousand dollars that she'd cashed out without telling her siblings . . . Maybe that was it. Maybe the NYPD was going to arrest her for bank fraud.

She thought about running. RBR was on the thirty-seventh floor of a Midtown office building, but there was an emergency stairway. Who could she turn to? Certainly not her brother, Will, or her sister, Angelique—one of them might have turned her in. Her friends wouldn't shield her from arrest.

Finally she realized that Martin Hull was the only person she knew who might help. He liked her and would probably drive her to another state if she asked.

The idea that Martin was the only person she knew to turn to was sobering. He was the closest person to her, and she was already planning to break off that relationship. What did that mean?

This dose of inexplicable reality somehow steeled Marilee. She decided to go to reception and face the music.

Odell Wade was sitting on one of the three rose-colored sofas across from Viola's desk in the kidney-shaped room with walls of blue-tinted glass.

"Detective Wade?"

"Miss Frith-DeGeorgio?"

The policeman stood up. Marilee's first impression was that he was devastatingly handsome. Tall and tan, with sandy hair and auburn eyes; his straw-colored suit hung very well on his lean and probably powerful frame. His smile seemed genuine.

"How can I help you?" she asked.

The policeman glanced over at the dark-skinned, wary-eyed receptionist and said, "Is there someplace where we can talk privately?"

*   *   *

Marilee's office looked out over Central Park. It was a balmy August day, and they could see all the way to Yonkers.

"What do you do here?" Wade asked, sitting next to her in one of the two chairs designated for clients and visitors. Marilee was appreciating his lips, which formed into the shape of a partly flattened Valentine's heart.

Seated upon the other chrome-and-orange padded chair, she squirmed a bit, thinking that there was something wrong with the cushion. It was then she realized that her dress was tight.

"Social media for the advertising arm of the firm," she answered, thinking, *Am I getting fat?*

"Like Twitter and Facebook?"

"And MyTime, Get It, Lost Treasure, and about a hundred more platforms."

"You like the work?"

"Not really. I used to run my own business, but now I'm just paying the rent."

"I don't want to take up too much of your time, Ms. Frith-DeGeorgio—"

"You can call me Marilee."

"Marilee. Do you know a Dr. Martin David Hull?"

"Yes."

"I'm investigating him, the NYPD is."

"About his wife?"

"He told you?"

"He said that his wife and some doctor guy ran away and the police were looking into it. But they showed up in Europe somewhere and the case was closed."

Detective Wade sighed and, with his eyebrows alone, denied Martin's claim.

"He brought us a letter," the detective said. "A letter he claimed came in an envelope postmarked from Amsterdam. But he didn't have the envelope, and there was no fingerprint other than his, nor were there any DNA markers to say that the letter actually came from his wife."

"Didn't she write the letter?" Marilee asked. "Couldn't you check the handwriting?"

"The body of the letter was printed by computer, and the signature was close but different enough to cause concern."

"And did you look in Amsterdam?"

"We found an address that a Sonora Simonson and Philip Landries had once possibly stayed in. But it was in a transient area, and there was no one who could identify their photographs. We have no evidence that they ever left the country."

"So you think that Martin murdered them?"

"We don't know what happened. Has he said anything to you?"

"Only what I already told you," Marilee said. "Why are you only asking now? I mean, I've been seeing Marty for two months. He thinks the investigation is over."

"My father had a stroke in Denver," Odell Wade said. "I went to take care of him until he died. Another detective had the case, but he didn't do much."

"I'm sorry, Detective Wade, but I don't know anything."

The policeman gave her a slightly pained look and said, "Are you going to see Dr. Hull again?"

"Is it safe?"

"I really don't know. But if you do talk to him or he calls you, I'd appreciate it if you would contact me."

4.

"Marty," Marilee Frith-DeGeorgio said to her lover at 3:03 in the morning. "Are you asleep?"

"I never sleep."

"Never?"

"Now and then I close my eyes and stop thinking for ten minutes or so, but life is very short, and we have a duty to future generations to make this a better world. So I stay awake as much as possible trying to finish my work before the dictum of mortality claims my soul."

Before, when Marty made pronouncements like this, Marilee found them fetching, the thoughts of an awkward little man thinking too much of himself. But this time she got nervous. He might be a murderer; that's what the handsome homicide detective, Odell Wade, had said.

After her meeting with the detective, Marilee cancelled her subscription to PFP and began seeing Martin almost every day. Her fear enhanced their sex life, and now she listened to him as closely as she used to heed her father when she was a little girl. The intensity with which she paid attention to the plastic surgeon brought about a feeling akin to love.

"What did you want?" Martin asked.

"Do you have a laboratory where you do your neuronal studies?"

"Yes, of course."

"Can I visit it?"

"I'd love that."

"You would?"

"Yes." Martin sat up in half lotus, looking down on his naked lover. "A couple of weeks ago I thought that you were going to drop me. I mean I'm not much to look at, and brain surgeons make a lot more money."

"Can you tell me something?" Marilee asked.

"What?"

"Would you have killed Sonora if you knew that she was having an affair with the gut doctor?"

"Philip," Martin said, obviously pondering the question. "No. Given time I would have fixed her."

"You mean hurt her in some other way?"

"Not at all. Sonora is an unhappy woman. When I met her she was fat and shy. When we got together, I paid for a personal trainer, and she turned her physical life around. She lost weight and looked great. But she was still unhappy. She will always be dissatisfied."

"How could you fix something like that?"

"Long-term unhappiness is mostly a chemical and glandular imbalance. I mean, you might be unhappy on any particular day, because you lost a job or a favorite pet ran away, but continual sadness is something else. Most of us cannot live up to our potentials because there's a biochemical war going on in our bodies—that and the fact that our knowledge of the world in which we live is usually subpar."

"What's the connection between sadness and knowledge?" Marilee asked. She enjoyed these talks with Martin, even though she was spying on him, trying to discover what had happened to his wife and her lover.

"Why would you put yourself in danger like that?" Angelique asked. Marilee had called to tell her sister to get in touch with Detective Wade if she went missing.

"I'm not really sure," Marilee replied. "When we were just together, I liked him, but it wasn't serious. I wanted to leave. But after talking to Detective Wade, the fear I feel gets me excited . . . in the bed."

"That's perverse."

"And," Marilee said, reaching for some knowledge she'd not yet articulated, "and for some reason his talk is making more and more sense. I don't know . . . sometimes when we're talking about his work I feel like we're colleagues.

"The only problem is that I have less time to exercise and I'm putting on weight."

"Knowledge is a form of culture," Martin said that early morning, answering his informant's/lover's question. "Not what we know but how we perceive the forms of knowledge brings us closer together. And belonging almost always trumps sadness. Why, I don't think I've had one sad moment since I met you."

"But that's love," she said, feeling ashamed of using the word. "Knowledge comes from education."

"That was once the case, certainly, but less so, and soon—no more."

"But the only way you can learn is by applying your mind to that task," Marilee said with conviction.

"But there are two types of learning," Martin said, showing his gapped teeth. "One is just the simple concatenation of facts, data. But there is a part of the brain that contains geometric forms that are designed to prepare the mind to apply the endless list of facts. One day we will be able to stimulate these forms intravenously."

"What are you talking about?"

Martin stood up and walked off of his low platform bed.

"You'll see when you come to my lab," he said. "I'm going down there now to get ready for your visit."

"It's three in the morning."

"I'll take a cab. I'll leave the address on the kitchen table. Come by around eleven. I'm sure you'll be amazed."

"Hello?" a woman's voice said over the phone at 4:09.

Marilee had waited as long as she could, but finally she just had to call.

"May I speak to Detective Wade?" Marilee asked.

"Who is this?"

"Marilee Frith-DeGeorgio."

"And why are you calling my husband in the middle of the night?"

Marilee wanted to say that it was morning but didn't. She suddenly imagined the entire globe of Earth dancing through the plane of sunlight, an intangible but still physical thing joining in that dance.

"I'm, what do you call it? I'm an informant, and he told me to call when I had information."

The receiver banged down, and Marilee waited. A few minutes later he answered.

"Ms. Frith-DeGeorgio?" Odell Wade said over the line.

"I've searched his house when he was out," she said. "I've checked every file in all of his computers and smartphone. I've been through his closets, pockets, drawers, and behind and under each piece of furniture. There's not one thing about his wife or partner that's incriminating.

"I asked him point-blank if he would have killed her if he knew about her infidelity, and he basically said that he felt sorry for her."

"Is there some reason you need to tell me all this at four in the morning?" Detective Wade asked.

"I'm going to his laboratory today."

"Oh." Wade hadn't even known about the lab until Marilee unearthed that knowledge. "That is important."

"What should I be looking for?" Marilee asked.

5.

The lab was in the basement underneath a six-story apartment building near Tenth Street and Avenue C in the East Village. The door was solid oak and fifteen steep steps down from the street. There was no knob or handle, only a big yellow button to the left of where the knob should have been.

Marilee pressed this button and waited.

A minute later the door swung inward, and there, standing before her, was a god.

He was tall, six six at least, and darker-skinned even than Martin. He wore a tan T-shirt, black trousers, and no shoes or socks. His demeanor exuded something like power or confidence, knowledge, and intense joy. His eyes were light gray, like those of some cats, and his hands seemed as if they were designed to perform miracles.

"Ms. Frith-DeGeorgio?" the earthbound deity asked.

For the moment Marilee was speechless.

"Are you all right?" the godling wondered.

"What are . . . I mean who are you?"

"Lythe Prime."

"That's your name?"

"And designation," he said. "I was born LeRoy Moss, but that was a very long time ago."

He didn't look a day over twenty-five.

"Come on in, Ms. Frith-DeGeorgio. Velchanos is waiting."

"Who?"

"He still goes by Martin Hull out there, but down here he is Velchanos."

The man calling himself Lythe Prime turned then, leading Marilee into a large empty room with high ceilings crisscrossed with ancient wooden beams overhead and a concrete floor underfoot.

"This isn't a laboratory," Marilee said, feeling a pang of fear.

"No," the divine youth replied.

He pressed a place on the white plasterboard wall opposite the entrance, and a panel slid aside, revealing a cavernous stairwell.

While Lythe Prime descended, Marilee took a moment to wonder whether this could possibly be where Martin had murdered his wife.

"Coming, Ms. Frith-DeGeorgio?"

The beautiful voice seemed to be calling to some hitherto unknown part of her—her soul.

The chamber below the first basement level was immense, at least eighty feet wide and half that in depth, with twenty-five-foot-high ceilings. There were eleven long metal tables, most of which held hundreds of multicolored beakers and vases that reminded Marilee of some fantasy palace. One wall held at least six dozen computers on various shelves and ledges. And at the far end of the room, there was a huge metal door that looked like the portal to a big bank's vault.

"Velchanos," Lythe Prime hailed.

That's when Marilee saw her lover/prey, in a classic white smock, sitting behind an old-fashioned walnut desk in a corner beside the vault.

He stood and said, "Hi, Marilee. I'm so glad you could make it. Come in. Come in."

She realized that she hadn't taken the last step from the stairs into the subbasement.

Lythe touched her arm. This sent a jolt through her like static electricity, only it was a pleasurable sensation. Almost involuntarily she took in a deep breath and walked toward the man whose chosen name was that of a precursor to the Greek god Vulcan.

How did I know that? she wondered.

"Come, sit," Martin said, giving her that goofy grin. "You met LeRoy."

"Lythe," she corrected.

"What's in a name?" Martin quoted. "Sit."

Marilee did as he asked, looking around the room. There was a scent in the air, something wonderful and fresh.

"I'm sure you want to know everything," Martin said.

"I just wanted to visit."

"I seriously doubt that," Martin replied, in a tone that was certain, almost hard.

"What do you mean?"

"Odell Wade convinced his superiors to reopen his investigation of me. I think it was when he realized that I had a new girlfriend."

For some reason Marilee was not surprised at Martin's knowledge.

"He believes that you really did murder your wife and the doctor," she said.

"No doubt," Martin/Velchanos answered. "Modern men have externalized their thought processes and use their prejudices to divine guilt."

"How did you know about Odell?" Marilee asked, twisting uncomfortably in her chair. Even her old *fat* dress was beginning to feel tight.

"I have a friend that works as a male receptionist in his precinct."

"That's convenient."

"Not at all. Lon Richmond was bed-bound, suffering from a slowly progressive nerve disorder. His mother died, and no hospital would take him. He was the cousin of one of my reconstructive-surgery patients, and so I visited Lon and gave him five injections. After two months, he was out of bed and applying for the job."

"A plastic surgeon cured an incurable nerve disease?" Marilee asked. Behind these words she was trying to remember the significance of *five* injections.

"As I told you, plastic surgery is just my day job."

"You sent him in there as a spy?"

"Most definitely."

Not for the first time, Marilee wondered if Martin was insane. She glanced behind her chair and saw Lythe Prime standing there.

"What was in those injections?" she asked Martin.

He smiled and nodded.

"What are you grinning about?"

"You," he said. "I've just told you that I'm spying on the NYPD, and they have assured you that I'm a murderer. Here you are in a closed space with me and a man who looks as powerful as a professional athlete. All that, and you ask the only important question."

"So, are you going to answer me?"

"The human body recognizes categories of cells. I have discovered that if I place a small amount of a certain cell type in the HMT-1 hinny, that parasite will be ferried to the part of the body that resonates with the passenger cell type."

"You can target organs," Marilee heard herself say.

"The brain," Martin said, "the heart, spinal cord, liver, and any gland I choose."

"And what do you use these parasites for?"

"Open the vault, LeRoy," Martin replied.

He stood and ushered Marilee toward the stainless-steel door.

The man once called LeRoy Moss entered a combination on a number pad and then turned a great lever that looked something like the chromium wheel of an ancient sailing ship.

When the door swung open, a gust of very cold air flowed out. Just when Marilee started to shiver, the gray-eyed god draped a full-length fur coat over her shoulders. He handed a like garment to Martin.

The three then entered the vault.

"Don't you wear something?" Marilee asked Lythe.

"I don't get cold too easy," he said with a smile.

Along the left side of the vault was a twelve-foot-high glass-like cabinet with hundreds of shallow drawers.

"For seven years I did volunteer work for a medical facility in Cambridge, Massachusetts. It was an interuniversity research lab that did autopsies on people with exceptional qualities: scientists, savants, athletes, and those with odd bodily quirks—"

"Like people that are impervious to cold," Marilee suddenly realized.

"Just so," Martin said. "When I became a trustee of the lab, I began harvesting cells from the best, the brightest, and the strangest specimens that humanity had to offer.

"I brought those harvests here and began to create cocktails for the next step in human evolution."

"You experimented on poor people who came to you as a plastic surgeon," Marilee accused.

"I started with dogs. Once I was able to transplant memories and thought processes, once I was able to successfully alter breeds, sizes, and senses—only then did I begin my work on humans."

"But there must have been many failures," Marilee challenged.

"Yes," Martin Hull agreed. "And some of them suffered; some died. But as a rule they were people suffering serious ailments, like Lon Richmond. I always told those first guinea pigs what the potentials were—and what the dangers."

"You call them 'guinea pigs'?"

"What else can I say? I used them as test subjects, and a few score of them died."

"Is that what happened to your wife?"

"She left before my tests began. I would have injected her in her sleep, but she ran off looking for happiness in Europe."

"My mosquito bites," Marilee said.

"You're at least an inch and a half taller," Martin said. "And that dress looks very tight on you."

Before she knew what she was doing, Marilee slapped Martin, hitting him with such force that he fell to the floor of the vault. Then she reached down and lifted him with strength she'd never had before.

That's when LeRoy/Lythe Moss/Prime grabbed her and pulled her out of the big repository of cadaver cells.

6.

They met at a coffee shop on Prince Street in Greenwich Village. Marilee had left a simple message on Detective Wade's home phone—"I have something"—and gave the address of the coffee shop.

"He has the cellular remains of dozens, maybe hundreds of corpses in his basement," she said. "And, and, and he's experimented on people, many of whom have died from his experiments."

"What kind of experiments?" Wade asked.

"He injects them with parasites."

"Oh my God."

"He's a monster."

"Did he do anything to you?"

"No," Marilee said. She was afraid to confess about her expanding body, about her once hazel eyes that were getting lighter each day.

"Will you sign an affidavit about what you saw in his basement?"

"Yes. Yes I will."

The day that Dr. Martin David Hull was brought to trial, Marilee Frith-DeGeorgio crossed the Canadian border headed for Montreal. She was now six foot two, with pearl-gray eyes and skin the color of alabaster. When she moved into the small studio apartment in Montreal-South, she opened a document on her PFP web address. There were seven e-mails in her virtual mailbox. Six of these were from lovers who wanted to see her again; one was from lytheprime@everchanging.uk.

Dear Valhalla,

Velchanos has directed me to inform you that he bears you no ill will; that he understands why you had to betray him. He also wanted me to answer one question you asked and two you didn't.

About the five injections: 1) is a collection of data-cell clusters culled from some of the most brilliant minds in the world, 2) are similar clusters that contain the equations to best manipulate this information, 3) is a growth formula that allows the body to reach what he calls our god-potential, 4) is a small cutting from a Miss Ota Wangazu who is the only known adult to have produced viable stem cells, and 5) are a few liver cells from different donors who never experienced a sick day in their lives.

Your first unasked question is: Why did he decide to become so involved with you? Velchanos says that he needed passion in his life; that he was guilty of playing God and needed the chance for forgiveness. On his first date with you he was only looking for temporary companionship, but after a month he saw in you his salvation. He hoped that by exposing you to his treatments and telling you what he'd done that you might, after considering everything, send him a card telling him your verdict.

And finally, a question you didn't ask and maybe never even thought of: Why hasn't Martin Hull grown and developed our gray eyes? He knew that he would be arrested and that there would be a worldwide witch hunt for his patients. He wanted no markers for treatments to be lifted from his body.

Yours, LeRoy/Lythe Moss/Prime

P.S. There are 12,306 surviving patients that received Velchanos's treatments. They have all gone into hiding, both to keep away from the official investigation that must come and to continue the Revelation—our name for the great change that this process will ultimately cause. You should stay in hiding. Your betrayal will not protect you from detainment, interrogation, and ultimately vivisection.

I have destroyed the lab. Only the living bodies of our tribe can be used against us.

Rereading the letter, Marilee realized that it had been written, almost wholly, in Latin. She migrated to Australia, kept her ex-husband's last name, and adopted Valhalla as given forename. She moved to the outskirts of Melbourne and there studied her mind and her body, looking for the deliverance of the human species.

BETWEEN STORMS

After the storm had passed, Michael Trey just didn't want to leave his apartment anymore. There was something about the booming thunder and the dire news reports, the red line across the bottom of every TV show warning residents to stay inside and away from windows, even if they were closed and shaded. Subway tunnels were flooded, as were the streets. The airports would be closed for the next four days, and the Hudson had risen up over the West Side Highway, causing millions of dollars in damage in Lower Manhattan.

The mayor interrupted TV Land's repeat of an old Married . . . with Children episode to report that the National Guard had been called out.

President Obama had taken a train (a train!) to Manhattan to address New Yorkers everywhere, telling one and all that he had declared them a disaster. He wore a white dress shirt with thin green and blue pinstripes. He didn't wear a tie, because he was getting down to business—that's what Michael thought. Even the president was afraid of the havoc that nature had wrought.

It didn't matter that the sun was shining the next day or that the skies were blue and cloudless. The storm, Michael knew, was hiding behind the horizon. And there with it was a hothouse sun, crazed terrorist bombers, and women with HIV, hepatitis C, and thoughts of a brief marriage followed by a lifetime of support. In North Korea they were planning a nuclear attack, and there was probably some immigrant on the first plane after the storm infected with a strain of the Ebola virus that would show symptoms only after he had gotten past customs.

Michael didn't go to work the next morning. The radio and TV said that most public transportation was moving normally. Traffic was congested, however. Three sidewalks in Manhattan had collapsed from water damage. Just walking down the street someone might get killed or paralyzed.

Europe's economy had almost failed again, except that the Germans bailed out the Greeks with money that neither of them had. China was going to take over the American economy and make Michael and everyone he knew into Communist slaves living in dormitories and eating boiled rice.

But if no one could buy the goods, then China's economy might fail, and it would engage its two-hundred-million-man army to reclaim all the money we borrowed to pay for the health insurance of undocumented, Spanish-speaking, job-stealing illegal immigrants.

There were microbes in the water after the storm. Militant Muslims had used the cover of the downpour to plant explosives under churches and big businesses. They weren't afraid of the rain, like Michael and other poor Americans who just wanted to work until retirement . . . never came.

*　*　*

The phone rang on the morning of the third day that Michael had not gone in to work at Prospect, Farr, Grant, and Heldhammer.

Michael picked up the receiver but did not speak.

"Mike?" someone said. "Mike, is that you?"

"Michael is not here," Michael heard himself say. Immediately he felt warm and safe behind the subterfuge of those words. He wasn't at home and therefore couldn't be reached, couldn't be touched, burned, infected, blown up, or experimented upon by sales scientists working in subterranean desert laboratories for the superstores.

A lifetime of the nightly news and conspiracy theories woven into TV shows, movies, and even commercials; of the racist/sexist/classist schemes of Big Business and its political candidate shills; the private prisons, police, billionaires and millionaires, movie stars and pop stars and country stars and serial killers: all this came together in Michael's mind in his apartment three days after the disaster that he finally understood would never end.

"Mike, it's Finnmore, Ron Finnmore. Mr. Russell is wondering where you are."

"I'll leave Michael the message," Mike said, and then he cradled the phone.

After hanging up, Michael had the urge to giggle but suppressed it. He knew that if he showed any emotion, soon they'd say he'd gone crazy and take him away.

"Yes," he said, when the secretary answered the phone. "I'm calling for Mr. Trey. He's not coming in today because of inclement weather."

It *was* raining, and so Michael felt justified.

"It's just a few showers," Faye Lesser, Thomas Grant's assistant's secretary said.

"That's how the last storm started. What if he got there and it came down like that again? Who would feed his cat?"

Michael didn't have a cat. He didn't have a fish or even a plant. If he had had a plant it would have died, because he hadn't put up the shades since the storm.

The television spoke of conspiracies and of disasters both domestic and foreign that were increasing in severity, like the storm that had raged over New York. There were mad cows and rampant use of hormones and antibiotics. The Y chromosome in men had shrunk to the point that soon men might cease to be men and would have to learn how to be women-without-wombs.

There were prisons across the country that together released at least a hundred convicted killers every week and banks that created bad debt (Michael was never sure how they did this) and then sold the nonexistent interest to pension plans that subsequently failed.

Michael started taking notes. He had five folders that he had bought for his financial records but never used. He labeled these folders: DISEASES, NATURAL DISASTERS, MAN-MADE DISASTERS, FINANCIAL DISASTERS, and HUMAN THREATS. Five folders were just right for the notes he needed to compile. He saw this as a sign that he was meant to stay in his fourteenth-floor apartment and study the truth that so many people missed because they went to work and therefore, somehow, inexplicably, betrayed themselves.

He spent whole days looking up fires, floods, serial killers, and food additives on his cell-phone IP. He ordered hundreds of cans of beans and tuna, concentrated orange juice, and powdered milk from grocery delivery services. He made the deliverymen leave the foods at the door and collected them only when he was sure that no one was lingering in the hall.

He used his phone to pay his bills until his accounts went low.

The super brought up his mail and left it at the threshold for him.

He had been fired, of course. His girlfriend, Melanie, told him that either he would meet her at the Starbucks on Forty-Second Street or she was breaking up with him. His mother called, but Michael fooled her by saying that Michael wasn't home.

And he was getting somewhere with his research.

At first he thought that the problem was that there were too many people, but he gave up that theory when he realized that people working together would be benefited by great numbers. Finally he understood that it wasn't the number of souls but the plethora of ideas that bogged down the world. It was like the old-time Polish parliament, in which nothing could be decided as long as anyone held a contrary point of view.

The problem with the world was a trick of consciousness: people believed in free will and independent thinking and were, therefore, dooming the world to the impossibility of choice. Yes. That was the problem. Together all the peoples of the world—Muslims, Hindus, and Jews; Christians, atheists, and Buddhists—would have to give up disagreements if they wanted the human race to survive the storm of incongruent consciousness that was even worse than the weather that had brought New York to its knees.

Michael felt that he was making great progress. He was beginning, he was sure, to articulate the prime issue at the base of all the bad news the *New York Times* had to print. He was trying to imagine what kind of blog or article he could author, when the eviction notice was shoved under his door. It had only been six weeks . . . no, no, nine . . . no, eleven. Just eleven weeks, but he was rent-stabilized, and the collusion of city government and greedy landlords made it possible for prompt evictions when there was potential for rent that could soar.

Working after midnight for days, Michael drilled forty-eight holes along the sides, top, and bottom of his door and similarly placed holes in the doorjamb and along the floor. He used a hand-held cordless drill to do this work, and it took him seventy-seven hours and twenty-nine minutes. Through these connective cavities he looped twined wire hangers, two strands for each hole. This reinforcement, he figured, stood a chance of resisting a battering ram if it came to that.

He also used melted wax to seal the cracks at the sides of the door so that the police couldn't force him out with tear gas.

His beard was filling in, and his hair had grown shaggy. He looked to himself like another man in the mirror: the man who answered the phone for the absent Michael.

He filled the bathtub to the overflow drain in case the super turned off the water.

On his iPhone he read the newspapers, studied the Middle East, Central America, and the Chinese, who, he believed, had gained control of capitalism without understanding its deteriorative quality.

Finally all those boring political-science courses that he took when he thought he might want to be a lawyer had some use.

He was well on his way to a breakthrough when the landline rang.

He always answered the phone because, in a discussion with the man in the mirror, he inferred that if no one answered, they might use the excuse that there was some kind of emergency behind his coat-hanger reinforced door.

"Hello?"

"May I speak to Michael Trey, please?" a pleasant man's voice asked.

"He's not here."

"Then to whom am I speaking?"

This was a new question, and it was very smart—very. This was not just some befuddled contrarian thinker but one of those unofficial agents that pretended to protect freedom while in reality achieving the opposite end.

"My name is X," he replied, and suddenly, magically, Michael ceased to exist.

"X?"

"What do you want?"

"My name is Balkan, Bob Balkan. I'm an independent contractor working for the city to settle disputes."

"I don't have any disputes, Mr. Balkan Bob. As a matter of fact, I might be one of the few people in the world who does not disagree."

"I don't understand," the independent contractor admitted.

"I have to go, Bob."

"Can you tell me something first, Mr. X?"

"What's that, Bob?"

"What do you want?"

The question threw X out of Michael's mind. The man that was left felt confused, overwhelmed. The question was like a blank check, a hint to the solution of a primary conundrum from an alien, superior life-form. It had ecclesiastical echoes running down a corridor heretofore unexplored in Michael's mind.

"What do *I* want?" Michael repeated the words but changed the intonation.

"Yes," Balkan Bob said.

"I want," Michael said. "I want people everywhere to stop for a minute and think about only the essential necessities of their lives. You know, air and water, food and friendship, shelter and laughing, disposal of waste and the continual need for all those things through all the days of their lives."

Balkan Bob was quiet for half a minute, and so Michael, not X, continued. "If everybody everywhere had those thoughts in their minds, then they would realize that it's not individuality or identity but being human, being the same that makes us strong. That's what I've been thinking in here while the rain's been falling and the landlord was trying to evict me."

"But Michael hasn't paid the rent, Mr. X."

"I have to go, Bob," X said, and then Michael hung up.

Eight days later the electricity was turned off. The grocery delivery service had brought him thirty fat, nine-inch wax candles, so he had light. It was all right to be in semidarkness, to be without TV, radio, or Internet. Michael had his five folders and the knowledge of a lifetime plus four years of college to filter through.

Two days after the electricity went off, it came back on. Michael wondered what bureaucratic and legal contortion had the man with his hand on the lever going back and forth with the power.

Just after the lights flickered back on, the phone rang.

When it sounded, Michael realized that there had been no calls for the past forty-eight hours—not his mother and not Melanie, who worried that her demands had brought him to this place.

He always answered the phone but rarely stayed on for more than a minute.

The phone didn't depend on the power system. Maybe the phone company had cut him off for not paying his bill and then, at the behest of the city, had turned the service back on.

"Hello," X said.

"Mr. X?"

"Bob?"

"How are you?"

"Things are becoming clearer all the time, Bob," X said. "I just don't understand why you cut off the power and then turned it back on again."

"I didn't do it," he said.

"But you're working for the people that did, or at least their friends and allies."

"Do you feel that you are at war, Mr. X?"

"I'm just an innocent bystander who has made the mistake of witnessing the crime." X was much more certain about things than Michael was.

"I recorded your statement about what you wanted. Someone in my office released the recording to the media. You have lots of friends out here, Mr. X. If you look out your window you'll see them in the street."

"I'd like to, but there might be something there I don't want to see. And I don't want anyone seeing me."

"No one wants to hurt you," Bob said in a very reassuring voice.

"No one wants to kill children in Afghanistan either, but it happens every day."

"You haven't come out of your apartment since we got hit by Hurricane Laura."

"And here I don't know anything about you."

"What do you want to know?" Bob Balkan offered.

"You ask good questions, Bob."

"And?"

"Do you think that we're equal to our technology?"

"Maybe not."

"So why are you on my ass? That's all I'm saying."

"Let me ask you a question, Mr. X."

"What's that?"

"Do you think that we're equal to our biology?"

Neither Michael nor X was ready for that question. It got down to the crux of what they had been trying to figure out. If the human mind, Michael thought, was the subject of biological instinct, then there was no answer, no agreement, nor any exit from madness.

Stroking his beard, Michael forgot about the phone call and wondered if his own body was an unconscious plot against the idea of humanity, humanness. Machines and techniques could be torn down and abandoned, but what about blood and bone, nerves and hormones? Was he himself an aberrant machine set upon an impossible mission amid the indifferent materials of existence? Was his resistance futile?

While he was considering these questions, the phone went dead and the lights cut off. There came sounds of heavy footfalls in the hallway. Suddenly there was a great thumping wallop against his fireproofed, steel-reinforced, hanger-looped fire door. The police battering ram hit the door nineteen times by Michael's count. The locks and hangers, doorjamb and metal infrastructure held. The pounding ceased, and voices sounded up and down the outside hall.

There were shouts and curses. One man suggested that they break through the wall.

Michael armed himself with a butcher's knife and then put the cooking weapon down.

"I can't hurt anybody," he said to no one.

That night Michael slept on the living room floor in front of the door. His iPhone was dead and the lights were cut off, but under candlelight he read *Man's Fate* by André Malraux. He felt for the characters in the novel, though for the most part he did not identify with them. Revolution, Michael thought, was both personal and shared, and everyone, and everything, had a part in it. His only affinity was with the feeling of doom and dread threaded throughout the book. He believed that soon he would be killed because he had decided to stop moving forward with the herd toward slow but certain slaughter.

"Mike. Hey, Mike," a voice hissed.

· Michael had fallen asleep. He believed that his name was part of a dream, but he didn't know why someone calling out to him would be important.

He tried to lift his right hand, but it wouldn't move.

"Mike!" The whisper became more plaintive.

Suddenly afraid that people had secretly come in and bound him, Michael lurched up, jerking his right hand from whatever held it.

His fingers were encased in wax. The candle had burned unevenly, and warm wax had pooled and dried around his hand. Michael laughed to himself, relieved that he was safe. He blew out the burning wick.

"Mike!"

The ventilation plate in the living room had a faint light glowing between its slats.

Michael's first impulse was to cover that opening with plastic and masking tape, but he hesitated.

He pulled a chair to the wall and got up on it so that he could stand face-to-face with the brass plate.

"Who is that?" he asked.

"Mike?"

"Yeah."

"It's Tommy Rimes from the apartment next door."

"The tall guy with the mustache?"

"No," the voice said. "I'm the guy who goes bowling all the time."

Michael remembered the squat middle-aged man with the potbelly and the red bowling-ball bag.

You wanna go run down some pins? he'd once asked Michael.

"What do you want, Mr. Rimes?"

"They got you all over the news, Mike. From Occupy Wall Street to the *Wall Street Journal*, they all been talkin' about you. You went viral on the Internet now that the cops couldn't beat down your door. Fisk, the guy with the mustache on the other side a' you videoed it and put it up on YouTube. You're a celebrity."

Michael was peeling the wax from his fingers and wondering what notoriety would get him. Would it hold the hurricanes back or keep the Communists from conquering themselves with capitalism? Would it get Melanie to take him back?

"Mike?" Michael had all but forgotten that Tommy Rimes was there.

"What?" the newly minted celebrity asked.

"Can you take off the ventilation plate?"

"Why?"

"I'm gonna push through a power strip and this aquarium hose I got. That way you can have power again, and if they cut off your water you can have that."

"Why?"

"This rich guy from uptown put what you said to the city psychologist up on a billboard down the street. I like it. I mean, I think you might got somethin' there. And even if you're wrong, I like it that you're stickin' it to the landlord."

By morning Michael had light, and once he powered up his phone he found that it was still working. There was an e-mail from Melanie telling him that she had paid his phone bill. On his tiny phone screen he could see newscasts covering a thousand people in the streets outside of his apartment building protesting the police, the mayor, the landlord, and everyone that uses the law to keep people apart.

"I believe that Mr. Trey is trying to speak for all of us," a young black woman with braids that stood out from her head like spikes said to an interviewer. "I mean, here we are working hard and barely able to live. We eat junk food and watch junk TV and our schools are being closed down because they're so bad. The police will frisk anybody, except if they're rich or something, and we're fighting a war without a draft. Mr. Trey has just stopped. He's saying that he doesn't want to be a part of all this [*bleep*] and that we should all do the same."

"I'm a conservative," a white man in a dark blue suit told a camera. "I believe that we have to fight the war and bail out the banks, but I still wonder about what this guy says. I think he's crazy, but you can't deny that there's something wrong with the world we're living in."

Both the liberal and conservative press praised Michael. They called him a people's hero who was refusing to take one more step before the other side made changes. They bent his words, however —that's what Michael thought. They didn't understand that the whole idea was *not* to have a hero but to discover a natural credo to unite people and keep them from destroying themselves.

"We love Michael Trey!" two beautiful young women shouted at one camera.

The city or the landlord cut off his water; Tommy Rimes turned it back on through the aquarium hose.

The iPhone sounded.

"Melanie?" Michael said, after seeing the screen and answering.

"They've closed down the street in front of your building," she said.

"The police?"

"No, the protesters. They want the city to leave you alone. One group is raising money for your rent, and four lawyers are working for injunctions against the landlord. Other tenants are making complaints against health and safety infractions. A journalist asked President Obama about you, but he refused to comment and it's been all over the news."

"What has?" Michael asked his ex.

"Obama not saying anything."

Michael tried to remember why he had decided to stay in his apartment. It was the storm. He was just too afraid because of the threat the news media made out of the storm. He was afraid, not heroic.

"Michael?" Melanie said.

"Uh-huh?"

"Max Strummer, who owns Opal Internet Services, wants you to do a daily podcast from your phone. He wants me to be the producer. Isn't that great? You could make enough money to pay your rent and lawyers. He said that if you couldn't think of anything to say that we could send you text files that you could just read."

"I have to go, Mel," Michael said.

"What about Mr. Strummer?"

"I'll call you later," Michael uttered, and then he touched the disconnect icon.

After turning off the sound on his phone Michael went to sit in his favorite chair. It was extra wide, with foam-rubber cushions covered in white cotton brocade. There was a lamp that he'd plugged in to the power strip hanging halfway down his wall from the ventilation grate hole. The light wasn't strong enough to illuminate the whole room, just the area around his chair.

Reclining in the oasis of light, Michael tried to make sense of the storm and his street being closed down, and of the young women who loved a man they'd never met and Melanie who had changed from an ex-girlfriend to a maybe producer.

When no ideas came, he turned off the lamp, hoping that darkness would provide an answer. It didn't. He was trying to recapture the moment when everything had made sense, when he took action without second-guessing his motives.

Feeling lost, he looked across the room and saw a blue luminescence. It was the phone trying to reach out to him.

Half an hour later he went to see who was calling. There had been a dozen calls. Most of the entries were unfamiliar, but one, instead of a number, was a name that he knew.

"Hello?"

"Mr. Balkan?"

"Mr. X?"

"No, no, this is Michael."

"Oh."

"Did you call me on city business?" Michael asked.

"They wanted me to call, but this is your nickel."

"I've been looking at the Internet," Michael said. "People all over the place want to protect me. They're offering money and legal support. One guy named Strummer wants to hire me and my ex to do a podcast for him."

"That's what you wanted, isn't it?"

"No."

"I thought you said that you wanted people to realize what they had in common."

"But between them," Michael said, "not through me."

"I don't get you."

"Not like a natural disaster or some enemy," the young bearded man replied. "I don't want to be the discounted meal at the fast-food chain that you can buy in Anchorage or Dade County. I don't want to be anything except an idea."

"But you're a man."

"Thanks for that, Bob."

"For what?"

"I needed to talk to somebody about these thoughts in my head. I couldn't get them out if I didn't have anybody to talk to. I know that you're working for them, but right now they don't know what to do. In that little window you helped me. You really did."

"Helped you what?"

"I got to go, Bob."

"Where can you go, Michael?"

"You always ask the best questions."

The next morning Michael was standing in his kitchen eating from a can of pork and beans with a teaspoon when he noticed that the spigot had a slow drip. Michael wasn't sure if it was the dripping or his talk with the city psychologist that made up his mind.

He tested the hot water and then called Melanie. She was surprised to hear from him and happy that he had decided to do his first podcast. He was careful, and she was too, not to talk about love.

At four in the afternoon Michael was ready. He had refused to allow Strummer to dictate what he said. He ignored the checklist of subjects his Internet listeners might want to hear about.

Michael had the bathtub draining when he started recording and had to close the bathroom door to keep out the noise.

*   *   *

"My name is Michael Trey," he said into the receiver, with no notes or even a notion of what exactly he'd say. "I have lived in Manhattan for seven years, and I was scared about Hurricane Laura—so scared that I haven't left my house since it broke. Because I wouldn't go out, I lost my job and my girlfriend, and the landlord has been trying to evict me. I'm broke, and they keep turning my utilities on and off. I have hot water right now, and so I'm going to take my first real bath in weeks.

"My neighbor, Tommy Rimes, pushed a power strip and a little hose through the ventilation duct, and so I've been able to get by. I've seen videos of people down in the street supporting me. I like that, but it's misguided. What they should do, I believe, is lock themselves into their own houses and turn off the world outside. I don't know if this would be possible or if it would make any difference at all, but that's all I've got.

"What I'm saying is that the president didn't talk about me because there's nothing to say. It is us that should be talking to him. It's us that need to get the red lines out of the bottoms of our screens, because we're in it together as far as we go. But maybe, maybe that's impossible, because we do things primarily as mammals, not men and women.

"That's really all I have to say. I know there are people out there that want a daily report from my musty apartment, but really all they have to do is listen to this, what I'm saying right now.

"Goodbye."

Michael turned off his phone before running the hot bath in the deep iron tub. It was this tub that made him take the apartment in the first place. The hot water felt so good that he groaned when he first sat back. The stinging in his wrists subsided, and he wasn't frightened except when he concentrated on the hue of the water.

He was exhilarated at first and then tired, in the way he used to be as a little boy getting in his bed. He wondered if anyone would ever make sense out of the fear-herding that all the people, and maybe all other creatures, of the world lived under.

He would have liked Melanie to say that she loved him, but only if he didn't have to ask.

THE BLACK WOMAN
IN THE CHINESE HAT

I meant to spend Saturday walking from Lower Manhattan back up to my neighborhood in Washington Heights, but I didn't make it very far.

I took the IRT from 157th down to Battery Park late that morning, then headed north on foot. I made my way up the promenade, such as it is, on the West Side. It was hot, and so there were lots of swimsuited skaters whizzing past. Most had nice bodies, almost everyone with a date. Men and women, men and men—hand in hand. There were some female couples, but most of them seemed more like just friends.

There was a sprinkling of solitary skaters and joggers, even one or two walking alone. Almost all of the singles wore earphones. Some danced to the silent music, others stared doggedly ahead.

It's not that I would have talked to anyone not listening to music. I was hiding under my hayseed straw hat and behind mirrored sunglasses. I wouldn't have been able to pass more than three sentences with a stranger on the street. Making friends has always been hard for me. Even after four years at Hunter College I had only two friends from there—Eric Chen, a history major from Queens, and Willy Jones, a psych major from Long Island City. Both Willy and Eric lived in Brooklyn. I liked them, but spending time with them was always the same. We'd talk about women and movies at coffeehouses until we got hungry and went for junk food. It was always the same. So that Saturday I decided to walk around and look at people and places that I hadn't seen before. Anything would be better than a day at home alone or with Willy or Eric.

Just a few blocks north of the Financial District was a large lawn filled with the prostrate bodies, primarily white, of sunbathers. Men with bulging muscles and women with the top straps of their bikinis undone to get a smooth tan. It didn't look comfortable. There was no ocean or nice air, just the filthy Hudson on one side and a line of brick-faced office buildings across the West Side Highway on the other. And it was over a hundred degrees. Actually it was ninety-six, but the weather man said, from a sunbather's radio, that the heat index, whatever that is, made it "feel like" a hundred and two.

There was a black woman, medium-brown really, lying amongst the others. She had on a one-piece fishnet bathing suit that, being almost the same color as her skin, gave you the idea you could see more than you really could. She was lying on her back with her head propped up, wearing a Chinese peasant hat and rose-colored sunglasses. I looked at her at first because she was the only Negro in a sea of white bodies, and then I noticed how good-looking she was.

I stared longer than I should have, and she noticed the attention. She propped up on an elbow and smiled. She had a good-size gap between her two front teeth. My heart skipped, and I felt a chill in spite of the heat.

She pointed at her hat and then at mine, as a kind of recognition, I guess, and then she waved for me to come over.

I didn't move. She smiled again and waved more insistently. I found myself walking over, between the five or six lengths of sunbathers, to get next to the black woman in the Chinese peasant hat.

She pulled up her legs to make room for me to sit down next to her.

I'm a very uncomfortable person. I'm big, not quite portly or fat but large enough to make simple motions like running or sitting on the floor difficult. I negotiated the maneuver as well as I could, managing not to step or sit on anyone.

"Hi," the woman said. She was young, some years older than I but not yet twenty-five.

"Hey."

"I got to go to the bathroom," she said with a grimace.

"What?"

"I got to go, but if I leave, one a' these white people gonna take my spot. But if you could hold my place while I run over there." She pointed at a squat concrete structure about a hundred yards away.

I nodded. She grinned and reached over to squeeze my wrist. Then, with the slightest pressure against my arm, she was up more gracefully than I could ever manage. I watched her lope away toward one of New York's few public toilets.

After she was gone, I stretched out to save her place, relaxing into my job. That's why I liked work and school; there you had something to do and someone to be, and people treated you in a certain way that you didn't have to think about. I mean, even if the boss didn't respect you, he still had to ask you a question now and then. And whenever I was asked a question, I knew the right answer. And as far as girls and women were concerned, even the prettiest ones had to say hello if you were in the same class or worked on the same floor.

I felt a sense of purpose on that lawn, even though anyone looking would have thought I was out of place.

I say that because I wore a heavy pair of black jeans with a lightweight gray jacket cut in the military style. I didn't wear a shirt that day. Everyone near me was nearly naked. One man, in the middle of a group of men, had taken down his trunks and was lying facedown, naked. *Butt all up in the air,* my mother's voice screeched in my ear.

I heard a sound behind me. It was a young woman's voice. I turned my head and saw that the woman wasn't complaining, as I had at first thought. Her boyfriend had gone beyond kissing and had his hand down in the towel that barely covered their lower bodies. She smiled at me over his head and then made a face that said something felt good.

A broadcast reporter was saying that a policeman had been shot while sitting in a car out in front of his house. I was wondering why he'd been sitting outside rather than in his house. I was still facing the girl but thinking about the man in his car.

"Hey! What you lookin' at?" The woman's blond-headed boyfriend had noticed her looking at me. His face was red. I didn't know if it was colored from anger or the sun.

I turned around quickly and raised my knees to my chest. My back felt vulnerable to attack. I didn't know if he was going to get up and hit me. I would have walked away, except for the black woman in the Chinese hat.

I had been sweating all morning, but now I could feel the moisture gathering under my arms and across my thighs. Thoughts kept coming in and out of my head. *He wouldn't be so tough if I had a knife . . . I should go . . . I should carry a kitchen knife with me . . . Where*

*is that woman? . . . Is a kitchen knife legal? . . . Is that him standing up behind
me? . . . Where is that woman? . . .*

I felt a hand on my shoulder and let myself fall sideways, thinking that I could kick him from the ground. I fell against a man's
hard body.

"Hey, guy, what's wrong with you?" the man I toppled on
complained.

Hovering in the sun above me was the woman I waited for.

"I knocked him over," she said to the balding bodybuilder. "I
hit his tickle spot by mistake."

While the muscle man groused, I saw that the lovers had gone.
My heart was thumping, and sweat was stinging my eyes. The black
woman in the Chinese hat descended to her knees and said, "Hey,
you OK?" in a tone that I'd never heard addressed to me before.

It was like she was my oldest friend or my wife or one of those
social workers who put their life on the line to help someone they
don't even know. I saw that she had some kind of leotard on under
the fishnet bathing suit.

"Yeah," I said, sitting upright. "I'm OK."

"You fell over just like a stack a' bananas."

"Yeah."

"My name's Chai," she said.

"I'm Rufus."

"How come you wearin' all them hot clothes, Rufus?"

"I thought it was gonna be cold this morning."

"I don't know where you comin' from. It's been hot every day
this summer. Real hot." Chai licked her lips. My eyes were drawn
to her mouth. I wanted her to say something else that sounded
like before.

Chai smiled and took a water bottle from her oversize bag.

"It's hot," she complained.

"Yeah, it sure is."

"I thought it would be nice to sit out here, but it's too hot."

"Today's a good day to be in air-conditioning," I said. "That's for sure."

"You got air-conditionin' at home?"

"No. But they have it at the World Trade Center."

Chai frowned. All I wanted to do was to keep her talking.

"Want to go down to the World Financial Center and get some lunch?" It took all the breath in my lungs to get those words out.

"I don't even know you, Rufus."

"There's air-conditioning down there."

"You got money?"

"Enough for lunch."

"Enough for a taxi to take us down there?"

"Wow, this is nice," Chai said, when we entered the glass-walled hall of palm trees in the lower court of the financial center. My friend Willy calls it the hall of palms. In the center of the vast room there are eighteen slender palm trees that reach thirty feet. Between them are benches like you'd find in a park. The benches were all occupied by people trying to escape the heat.

"I never even knew this place was here," she said, taking my arm.

I could feel her breast against my shoulder. I wanted to swallow but couldn't make my throat cooperate.

"I'm hungry," Chai said.

We went under the Merrill Lynch mezzanine into the upscale food court. Past the Rizzoli bookstore and behind a yellow pillar was Pucci's Two, an Italian restaurant I sometimes went to on my lunch break from Carter's Home Insurance.

"No swimwear inside the dining room," said the slender host at the podium that led into the restaurant.

Actually, there was no *inside* to the restaurant. There was just an area where there were about thirty tables cordoned off by a thigh-high green fence. The only inside was the kitchen.

"How's this?" Chai said. She pulled a large piece of brown cloth from her bag and wrapped it around her waist. The skirt accented her figure, made her seem more womanly.

The host was obviously perturbed to see a woman dressing right there in front of him. He was an older white man with a full head of white hair. He stared at Chai for a moment and then a moment more. Finally he got two menus from a slot on the side of the podium and strode toward our seats.

It was just noon, and so the restaurant was nearly empty. He led us to a small table for two in the back.

"I don't wanna sit in the back," Chai said, when he held a chair for her.

"I thought you wanted privacy," the maître d' replied.

"Ain't nobody here," Chai said. "All you could have is privacy."

We ended up at the thigh-high fence watching people walking by.

"Anything to drink?" Our waitress was a black woman with seven silver studs in each ear, a gold ring at the outer corner of her right eye, a tiny silver circlet at the left corner of her lower lip, and a blue stone in her nose. She laid down our menus and smiled.

"Red wine," Chai said.

"We have a Merlot and Beaujolais," the waitress replied. She was looking somewhere beyond the confines of the restaurant.

"Whatever."

The waitress looked at me. I'm only twenty. I went to college early, at sixteen, but I look older.

"Beer," I said. "Whatever you got on tap."

The waitress moved away.

The maître d' seated a couple at the table next to us. There was already a line of couples waiting to get in.

I noticed that Chai was still wearing her rose glasses and peasant hat. I removed my hat and glasses, hoping that she'd do the same.

Instead she reached across the table to caress my cheek.

"You have a nice face, Rufus." Her hand slid from my jawbone and across my lips. "Nice lips too."

"They have really good pasta," I said, opening the menu.

Chai smiled at me and leaned forward.

The maître d' sat another couple on the other side of us.

"How old are you?" Chai asked.

"Twenty-three."

"You in school?"

"No. Uh-uh. I just graduated from Hunter a few months ago. Now I work at an insurance company down here."

"I used to work down here," she said. "At Crystal and Pomerantz. I typed and stuff. But I don't do that anymore."

"What do you do now?"

"I do clothes for a couple a' black magazines. Clothes, and I help out on the photography shoots."

The waitress came with our drinks then.

"Are you ready to order?"

"Do you have specials?" Chai asked.

The waitress frowned and then produced a pad from the pocket of her blouse.

"Angel hair pasta with a sauce of fresh tomatoes sautéed in olive oil with garlic, kalamata olives, fresh basil, and finished with crumbled goat cheese. Broiled scrod served with an anchovy sauce . . ."

"Ugh! Anchovies is nasty," Chai complained.

" . . . and a thick veal chop," the waitress continued, "flattened, breaded, and fried in olive oil, served with broccoli di rape."

"I want the pasta," Chai said.

I ordered the blue-cheese cheeseburger with a baked potato and salad.

"If you lost some weight," Chai said, when the waitress was gone, "and did some weight liftin', you'd be fine."

"I'm gonna start my diet next week," I said. "Monday morning. I got Special K for breakfast and seven grapefruits."

"What kinda milk?"

"*Milk* milk."

"If you gonna diet it's got to be skim milk, fat-free."

"Oh. Uh-huh. That's why I was walking on the promenade today."

"Why?"

"Because I'm starting to get healthy. I'm gonna walk up to my house on One Fifty-Eight."

"You better walk up to one thousand fifty-eight if you gonna eat that hamburger."

"Yeah," I said. "I know."

"I want to be a nutritionist," she said. "But first I'm gonna get into clothes design. I made my bathing suit."

"You did?"

"Uh-huh. Made it fishnet to make you think you could see sumpin' and then lined it so you couldn't. You like it?"

"It's beautiful."

That was the only moment that Chai was at a loss for words. Her head moved back slightly, and her eyes opened wide enough that I could see them clearly through the flush of her plastic lenses.

"Where you from, Rufus?"

"I was born in Baltimore," I said. "Then we moved to Portland and Oakland and then LA . . ."

"I wanna move to Atlanta," Chai said. "Then go to LA after I get established. 'Cause you know they say LA is a hard town, and somebody black got to be ready if they want to live out there."

"I don't know," I said. "I was only there for a year before my mom brought me to Brooklyn."

"And then you moved to Washington Heights?"

"Yeah. My mom made sure that I was in school at Hunter, and then she moved back to LA to live with my uncle Lon."

The food came then. I regretted every bite of my burger. I wanted to leave some, to start my diet a few hours early, but I couldn't stop eating. I couldn't even slow down.

"So you alone out here?" Chai asked me.

"My aunt Beta," I said, shaking my head, mouth full of meat. "She lives in Brooklyn."

"What kinda name is Beta?"

"Mom is Alpha, and her sister is Beta," I said.

"What's that mean?"

"It's the beginning of the Latin alphabet. *A* and *B*."

"They named two little girls after letters?"

"My grandfather. He's like an inventor. He said that he thought all children were like experiments, that every child born was a test of nature to make a better human being."

"Huh. That's weird."

"Yeah. He said that all the tests so far had failed, mostly, and that we should keep track of the failures, that one day the government would agree with him and start naming every person so that they could see how the process was coming along."

"He sounds crazy."

"That's what my grandmother thought. That's why she left him and moved to Baltimore."

Chai had pecan pie and chocolate liqueur for desert. I had a bite of her pie. After that I showed her all around the World Financial and World Trade Centers. She'd been in them before but didn't know all the ins and outs the way I did.

There was an award-winning exhibit of news photography in the sky tunnel that connected the two centers. The scenes were mostly of suffering in other parts of the world. The one I remember was an African soldier raising his machete to deliver the killing blow to an unarmed man that he'd been fighting. The man was already wounded, and this was obviously the last moment of his life. I was sure that there was another photograph—a picture of the murdered man, evidence that his attacker was a murderer—but that photograph, wherever it was, was not an award winner. Chai spent a lot of time examining each picture. She was interested in photography too, she said.

I kept close to her, waiting to hear that tone in her voice again, the tone that made me feel like I had always known her.

We went to J&R Music World, and she bought CDs for her sister. And then we went to the building where I worked. She said that she wanted to see it.

After that we walked some more, and then we had tempura at Fukuda's Japanese restaurant.

"I don't have just one boyfriend," she told me when we were walking down Broadway in the early evening. I hadn't asked her, but I did want to know.

"Right now I see two guys. One's a cop, and the other's a ex-con. I like the cop 'cause he know what to do, and I like my convict 'cause he make me feel it when we together."

"They know about each other?" I asked, as practical as my grandfather.

"Uh-uh. Strong men like that cain't share without fightin'. So I just don't tell 'em."

It was then that she took my hand.

"Take me to the movies, Rufus. Take me to see *The Thomas Crown Affair*."

"I only have enough for two subway tokens."

"You don't have a bank card?"

"I don't have any money in the bank."

"I thought you said that you work for that insurance company?"

"I do, but I just started and I haven't been paid yet." This was mostly true. Actually I had worked at Carter's Home Insurance for three months, but I was just promoted to my new position two weeks ago. Before that I had only made minimum wage.

Chai let my hand go. I thought that she would leave now that she knew I was broke.

"I know somethin' we could do, don't cost but fifty cent," she said.

"What?"

Again she took me by the hand. We walked farther downtown, our fingers interlaced. My hand was sweating, and even though I always thought that holding hands meant something close and special, I didn't feel the closeness that I had on that sunbathers' lawn. It was just two hands and some fingers pressed together on a day that was too hot.

"What's this?" I said, holding back at the outside escalator.

"The ferry," Chai said. "The Staten Island Ferry. It only costs fifty cent. Don't worry, I'll pay for it."

We held hands up the escalator and through the swinging glass doors. She had to let go in order to pay at the kiosk. We came into a cavernous room that was over a hundred feet across, and just as long. There was a magazine stand in the center of the room and wooden benches along the walls.

"Good, it's pretty empty," Chai said.

Now she held my arm. I still didn't feel that closeness I craved, but there was security in the touch. I'd never been to Staten Island and said so. She told me that her cousins lived out there in Saint George. She used to visit them when she was a girl.

At the far end of the large waiting room was a huge door that sat on wheels. Through the door we could see a crowd of people all walking in one direction, toward the exit and the city.

"That means the ferry is unloading. When they're finished and when the cars are all off, then we can get on."

"They take cars?"

"Uh-huh. Right down below us."

The door was pushed open from the outside by an older, red-faced white man. The color reminded me of the man who was so angry when his girlfriend looked at me.

"Great, it's one of the old ferries," she said as we walked up the ramp.

It was like one of the old barges that my uncle Lon used to take me on off of Redondo Beach. Lots of old wooden benches and a galley where you could get hot dogs and sodas.

Chai ran, dragging me along, to the front of the boat. There we looked out over the watery expanse.

"I used to love this when I was a kid," she said. "Thanks for coming with me."

The horn sounded, and the big boat lurched out into the water. Six or seven others came out onto the prow with us.

Chai grabbed my hand again and said, "Come on."

She led me back into the boat and up a flight of stairs that went above the galley. Up there was another room full of old built-in benches. On either side was an outside area with a long bench that looked out to the water. On one side an old couple sat, and on the other two little kids looked out from the front.

Chai took me to the aft part of the side where the children were. We sat and looked out for a moment or two. We were going to pass Ellis Island and the Statue of Liberty. I was about to say how great it was when Chai kissed me.

What I remember most about it was her tongue. It was very large and muscular. My old girlfriend, the only girlfriend I ever had, Rachel, had a small tongue. When we kissed, Rachel opened her mouth, but her tongue didn't do anything. But with Chai it was a real physical experience. The boat ride was smooth, but that kiss was like stormy seas. It still wasn't the intimacy I had experienced on the promenade, but it was overpowering.

Chai laid a hand on my thigh, right on my erection. She didn't move the hand or squeeze but just let the weight sit there. After a moment I was kissing back. Every time my tongue pushed into her mouth it was pressed back. It was almost like the tongues were engaged in a war or maybe a war game. My chest started to hurt, and there were sounds coming from my throat. Chai used her other hand to caress the back of my neck.

When I started to come, Chai moved back from the kiss to watch my face. Her hand was still just weight, but it was enough. I struggled not to make too much noise. I could see that there was someone down on the other end of the bench; I could see their form in my peripheral vision.

My body tensed, and my legs went straight. I wanted to cry.

It was then that Chai whispered, "So much." Then she leaned closer and spoke right into my ear, "Don't stop," and I had another orgasm and I thought I was going to die.

There it was, cast in something stronger than stone, the intimacy, and the closeness I had always wanted but never suspected until that day. I panted like a dog, and Chai grinned broadly. My body was still shaking.

"That was good," she said, and then she curled up beside me and put her head on my shoulder and her hand upon my chest. We sat there looking out at the water. The ferry slowed for landing and then jarred against the wooden pylons of the pier.

Whoever it was at the other end of our bench got up and left. I think Chai fell asleep. I did too.

"So I told my mothah I didn't care what the hell he told huhr," a woman said. It was real, and I heard it, but I was still asleep.

I felt a forward pitch of the boat and awoke. An old woman was sitting next to me. A man in some kind of uniform was next to her. Two young women were standing at the railing looking out over the water. It was one of them who had been talking about her mother.

Chai was asleep. Just seeing her seemed to fill my lungs with air. This time I watched the water and the sights.

It might have been eight o'clock. The sky was still light, and the ferry was full of Staten Islanders going out for the night in Manhattan. I stayed still, hoping that Chai wouldn't rouse.

"Hey," she said, when we were close to shore.

"Hey," I said in a new voice, one that echoed the intimacy I craved.

She sat up and said, "I got to get home."

"Can I call you?"

"I don't really have a private line. But you give me your number, and I'll call you, OK?"

There was a yellow nub of a pencil in her bag and the inner side of the ingredients flap from an empty package of trail mix that had been thrown away in the terminal building. There I wrote my full name and the phone number of my temporary desk at work. I hadn't gotten a phone in my house yet. I didn't have the deposit.

"Goodbye, Rufus Coombs," Chai said after she kissed my cheek. "I'm gonna call you and see how your diet's comin'."

I wanted to walk her to her subway station, but she said she needed to walk alone.

The first time I woke up it was because of that pain in my chest. I guess I got excited in my sleep. The pain turned into fear of a policeman who found out that I had been kissing his woman. That fear gave way to fear of an ex-convict, a murderer, who would kill me for the same reason. I fell asleep again only to awaken to a phrase, *AIDS kiss*. I wondered if I had heard those words on the radio or read them somewhere. The thought of the disease crawling through my veins got me up out of bed. I went to my tenement window and looked out over New Jersey. I wondered if she would call me. It would have to be within the next six weeks, because that was how long I'd be in the claims department.

I sat in my heavy chair waiting for the sun, wondering if she would call and if I saw her would one of her boyfriends kill me. I wondered if she might die from AIDS and never call to warn me. Somewhere in the tangle of fears I fell asleep again.

LOCAL HERO

My grandfather, and Sherman's, was Theodore Brownley from Spiritville, Louisiana—a town that no longer exists.

Theodore moved to Brooklyn soon after the flood that washed Spiritville into the Mississippi in November 1949; at least that was what my cousin Sherman said that our grandfather told him. Grandpa Theodore came to Flatbush, bought an empty lot, built the house that Sherman was later born in, married Florida James from Brownsville, New York, and fathered three sons: Isaac, Blood, and my mother's husband, Skill.

Florida bore their three sons in the first four years of marriage. The brothers Brownley courted three sisters born to Lucinda Cardwell, who lived with her brood across the street and down the block from the Brownley clan.

Three brides for three brothers, and, if you believe the rumors, there was some cross-pollination too.

My father, Skill Brownley, was married to Mint Cardwell. Our first cousin Theodora's mom was Lana, and her father was Isaac.

Blood married Nefertiti, then got killed in a bar fight just a year after she bore his son.

These names are very important because they are the stakes that hold down the billowing tent of my story, my lives. I am Stewart Cardwell-Brownley, born into the family of Skill Brownley—Grandpa Theodore's youngest son. I have two brothers and one sister. Theodora had one sister and one brother. The three sisters that the Brownley brothers married had five other siblings. But the rest, even though I love them dearly, don't figure much in the telling of my tale.

What matters is that Sherman, like his father, Blood, was killed in a street fight not three blocks from the house Theodore built. My first cousin Sherman did all things good and bad. He was a straight-A student, a Lothario of mythic proportions, nationally recognized for high school baseball and basketball, a devout Christian, a sometimes heavy drinker, and a street fighter. His hunger for truth was equaled only by his thirst for life. He could never get enough, and his heart was all over the place. I was closer to him than to anyone else in the Brownley clan. Partly because, even though he was only a year older than I, Sherman was my protector and teacher; he taught me almost everything I knew, including, though it seems unlikely, most things I learned after his death.

As a youth I was never very good in school or at athletics; neither was I popular. My parents never pushed me much, but they always offered to help me with schoolwork, and my father played catch with me and my younger brother Floyd on fair days in Prospect Park, when he wasn't putting in overtime at the machine shop.

I had three friends through all the years of public school. Bespectacled Mister Pardon, Fat Jimmy Ellis, and Ballard "the Perv" Ingram. We would hang out on the lunch court before and after school, trading comic books and gossiping about the sex exploits of everyone else.

Every now and then Sherman would join us, usually waiting to hook up with some girl. We liked him because he was the best of us, all of us. He ran faster, stood his ground no matter the odds, and he could recite every school assignment by heart. At church he sang with the gospel choir, and afterward he'd make out with one of the church daughters in the storeroom behind the dais upon which the choir performed.

But even though he was a blazing star among assorted lumps of clay, Sherman would join me and my friends on the lunch court just as if he was one of us, talking about the X-Men and teachers he couldn't stand.

I remember one day he asked short, squinty-eyed Ballard the Perv what comic book character he wanted to be.

"Not," Sherman stipulated, "the one you like the most but the one you would be if you could be."

Ball, which is what we called Ballard sometimes, scrunched up his eyes and stared at my first cousin like he might be a cop who needed the right answer or else he would kick some ass.

"The Thing," Ball said at last. "The Thing from the Fantastic Four."

Sherman smiled and winked at me.

"He's ugly," Fat Jimmy said.

"Yeah," Ball replied, "but he's got a secret power."

"What power?" Mister asked. Mister Pardon was dark-skinned, like the rest of us, and named Mister, in the Southern black tradition, so that no white man could disrespect him. He was an exceptional student, though he stuttered when talking to anyone but us three and sometimes Sherman.

"His dick," the Perv said. "It's rough the way my uncle Billy says that girls like it, and it's really big 'cause of those cosmic rays."

Ball's voice was so filled with wonder and desire that I was afraid Sherman might turn mean and make fun of him. I and my friends were all around thirteen, while my cousin was fourteen going on forty. Sherman could be cutting, and I had the urge, but not the nerve, to stand between him and Ball.

Sherman bit his lower lip and cut his eyes at the Perv.

"Yeah, right?" he said with a smile. "That's what I always thought about the Hulk. You know like if the madder he get the stronger he is, then maybe the hornier he get the bigger his dick is."

Ballard the Perv's eyes opened wide, and I believed that he'd dream about being the Hulk for the next year.

One afternoon, more than a year after the bio-philosophical talk about the sexual prowess of superheroes, Sherman came up to me and my friends on the lunch court. This was unusual, because my cousin had graduated to high school and didn't come by very much anymore.

Sherman sat down and greeted me and my friends. He told us about a fight he'd got in with a cop's son. The kid was named Carl and was in the eleventh grade.

"I got beat down," Sherman said, with a wry grin, "but I gave him a black eye and chipped his front tooth."

Mister, Jimmy, and Ball had a hundred questions, but Sherman said, "We can talk about all that later. Right now I need Stew here to help me with somethin'."

I was due home in less than an hour. My mother and father were very strict, and even though I hadn't done very well at anything in particular, I always obeyed them and showed up on time. On the other hand, Sherman had never asked for my help before. He made sure to spend time with me a day or two each month. Once in a while I stayed over at the apartment where he and his mother, Titi, lived. At night, after she was asleep, Sherman would take me up to the roof, where he smoked cigarettes and drank sweet wine.

"You see down there in the alley?" he once asked me.

"Yeah, I see."

"All kinds of things happen down there in the nighttime. People fuckin' and fightin', and sometimes they die. Right down there in the open but in the dark."

I peered into the night, which was broken now and then by fluttering moths or the passing headlights of some car. If I had just looked into that abyss by myself I wouldn't have seen a thing; but through Sherman's eyes I could imagine the way the darkness, with the partial architecture of the urban night, was magical, alive. When I inhaled it felt as if that night was coming inside me.

And so, when Sherman came on that lunch court and said that he needed me—I went.

On the A train to Manhattan we sat on a bench for three, and he looked me over.

"Your hair is all right," he said, after a minute-long inspection, "but you gotta button that shirt to the top and tuck in those tails."

I did as I was told.

"Did you brush your teeth this morning?" Sherman asked.

"Yeah."

"How about a shower?"

"I took one after gym class."

Sherman was still studying me. He seemed more like a teacher or a young father than my cousin and friend.

We were passing underneath the East River when he said, "I met this girl from California goes to a private school on Seventy-Second

Street. Her parents are out of town tonight, and she said she wanted me to come by, only she had already planned to have one of her girlfriends come over, and so she asked if I could bring another guy."

"Girls?" I was pretty sure that half the subway car could hear the fear in my voice.

"Don't worry, man. Tanya—that's my girl—Tanya said that Mona is fine. So you don't have to worry about me puttin' you with no ugly girl."

I swallowed hard again and tried to think of some way out of that train, that destination. I had hardly ever kissed a girl, and when I had it hadn't seemed so great—for her.

"When you kiss," Sherman said, as if he could read my thoughts, "you got to give her some tongue. Girls like that, and you will too."

We got out in lower Manhattan south of Canal. From there we walked west. On Washington we came to this modern-looking apartment building that had glass walls and a doorman seated behind a high desk.

Sherman walked right up to the desk, and I followed a few steps behind.

The doorman had bright copper skin and an accent from somewhere in the Spanish-speaking New World.

"Can I help you?" he asked, dubiously.

"Tanya Highsmith," Sherman said. "Apartment fourteen twenty-seven."

That was the most impressed I ever was with my cousin, in this life. *Tanya Highsmith, apartment fourteen twenty-seven.* He spoke clearly, with no hesitation or shame. He wasn't some young tough from the 'hood but a man coming to see a woman.

The doorman nodded and picked up a phone.

*   *   *

The next thing I knew I was standing at an off-white door on the fourteenth floor in a wide hallway that had avocado-colored carpeting and muted rose-red walls.

When Sherman pressed the doorbell I got a little dizzy. Standing there I worried that I'd fall on my face. I do believe that the only reason I didn't faint was so as not to embarrass my cousin and best friend.

The door swung inward, and I was surprised at the young woman who stood there. The beautiful teenager wore a gray silk T-shirt under an emerald cotton vest that had little red eyes stitched into it. Her skirt was a gold color with a blue hem, I remember. She was barefoot and a little breathless. But none of that mattered at first glance. What struck me was that she was a black girl; well, not really black but rather a creamy brown. At any rate—she wasn't white. I figured that in a building that nice, with a girl from a private school, that Sherman must have found him a white girl to visit.

"Hey, Tanya," Sherman said.

"Oh my God," she exclaimed. "You two look exactly alike."

I'd been told before that Sherman and I bore a strong resemblance. I couldn't see it; I think that was because he was so powerful and brave and cool, and I was just barely normal.

"They do!" another girl said. This one was also under the category of our race, what people nowadays call African American. But where Tanya was slender of face and body, her friend was a curvaceous girl with skin just a touch darker.

They were Sherman's age, maybe even a little older.

"Mona," Tanya said, "this is Sherman and his cousin Stewart."

"If we look just alike," Sherman said, "then how you know I ain't Stew?"

The skinny girl grinned, cocked her head to the side, and said, "Because I know what I like. Come on in. I got it all ready."

Tanya took us through the living room into a yellow-and-red-tiled kitchen. Past the stove there was a little nook of a room with no door, in which sat a small, square, orange table-booth. There she had set out a crystal decanter filled with amber liquor and four bulbous drinking glasses.

"Cognac," Tanya said. "Like I told you."

Sherman and Tanya sat on one side of the table, her in and him out. I climbed into our side, and Mona pulled in close beside me.

Tanya explained to her friend and me that she met Sherman on the F train and that the first thing he said to her was to ask if she had ever had champagne.

"I asked him why," she said. "And he told me that I looked like I was rich and so I must have had some."

"What did you say?" Mona asked. At the same time she laid her left hand on my right.

"She said that there was something better than champagne," Sherman answered.

"Cognac," Tanya finished, gesturing at the contents of the tabletop.

She poured us each a generous dram and warned us to sip it because the cognac was strong.

When Mona let go of my hand to reach for her glass, I felt both bereft and relieved. She got my glass too, turned toward me on the small bench, and clinked hers to mine. She smiled at me with lips that I will always think a woman's lips and smile should be.

"Cheers," she whispered, and we all sipped.

"Damn!" Sherman said. "This feels warm all down in my chest."

"That's what it does," Tanya said, a note of triumph in her voice.

"This how rich people feel all the time?" my cousin asked.

Tanya's reply was to lean forward and kiss him.

Sherman already knew how to kiss. After a moment with her mouth, he moved to the side of her neck. This caress brought out a smile, and the next thing I knew Mona gave me a peck on the mouth. My tongue was ready, but her lips moved quickly to my ear.

"We should go in the other room and leave them alone," she whispered.

Mona poured some more brandy into our glasses and then led me by the hand into the living room. There we drank and whispered and kissed—a lot. Toward the bottom of the snifters my trepidations evaporated. Mona showed me how and where to kiss and when to linger. In hushed tones she told me about her white boyfriend and how he would never let her guide him to her desire.

I was overexcited and so suffered two premature ejaculations, but Mona was more experienced and explained, between kisses, what was going on with me and how we could get back to where we wanted to be.

Somewhere in the night I looked up from the sofa and saw Sherman and Tanya, mostly naked, tiptoeing toward another part of the house.

"Kiss me, Stew," Mona said, to bring my attention back to her.

The couch Mona and I staked out was long and deep, like the sleep we tumbled down into. It was slumber in an upholstered hole at the side of a road in some fairy tale my mother might have read aloud before my siblings and I fell to sleep . . .

My mother. I came awake suddenly, so deeply afraid that even the loss of my virginity failed to buoy me. I sat up quickly and felt a wave of pain go through my head. I gasped, looked around, and saw Sherman sitting in a stuffed chair set perpendicular to the foot of our sofa.

Mona groaned and shifted under a blanket I didn't remember.

"I been waitin' for you to wake up, cousin."

"Does your head hurt this bad?" I asked.

"It'll go away in the air outside," Sherman explained.

"My parents are gonna kill me," I predicted, through pain and some nausea.

"Uh-uh, man. I got that covered," my cousin promised.

It was late May, and the sun was rising at around five that morning as Sherman and I made our way to the subway.

"What you mean you got it covered?" I asked Sherman for the sixth time as he handed me a subway token.

"While you was playin' makin' Mona moan I called Titi an' asked her to call your parents and say you was sleepin' ovah."

No magician ever impressed me as much as Sherman did.

"And she did it?" I asked.

"Sure she did. I told her that you and me were on a double date. She understands what men need to do."

For a week or so after the visit with Tanya and Mona, I avoided my cousin. I wanted to forget about cognac and sex and Manhattan too. I felt so guilty that I was even trying to do some homework one Wednesday evening in the bedroom I shared with my brother Floyd.

"Stew?" my mother, Mint Cardwell-Brownley, called from the hall.

"Yeah, Mom?"

"Phone. It's your cousin Sherman. If he wants you to come over, tell him you have to come back here to bed."

"Hey, cousin," he said, when I answered.

"Hi." I didn't want to be rude.

"Where you been, man?" he asked.

"Nowhere. Studyin' for finals is all."

"Well, come on ovah an' I'll help."

There was no way that I was going to see Sherman and Nefertiti. My soul was on the line; that's how it felt. I tried to think of some kind of reason that I had to stay and do my homework alone. Maybe it was some kind of spelling that I had to commit to memory, and Floyd was already testing me. That was a good excuse.

"What you thinkin', Stew?" my cousin asked.

"Nuthin'."

"So you comin' or what?"

"OK." And that was it. My soul was sold, and Sherman owned it.

That early evening we went down an alley past the back of a bodega. We stopped for a minute while Sherman looked around.

"You see that little window ovah the door?" he asked me.

"Uh-huh."

"That's what they call a transom, and Julio's ain't got no alarm."

"So?"

"I'm 'a break into that bastard an' steal one hundred dollars."

"Why?" I was so scared that even the spiritual devastation of sex seemed tame.

"'Cause I can. 'Cause I wanna do everything. Don't worry, Stew. I won't bring you into it."

The years passed, and Sherman and I were fast companions. Whenever he broke the law he did it alone, but later he'd tell me all about it—step-by-step. I spent lots of time with him and his mother, my aunt Titi, in their sixth-floor walk-up apartment. Titi was always nice, kissing me hello and goodbye.

My own mother rarely kissed me. I had never much thought about that until I became the beloved chattel of my aunt and cousin.

*   *   *

After high school Sherman was accepted to NYU on full scholar-ship, and then I, the next year, went to work on an early-morning paper-delivery crew for the *New York Times*.

Somewhere in that time our cousin Theodora decided to take the NYC civil service exam. She asked Sherman to help, and he did. I hung around because it felt better to be with him than my own parents and siblings.

Theodora and I studied together. I had no desire to take the test, but I liked her. We'd laugh and try to fool each other, and Sherman told me that she'd do better if I was there too. Theodora was slender and tall, and she told us on the third night of study that she liked women more than men.

"I just like the way girls kiss," she admitted between practice tests. "It's like I know something with them, when men keep their secrets."

I didn't care about who she loved. Theodora was my blood, and I had learned from Sherman and Titi that that was all that mattered.

A few years later, after Theodora had gotten a clerk job at the local police precinct, Sherman got into a fight with the husband of one of his girlfriends.

It isn't what it sounds like. Isabella Vasquez was a first-grade schoolteacher, who taught many of the kids that our siblings and cousins had produced. Sherman got to know her when taking our nieces and nephews to school on Thursday mornings.

Isabella's husband, Murphy, one night got drunk and knocked out one of her teeth. So Sherman kicked his ass.

Murphy got mad at that, and with two of his friends he beat my cousin to death. They jumped him in an alley and stomped his face and ribs. Nefertiti and I sat by his body in the mortuary all

Saturday morning, while Murphy Halloran and his friends were being arraigned and charged.

Nefertiti held the vigil in her sixth-floor walk-up. All forty-seven of the Cardwells, Brownleys, and Cardwell-Brownleys came. Our grandparents were dead, but Titi had brought out an old photograph of them and tacked it to the wall.

I was there from the beginning to the end, serving sweet wine with butter and salami sandwiches on hard rolls. My mother, Mint, when she first saw me there, sneered in a way that I didn't understand —at the time. Many others who knew how close I was to Sherman said how sorry they were and how much alike we looked.

I stayed to clean up after the wake. Titi watched me from the kitchen door.

"Sherman loved you," she said.

Her tone was sweet, but still I took it as an accusation. I castigated myself for failing to be there to fight side by side with him.

"He was my best friend," I uttered, trying not to cry, again.

"More than that."

"I know we're blood, but I always thought of him as something more, I guess."

"He was," Nefertiti said. "Your father and his are the same."

"My father, Skill?"

"No. My husband, Blood."

I stopped drying plates and turned to look at Titi. She's a dark-skinned woman with bright eyes and graying dreads. I could see that she had always loved her husband and son in me. That connection was the source of her kisses and kind words. It was why she protected me when Sherman and I spent the night with those fancy girls.

She took a light-brown snakeskin wallet from the pocket in her apron and handed it to me.

"It was Sherman's," she said. "I couldn't even look inside. They killed my boy. This world killed him. He was too beautiful, too beautiful."

"I can't, I can't take this, Titi."

"Please," she implored. "I'll sleep easier if I know he's with you."

The next day was the funeral. Six hundred people and more showed up.

Mister Pardon, Fat Jimmy, and Ballard the Perv were there. They told me how sorry they were and dredged up the old stories about Sherman's adventures at school. I liked my friends, but they seemed very far away. Or maybe it was me; ever since I'd heard that Sherman had died I'd felt that there was a wall between me and everyone else. Everyone except Nefertiti.

I sat through the ceremony thinking that Sherman was my brother, my brother.

My mother's husband—my uncle Skill—and I took opposite sides at the front of the casket.

The reception after the interment was held in the house that our grandfather Theodore Brownley had built. I hung around the corners, talking to people as little as possible. People talking and laughing and remembering things about Sherman just made me angry. Didn't they realize that someone who was so much more had been taken? Didn't they understand what Sherman was in this world?

That morning I'd broken up with my girlfriend of two years, Leora Dumas, because she said that Sherman had been a bad influence on me.

"He was crooked," Leora said. "And you couldn't see that he was holding you back."

I was living with Leora because I didn't make enough delivering papers to afford my own place. She wanted to get married, but I really didn't have any interest in that. I guess Sherman dying meant that I had to move on, no matter what Leora said.

So what if I gambled with Sherman sometimes or drank too much or bought things I couldn't afford? My cousin, my brother, made me feel that life was important, that I was important. Without him I was nobody.

"You look so much like him," a woman said.

It was Natasha Koskov, from Brighton Beach. She was a breathless Russian with a long neck and lips like Mona Tremont, the first girl I ever really kissed.

"That's what they say," I replied, wondering where the words and light tone in my voice had come from.

"He loved you," she said, looking into my brown eyes with her black ones.

"You wanna go get a drink?" I imagined Sherman asking.

"Yes," Natasha Koskov replied.

We drank and kissed, went to her apartment, and made love. She called me Sherman, and after the first round I didn't correct her.

I was another man that night. Natasha wasn't loving me but Sherman—Sherman, who could not be erased from this world or her heart or mine.

Sometime after three in the morning I was walking from the subway toward Titi's apartment building because I had no place else to go.

I hadn't lived with my parents for three years, and the thought that my father was not my father kept me from calling them. I wondered if he had known, if he and my mother had kept the truth from me. Maybe that was why my mother showed me so little affection.

"Hey, you!" a man said from somewhere to my left.

I turned and saw a rough-skinned, earth-toned man wearing a hoodie. He carried a small pistol in his right hand. I'd had a lot to drink, but I was sober. I was coming back from a night of lovemaking, but I was downcast, brooding.

"Gimme yo' got-damned wallet, main!"

He could have demanded anything else: my shoes, my baby finger, every cent I ever made. But it was Sherman's wallet in my back pocket. It was my brother's legacy this man was asking for.

I looked at him, and time slowed. Under a night-time lamppost his sludge-colored eyes were frightened, as mine should have been. I suppressed a smile, breathed in the darkness, and looked up suddenly as if seeing something surprising behind his back. It was just enough to cause him to falter and to give me time to reach out with both hands and tear the gun from his grip. He tried to grab it away, but I pulled back the hammer and steadied my right hand with my left. This was something Sherman had taught me with a pistol he kept in the top drawer of his bureau.

"Now I want *your* got-damned money, man!" I said on that dark and empty street. There were tears in my eyes.

The thief heard in my grief-stricken, strained voice that he was as close to dead as he was likely to be before that final breath. He reached into a pocket and came out with a wad of cash that he'd probably robbed from other brooding late-night strollers. He held the cash out to me.

"Drop it on the concrete and haul yo' ass outta here 'fore I shoot you dead."

It was the terrified look on the mugger's face that made me decide to kill him. I was outraged that a man who made his living robbing others would not be brave enough to face the consequences of his crimes. His cowardice negated any claim to clemency.

I was just about to shoot the mugger when a bright light flashed, a siren chirped, and a magnified voice called out, "Drop the weapon! This is the police!"

In that moment I argued internally about the action I should take. One side of my mind said that the mugger should die, no matter what some bright light and bullhorn said.

"No, cousin," Sherman argued. "You got to live for Titi and for me too. You could have killed him, but now you got to drop the gun, get down on your knees, and put your hands behind your head."

As Sherman said these things, I did them.

The mugger stayed on his feet, trembling.

The policemen, two of them, hurried over—their guns drawn, their eyes searching for trickery and deceit.

"Don't say anything, cousin," Sherman whispered. "Not a word."

They took us, me and the man that tried to rob me, to the precinct station. I was put in a small interrogation room and handcuffed to a metal hook anchored in the wall. A cop in a suit tried to question me, but I wouldn't so much as look at him.

A long time passed. During that period I thought about Sherman and the words he had spoken years before when talking about what he'd do if he were caught in some crime. I realized that he had been teaching me how to survive after he was gone.

When the door came open again, my cousin Theodora entered. She was the last person I expected to see, hastily clad in blue jeans and a long turquoise T-shirt. Her hair was wrapped up in a nylon stocking, and there were bags under her eyes.

She stared at me with a confused look on her face. Then, slowly, the answer to the riddle of who I was and who they thought I was, came to her.

She squatted down in front of me, her face not two inches away from mine.

"Stew?" she whispered.

I couldn't speak.

"Why you had Sherman's wallet on you?" my cousin asked.

"Titi," I uttered softly.

Theodora understood.

"Listen, Stew," she murmured. "They found me as the contact in Sherman's wallet. They think you're him. Tell me what happened, and I'll try and get you outta here."

"Man tried to mug me, and I grabbed away his gun."

Theodora was well known at the precinct. They looked up the mugger's records and Sherman's to find that my mugger, Chris Hatter, had been arrested for violent crimes many times. That, and the fact that his fingerprints and the ones on the bullets matched, got me released.

Titi let me come live with her.

Sleeping in Sherman's bed, waking up each day and putting on his clothes, made me feel . . . different, more and more so each day. I began reading his library of college books and the thirteen volumes of the detailed journal he'd kept since the age of ten. And, slowly, I made a plan for my future.

I applied to college, saying in my essay that I wanted another bachelor's degree, one in English literature because I wanted to teach.

*   *   *

Six months later I was in Greenwich Village at one of eight NYU registration tables. The table I stood in line for was specified for people with last names that started with letter *A*, *B*, or *C*.

I stood there thinking about the police captain who harangued me for not telling the arresting officers that I was the victim of the mugger I had disarmed.

". . . and we might have let him go," the captain said. "By keeping quiet you could have put a dangerous criminal back on the street . . ."

And now I was at the front of the line at registration.

"Name?" a blond girl with a wide face and rimless glasses asked.

Instead of responding I gave her the driver's license from my wallet.

She took the card and read it, looked up, and said, "Sherman Cardwell-Brownley?"

I sighed, smiled, and nodded. She smiled back and started going through a box of large envelopes sitting next to her. The young woman—her name tag read "Shauna"—found the name and handed me my schedule for the fall semester. I had been given a dorm room, a roommate named Lucian Meyers, and a laminated card with the photo of a face on it that looked a lot like mine.

OTIS

Crash Martin, christened Percival by his parents, left school in a hurry when he thought the truth had come out. The Martin family lived in the West Village neighborhood of Manhattan, in a three-bedroom apartment, with rent control grandfathered in through his father's father, both named Reginald, upon the elder's death in 1999. While Reginald Jr. had been born in that apartment, Mathilda Poplar-Martin, Crash's mother, hailed from Portland, Maine, and still owned her family cabin on Monhegan Island, population seventy-three.

"There are twenty-seven artists, forty-five fishermen, and me," she'd say of her island home away from home, "when I'm there."

Crash had an older sister named Albertha, a fraternal twin brother called Brother, and a cousin named Bob. Bob's parents had died in an automobile accident on California's Pacific Coast Highway. Claudia, Bob's mother, had been talking to Mathilda on her cell phone while Bob's father, John, drove the family from Santa Barbara down to LA. Mathilda didn't care much for her brother's wife or for him, for that matter, but she felt that it was providence that she was talking to them when they died and so told Reginald Jr. that Bob had to come live with their family.

Of the six residents living in the fourth-floor apartment on Gay Street, only seventeen-year-old Albertha had her own bedroom —for obvious reasons. The unlikely twins were both fifteen, and Bob was eleven, though he insisted that he was twelve. The three boys slept restively at night in their bedroom, which was also the smallest proper room in the apartment. Crash and Brother had mattresses set upon box springs in opposite corners, while Bob slept on a shelf Reginald Jr. had installed to make room for a study desk that only Crash used.

The study desk was Crash's province, because Brother was dyslexic, which Crash understood as not liking to read, and Bob had ADD, meaning that he could not concentrate on any one thing for very long. But even though Crash had the desk to himself, he didn't use it often, because his brother and cousin made loud noises at odd moments that would shock and distract him.

So Crash used his sister's desk, even when she was in the room, because Albertha didn't seem to mind his presence, and the noises she made were both consistent and benign. Albertha talked on the phone to her friends most waking hours.

" . . . and then Billy said that Principal Rivers knew that Mr. Eagles had been arrested for bein' drunk, and he said that Principal Rivers didn't get him fired because Eagles knew that Rivers had had sex with Mrs. Longerman's wife, Betty, before Betty realized that she was a lesbian . . ."

Albertha had long riffs of interpersonal explanations that went on and on and on. For Crash it was kind of like white noise playing in the background. While he wrote and read, Albertha explained the only things that were important to her and maybe her friends— what A did or didn't do with B, either against C or behind C's back.

The only thing that confused Crash was why his sister never stopped to listen to her friends, most of whom were girls. He decided that her friends were, like him, doing their schoolwork and found it soothing to hear his sister's soft chatter while delving calculus or unveiling the disturbing mysteries of biology.

Schoolwork came easily to Crash. His brother, Brother, cousin Bob, and Albertha all went to public schools, but Crash had a scholarship to Horatio Preparatory School, grades six to twelve. There were only 218 students at Horatio, and the education, everyone said, was one of the best in the nation.

What made Crash such a good student was that he could solve math problems by closing his eyes and allowing the equation to enter a place in his mind where it somehow solved itself, and also that he could read and retain a thousand pages in an evening's time. The years he attended public school, the teachers and counselors saw his odd quirks in learning to be symptoms of a mental disorder. When Mr. Martindale ordered Crash to write out the calculation to solve a long division problem, the youngster butted him in the nose out of sheer frustration.

"He's definitely suffering from a mild case of autism," the school's psychologist-counselor, Hannah Freest, told Mathilda Poplar-Martin at a special emergency meeting to discuss Percival's violent assault.

"But my son is happy," Mathilda said. "He's not suffering at all."

"He struck Mr. Martindale."

"A math teacher," the mother pointed out, "who does not accept that my son can do math problems in his head."

"Skirting processes," Hannah Freest argued, "which are part and parcel of the standardized education required by the state."

The phrase *standardized education* struck Mathilda. She realized in an unexpected instant that school for Percival was a factory, where he was a defective product soon to be discarded for more manageable material.

"Leave my son where he is for the rest of the semester," she said, "and I will have him in a private institution by January."

Horatio Prep tested Percival, called Crash for the rest of the semester by adoring fellow students. The private school accepted him, agreeing to waive tuition. That solved the problem of the young man's education for four blissful years. But by the time he reached the tenth grade, Percival had become bored with what the teachers had to show him.

Math and language gave him no problem. He understood the facts his teachers presented but was never, to his satisfaction, shown what lay behind the curtain of this so-called knowledge. Why did things happen? And what was responsible for why things were the way they were? On top of his own ennui, Crash could see that his classmates were often frustrated by the processes of acquiring knowledge and were rarely given what he thought of as truth. So he began to help his friends by giving them answers to the rote questions that a formal education asked over and over, like some monstrous dictator-parrot.

He taught his friends how to cheat on tests in ways that no one would suspect. He wrote papers and installed viral programs on their class computers, programs that would seek out the answers they needed.

One night he was lying in bed, only half-asleep, amid the clamor of Bob's nightmare cries over the deaths of his parents and Brother's rustling susurrations arising from the throes of yet another wet dream. At times like these Crash could drift, examining his mind without complete awareness. A thought would come into his mostly sleeping consciousness; birds' wings or World War II

Russian tanks, blood pulsing through vessels or words that rhyme. This was a state of complete ease, unencumbered by the limitations of time. Much later in life he would claim, "I do my best thinking when I'm asleep."

On this particular night, Crash suddenly realized that some student would betray him to the administration one day. This revelation forced him to recognize that in the eyes of the school he had been not helping but cheating. This meant that sooner or later he would be expelled from the one place where people believed in him.

Crash might have dismissed this dark epiphany as a bad dream if it were not for the note Alissya Progress brought to his first-period life-drawing class.

The model that day was Felix Neederman, a freshman from CCNY, who posed wearing nothing but briefs. He was reclining on a large wooden crate, propped up on one elbow, with what Crash's father would have called a shit-eating grin on his lips. Felix was pale-skinned and muscular, blue-eyed, with dirty-blond hair.

Crash sat on the high wooden stool at his easel with a stick of charred willow wood in his hand. He gazed at the burnt twig, which was quite a bit darker than his taupe-brown skin. The brown newsprint drawing pad hanging from the easel was closer to Crash's hue.

His father, Reginald Jr., was a deep brown color. Brother was a slightly darker brown than Crash, and Bob was that odd olive hue most people called white. Mother Mathilda had pale skin that she slathered with tan makeup every morning before facing the world. The only reason Crash knew his mother's true color was that they both liked to swim in the ocean, and her makeup, as she said, "could not survive the brine."

Thinking about skin and color, Crash had yet to make a mark on the pristine sheet of newsprint. While he pondered the colors ranging from charcoal to pale he noticed Alissya walking by. He arranged the easel so that he could see the paper and Felix Needer-man at the same time. He knew from previous classes that this binocular experience would end up with him tracing what he saw in the air upon the sheet of paper.

"Mr. Martin," Ernst Schillio said.

"Yes," Crash murmured, seemingly addressing his burnt willow stick.

"Miss Warren wants to see you."

Looking up, the tenth grader saw his teacher and Alissya staring back at him. He knew in an instant what was happening.

Crash placed the twig on the tray beneath the hanging pad of newsprint, hopped off the battered oak stool, and walked toward the exit. He was aware of the eyes of his fellow students watching as he made his way toward the classroom door. At public school the other kids would *ooh* at a student being called to the office. But at Horatio they only watched.

Percival was certain that his dream state the night before had predicted what was happening. Someone had turned him in, and now the principal was going to expel him for cheating.

By the time Crash made it to and through the doorway to the hall, his decision had been made. If he turned right, the principal's office was two doors away. Going left three doorways would bring him to Antoine Short's office. Antoine was what they called at Horatio the Student Advocate. If asked, Antoine would be required to go with Crash to the principal's office to protect him as much as possible from disciplinary actions demanded by school rules.

But Crash wasn't interested in the left or the right. Straight ahead were the double front doors of the school that opened onto Horatio Street and escape.

*   *   *

Bob, Albertha, and Brother were all at or on their way to school by the time Crash left Horatio. Reginald Jr. had been at work at Tourmaline Distributions since before the kids were awake, and Mathilda would be gone by ten to visit her ex-boyfriend Matthew Sinn in the hospice where he was dying from lung cancer.

Upstairs, in his parents' bedroom, on the high shelf in the big closet, Crash found his backpack among the others that Reginald Jr. and the boys used when they camped in the wilderness of Monhegan Island on summer vacations in late August.

Crash took jars of crunchy peanut butter and grape jelly along with a hard-crusted loaf of sourdough bread from the kitchen cabinet, a heavy afghan sweater from Brother's bottom drawer, and his father's Swiss Army knife. He dressed in canvas pants, a long-sleeved, heavy blue-and-white-checkered cotton shirt, and a light windbreaker. Clad in his makeshift camping wear and carrying the pack on his back, Crash set out for the E train. He took the subway to the Q37 bus, from which he transferred to the Q55. At noon, give or take a few minutes, he arrived at Forest Park in Queens and followed a rarely used path to Pine Grove, a place where his father took the boys camping now and then.

"What if they catch us?" Crash remembered his twin asking at the outset of one such outing.

"It's not illegal to camp in the park if it isn't posted," their father replied with a nonchalant shrug. "But if the park rangers or the police find us, they'll probably check our IDs and send us home."

Crash knew that the eastern white pines of the grove gave great cover and so was not worried about being found. His backpack contained a camouflage pup tent, a thin down sleeping bag, a butane hotplate with enough fuel for a week's worth of cooking, a pot and pan, a quart bottle of water, a battery-powered lantern, and six dried packets of onion and mushroom soup mix that came with a five-year guarantee of freshness. There were various other contents of the pack: three teabags, a tin cup, and a hunting knife designed, as his father said, for industry or defense.

Crash put up the tent and sat next to it eating a PB&J on sourdough. As evening came on, he began to wonder what would be happening between his home and the school. The principal's office would have called his parents, saying that they had to come in for a special disciplinary meeting. On the other hand, his parents would have called the administration office wondering what the school had done with their son. Sooner or later they would figure out that Crash had suspected why the principal called him to her office and, instead of facing the music, had run.

Down in a clearing below a scrim of pines, Crash saw three deer illuminated by an early moon. He'd turned his lantern on low to read *Demian*, by Herman Hesse, a book that had been assigned in Mrs. Schrodinger's World Literature class. Crash liked the book because it saw the world the way he did: not only good and evil but also light and dark mixing to make things so hard to understand. He liked the main character, Emil Sinclair, a lot. He was a misunderstood kid who couldn't solve the simple problems of life.

"Hey there, little brother." The voice was both rough and soft.

Crash peered in the direction from which the voice had come, but at first all he could see was darkness. He knew this was because of the blinding effect of the moon and electric light. He wasn't afraid, because Brother called him "little brother" due to a half-inch deficit in height; Crash had been born seven minutes before Brother, and his jealous twin always tried to make Crash seem the junior.

As Crash's vision acclimated, there appeared before him a tall and lanky young black man wearing black trousers and maybe a red T-shirt. The dark-skinned lad smiled brightly and said, "What you doin' out here readin' a book in the woods, man?"

"Reading," Crash said, though he knew this was not a satisfactory answer to the question.

"What's your name?" the young man asked. He took a step forward and hunkered down in an easy movement, right forearm on the knee, the knuckles of his left hand grazing the grass.

"My parents named me Percival, Percy, but everyone calls me Crash."

"Why Crash?"

"What's your name?" Crash asked.

"Otis." He said the word as if it were somehow a defeat. "Otis Zeal."

"That's a cool name," Crash said. It was the right thing to say.

Otis grinned again and asked, "Why you out heah?"

"They were going to expel me from school for helping about a dozen kids cheat on their homework and their tests."

"A dozen is twelve, right?"

"Yeah."

"So how much them other kids pay you to help 'em cheat?"

"Nothing."

"Nuthin'? You mean you helped them and didn't even get paid?"

"It was kind of like an experiment."

"Like a scientist, like on TV?"

"Uh-huh. You see, I thought that maybe my friends weren't learning because the teachers made the answers so much of a mystery. If they saw the question and then the answer, maybe that would help them know what they were learning about."

"You sound kinda crazy, Percy Crash."

175

"Why are you out here, Otis?"

"I always come out to here when I get in trouble too. My uncle used to take me here when I was kid like you, and now if I think somebody's after me I come here to hide."

"What are you hiding from?" Crash asked.

Otis embarked upon a meandering tale that made only a little sense to the sophomore from Horatio Prep. The story started with a girl named Brenda Redman. She was real cute, with a fat butt, and she could dance. Otis was a good dancer, and so every time he and Brenda met at a party at somebody's house in the Bronx, they danced to just about every other cut the DJ played. The problem was this guy named Lawrence. Lawrence liked Brenda, and she liked him some too, but he couldn't dance like Otis, and Brenda needed to be dancing when she was at a party and the music was playing—especially if there was wine involved. It was the wine, Otis believed, that made Lawrence angry. Brenda wasn't his steady girl or anything, but even still, Lawrence pushed Otis, and that made Otis mad.

"You don't wanna get me mad, little brother," Otis said, in the middle of his story. "When I get mad there's no tellin' what I might do."

Anyway, Otis got mad and stabbed Lawrence, who was a much bigger man, in the shoulder with a little paring knife. Otis always carried an edge—that's what he said.

"Did you kill him?" Crash asked Otis.

"I 'on't think I did. You know, sometimes people die when you don't hurt 'em much, but I don't think he woulda died. It don't matter though, because his cousin belongs to a gang, and they'll be lookin' for me for a long time."

There was a lull in the conversation for a while after that. Both young man and boy looked around, appreciating the relative silence of the city park. Then Otis began to shiver. The tremors started in his chest and radiated out toward the limbs. Crash crawled into the little pup tent and pulled out Brother's afghan sweater.

"Here," Crash said, "put this on."

Otis reached out and pulled the woolen garment over his head. He nodded, grinned, and then shuddered once before plopping down into a half lotus.

"That makes the difference," Otis declared.

Crash thought the words sounded like something a parent or some other elder had often said.

"You want a PB&J?"

"Wha's that?"

They talked about school because it was something they had in common. Otis had been kicked out so many times that they finally stopped expecting him to come back. Mostly these suspensions were because of his bad temper. Whenever Otis got angry he had to do something hard. He'd throw a glass against the wall, hit somebody, or something else like that. One time he pushed a girl named Theodora down some marble stairs.

"I was already sorry before she stopped tumblin'," he said. "But I didn't say it, because I had no right to expect forgiveness. I always keep thinkin' that maybe I could find a place where you nevah have to get mad, and then I'd be cool. My daddy told me before he died that that place was called *Dead*."

When it was Crash's turn to talk, he said that he felt like an outcast in school. Horatio Prep was better than public school, but still everybody thought that he was tricking them with the way he learned things.

"It's like when I read a book," Crash explained. "I turn the pages so fast that nobody believes I'm really readin', or when people just say a math problem and I know the answer."

"You didn't turn the pages fast when I saw you reading your book," Otis pointed out.

"That's because, um, after I read a book a few times I go slower and slower, because my mind is making up all this other stuff about how the people really felt and what they looked like."

"Like it was a TV show, but you have to see it ovah and ovah until you understand how what happened happened?"

"Yeah." Crash felt that no one had ever put into words the feelings he got while he was learning.

"Why don't you read me a couple a' pages?" Otis said.

Crash read nearly a dozen pages out loud, marveling at how good it sounded. He didn't trip and stumble over the words as he did when he read out loud in English class.

Otis started yawning after a while, and Crash stopped reading.

"Guess we should get some sleep," Otis suggested.

"Uh-huh."

Then Otis stood up on his knees and took three stump-like steps, bringing him very close to Crash. He leaned forward slowly and kissed Crash on the mouth. It was a wet kiss, not anything the sophomore had experienced before.

Otis leaned back and asked, "Is there room in yo' tent for me?"

The youths gazed into each other's eyes for a long moment before Crash said, "Uh-uh. It's too small."

Taking a long time before he spoke again, Otis finally said, "OK. I'll just curl up in this sweater next to it."

In his half-asleep state it came to Crash that Otis kissing him was the opposite of Otis getting mad. It made him happy that he was able to calm the angry young man down. He was smiling in the tent when somebody grabbed him by his shoulders and dragged him out.

"Who are you?" a man's voice shouted.

The sun was up and shining and hurting Crash's eyes.

"What are you doing here?" another angry voice wanted to know.

Crash held out his arms to show that he wasn't resisting them, but the man still lifted him from the ground and pulled him so close that Crash could smell bacon on his breath.

"Who are you?" Bacon Breath demanded.

"Percival Martin." He felt defeated because he used a name he no longer answered to.

"Where's some ID?"

"In my, in my, in my . . ."

"In your what?"

"In my backpack."

"Where is it?"

"Next to the tent."

Crash glanced at the side of the tent where Otis had been sleeping, but both the sometimes angry young man and the backpack were gone.

When Crash realized that Otis was gone with all his belongings —money and food, cookware and butane hotplate—he was giddy with the knowledge that he had helped his friend.

"You're going to jail, Percival Martin," one tall, treelike park man intoned.

They were all sitting around the dining table that night—the entire Martin clan plus Bob. It wasn't unusual for the family to gather over a meal, but this time there were no plates of food before them.

"What did you do?" Reginald Jr. asked.

Albertha was sitting next to her father. Crash imagined that his sister could hardly wait to get to her room, where she could tell everyone about her crazy autistic brother.

"I figured out how to help all the kids I knew get good grades on their papers and tests."

The police had called Reginald and Mathilda. They'd come down to the Queens police station and taken their son home.

"But why did you run away?" Mathilda asked.

Brother was peering at Crash with a crestfallen look on his face. This expression presented itself like a simple equation to Crash. It said that Brother realized that he would never be as much fun as him.

"I dreamed that . . . No, no, no. I saw that one of the kids would tell on me sooner or later. And then when I went to Mr. Schillio's class and he told me to go to the principal's office, I knew I was in trouble."

"The school didn't say anything about you cheating," Mathilda said.

Bob was studying his cousin.

"They didn't?"

"No," Reginald Jr. replied. "They called to tell us that you were going to be valedictorian of the second years."

"Oh."

"You have to stop cheating," the father continued. "Tell your friends that you can't do it anymore."

"Are you OK?" Mathilda asked.

Crash turned toward his mother but had no words to say.

"That goes for all of you," Reginald said to the other kids. "We never mention cheating again."

*   *   *

Years passed, but nothing happened that was as powerful or insightful or fulfilling as the day when Crash ran away. He'd kissed fourteen girls and a few boys, but nothing made an impression on him like Otis did amidst the pine trees and darkness, witnessed by lost deer and a few fireflies.

It was on this true adventure Crash had learned that the mathematics of life were ever so much more complex than counting up things in his head.

Albertha married her first boyfriend, Clyde Friarstone. She talked for both herself and her husband while Clyde smiled shyly at her side. Bob became a renowned artist and sometime opioid abuser. He still lied about his age.

Brother worked construction for six years, then he enlisted and did three tours of duty in Afghanistan. During his period of service he avoided the members of his family, most of whom were against the wars. But a few weeks after his last tour, Brother showed up at Crash's upper-Harlem apartment. Crash served his twin a glass of cabernet.

"When do you graduate, little brother?" Brother asked.

"Next year."

"You gonna work for the government?"

"I don't think so. Maybe I'll be a physics teacher at some small college upstate."

Crash thought that Brother didn't like this answer, but instead of saying so he asked, "You ever talk to Mom?"

"No," Crash said in a hushed tone. "She sends cards every once in a while but . . ."

"I throw 'em away," Brother said. "She was a bitch leavin' Dad. No explanation, just a note saying that it was over and she was gone."

"Why'd you join the army?" It was a question he'd always wanted to ask.

"To serve my country. To save people who got stuck under the Taliban."

"Did it feel like you broke outta prison and at least just for a little while you were free?"

Brother winced and said, "I got shrapnel in my chest. The doctors say that it's better to leave it."

They drank more and talked about old times in the bedroom with cousin Bob.

Crash didn't tell Brother that Mathilda had sent him her e-mail address or that he'd contacted her a few times. But something about Brother's visit made him decide to take the subway out to Queens. Her apartment was less than a mile from Forest Park.

He knocked on the sixth-floor apartment door and waited, nervous for the first time since he believed he was about to get expelled. The door came open. A willowy man stood there. He looked familiar, very much so.

"Matthew Sinn?" Crash asked.

"Hi, Percy. How are you?"

"I thought you were dead."

"I would be if it wasn't for your mother."

"It was really because of you, baby," Mathilda said to Crash at dinner. She'd made chicken and dumplings with almandine French beans and peach cobbler.

"Me?"

"You were so brave."

"What are you talking about?"

"Your whole life you were different. Nobody understood you. Your teachers were angry because you didn't need them. And then you ran away to the woods with a backpack and a book. You were only fifteen, and emotionally so much younger than that, but you took your life in your hands . . ."

"The day after you came back, she took my hands in hers," Sinn said. "She held on tight and told me I wasn't going anywhere. Before that everyone came to see me just to say goodbye, but Mattie held on tight. After three months I was in remission. In three years my cure moved in with me."

"Why didn't you tell anybody?" Crash asked his mom.

"I would have told them all," she said, "but no one replied to my cards except you. Reginald phoned me once, but before I could explain he called me vile names and hung up. I would have liked to remain his wife and just . . . be close with Matthew. But Reggie hated me for breaking the cord of our discord."

The last five words were often used by Mathilda's English professor father.

"But you just said you were gone," Crash argued.

"I said that I needed space."

That night Crash got on the Internet and entered an algorithm created to search for the name Otis Zeal. In a way, Crash thought, Otis was the one person who understood him like he intuitively understood long division.

The next morning Crash called his father. Minnie Saltworthy, Reginald Jr.'s live-in girlfriend, answered, "Martin residence."

"Hi, Minnie," Crash said.

"Hi, Percy. You want to talk to your father?"

"Hello, son," Reginald Jr. said. He'd retired from his sales job and now stayed home most of the time. He and Minnie, only fifteen years his junior, took vacations four times a year. They went on voyages and train treks, visited Mexico, and even went on a camping tour in the Italian Alps.

"Hi, Dad."

"You calling just to say hello?"

"I wanted to say that I love you, Dad; that I miss the days when we were kids living in that apartment and going to school."

"You can come home anytime you want."

That night Brother died of a heart attack. Skipping the funeral, Crash went the next day to the grave site. Brother was interred beneath a temporary plaster marker, upon which was written his birth name—Constant Stevens Martin. Crash wondered why he never knew Brother's real name. He wondered whether Brother had known it.

Soon after Brother's death, Crash dropped out of Columbia and started an online business that generated outlines for school papers and explained ways to take and take advantage of school tests. He made lots of money and often chatted, digitally, with his ever-changing cast of clients.

And then one night, while writing an e-mail to hornyowl297, he received a message from the Otis Zeal algorithm. He'd already read dozens of little reports of Otis being arrested, tried, and sometimes convicted. The not-so-young delinquent popped up all over the boroughs. He'd married Brenda Redman, but five months later she'd filed for, and been granted, a restraining order against him. Their divorce came soon after that.

But that evening, while trying to explain to the postgraduate hornyowl297 that all math existed before human understanding, he received the notice of Otis's death.

*   *   *

At a small graveyard called simply Final Rest, on the border of Queens and Brooklyn, the funeral and burial of Otis Zeal was held. The ceremony was scheduled for 7:15 A.M. Crash arrived at 6:27. The small chapel was empty, and so he took a seat at the back, in the third-to-last row. There he remembered the night he met Otis. There was the hello, the confession, and the kiss. It was a moment that happened outside of his head but was as important as the eternal resolution of pi.

"Who you, sugah?" a woman asked.

Crash looked up to see a dark-skinned woman wearing a black dress suit with a pale pink blouse underneath. There was a deep purple iris pinned to her lapel and a smile that Crash believed would never be far from her lips.

"Crash."

"Not Percy Crash?"

"Uh-huh. That's what Otis called me."

"I'm Zenobia Zeal," the woman said, taking Crash by the sleeve of his blue blazer. "You come up with me to the first row. I know that's what my son woulda wanted."

She dragged the shy professional cheater to the front of the first row of pews. The coffin had come while Crash was remembering.

"You know who I am?" the young man asked.

"Otis nevah stopped talkin' 'bout you. He said that you gave him all this stuff and read to him from a book called *Demon* and that he told you just about everything and you didn't laugh once."

"Really?" Crash asked. He'd thought that the older boy had probably forgotten him.

"I'll prove it." Saying this, Zenobia Zeal pulled Crash from the front row to the side of the open coffin.

Otis looked very much the way he had when Crash last saw him. Only now he sported a thick mustache. He wore blue jeans and a pullover afghan sweater.

"That there sweater was the onliest wrap he never lost," the ever-smiling mother said. "He told everybody that you was his best friend and that sometimes he'd come to see you on Horatio Street where you went to school. Nobody believed him though. We all thought he stole that sweater. But now here you are, his oldest friend, come to say goodbye to him."

Tears glittered in the older woman's eyes.

"How did my friend die?" Crash asked.

"Fightin'."

"Over what?"

"You never knew with Otis. He was just so sensitive. He always thought that people was laughin' at him or takin' advantage. He always said that you were the only one to treat him like a human being. Why is that?"

Crash stared into the dark woman's inquiring eyes and wondered about the question. He realized that she wanted him to share something intimate about her son, something uplifting.

"There's something different about my brain," Crash said, for the first time ever.

"Oh." A flash of concern moved across Zenobia's face.

"Not a disease or a condition," Crash interjected. "It's just that I think differently, and, in a way, Otis did too."

Zenobia nodded sagely.

"And so when we talked," Crash went on, "it felt like we understood each other. All the people in the world didn't understand us, but there we were, like brothers really. I knew him better than I did my own brother."

Zenobia took Crash's hand in hers, making him think about his mother and the life she saved and about Otis and his heartfelt kiss.

SHOWDOWN ON THE HUDSON

How the whole thing started is a mystery to most people, even the police. But those of us who were around 145th Street and Broadway, up in Harlem, knew something new was happening the day Billy Consigas came to town. His mother had moved to New York from southern Texas to escape an abusive husband. "A roustabout name of Henry Ryder," Billy told us.

And so Billy (who was fifteen at the time) was forced to leave his beloved Texas for Harlem. He didn't like New York at first, said that there was no place to stretch your legs or keep a horse. Some of us used to make fun of him, but that never amounted to much because Billy was an honest-to-God, one-hundred-percent bona fide black Texas cowboy. He wore a felt Stetson hat that was almost pure white. From the band of his hat hung a tassel of multicolored triple-string beads that he said was a gift from his Choctaw girlfriend when he had to leave Texas, *to come north*. He wore fancy bright shirts with snap buttons made from garnet, topaz, and quartz. His jeans were always well worn and rough as sandpaper. And he boasted that he had cowboy boots for every occasion—from weddings to funerals.

He got in good with the girls because, before long, he had a job for the NYPD training their horses in a special area of Central Park. He'd take young ladies up there in the early hours of the morning and teach them how to ride. Nesta Brown told me that if a man takes a girl riding that morning, he will most likely be riding her that night.

She actually said *most likely* with a dreamy look in her eyes and a kiss on her lips.

Girls our age flocked around Billy, and I never heard one of them call him a dog.

The black cowboy also had the most beautiful pistol any of us had ever seen. It was a silvery Cowboy Colt .44 six-shooter etched with all kinds of designs and finished with a polished horn handle. The holster for this ten-inch pistol was black with silver studs. And even though I am no fan of Westerns, when I saw how fast Billy could draw I downloaded fourteen cowboy films.

Billy drawled when he spoke and respected everyone he met. He'd always take his hat off inside or when in the presence of a woman or girl. And he could fight like a motherfucker.

One time, over by the Hudson, uptown, this big dude was chasing down some man that he claimed owed him money. The big man caught the little one and started beating him. The poor guy fell to the pavement and was bleeding from his mouth and forehead. That's when the big man started kicking him.

After two or three kicks, Billy Consigas walked up and said, "All right now, he's had enough."

When I tell you that the bully was big, I mean it in every way possible: he was tall and fat and had biceps almost the size of his head. But it wasn't only that he was big; he was fast too. He hit

Billy—who was five ten and 160 at most—right in the chest. Billy flew back and hit the wall behind him. We all thought that he was going to get himself killed.

The little man on the ground got up and started running.

Billy pushed off from the wall, took a deep breath, and then he smiled. Smiled!

"Fuck you, you grinnin' fool," the big man yelled, and then he ran right at Billy.

Billy kept on smiling. He didn't move until the guy was almost on him . . . and then he did this amazing thing. He jumped half a step to the right, so that his attacker slammed into the wall. Then Billy jumped up on top of the guy and clamped his left arm around his neck. We didn't know it at the time, but that was the end of the fight right there. The big guy was twisting and jumping around but couldn't throw Billy off, and Billy was steadily hitting him in the face with these wicked right uppercuts. He must have hit him two dozen times before the behemoth slumped down on the sidewalk. The bully tried to get up three times, but his legs were spaghetti and his shoes roller skates.

We never found out what happened to him because we heard sirens and scattered.

After that fight Billy became like a hero among the young men and women up around 145th. He didn't consider himself a leader, though, because of something he called the Cowboy Code. I never got all the ins and outs of that system, but it had something to do with being self-sufficient and treating all others equally. Leaders, he thought, were there only for the weak.

"Felix," he said to me one late afternoon when I was showing him around Times Square, "a man has to stand up on his own two feet. The only leaders they should evah have is parents, teachers, and generals during time of war. Other than that we all just people come from our mothers and headed for the grave."

Billy talked like that. He bought me a hot dog, and I paid for our tickets to the wax museum. We walked in the crowds of Times Square for hours. Billy was especially interested in the Singing Cowboy, who wore only a Stetson hat and underpants as he played the guitar and posed for photographs.

"What do you think about that?" I asked after Billy had stared at the street performer for at least three minutes.

"Like any other child's cartoon on the television."

It was somewhere past eleven in the evening when we decided to take the number one train back to Harlem. Billy had paid for our barbecue dinner. He told me that it was OK because the police gave him good money to train their horses.

When we were walking toward the train someone said, "I'll be damned, a nigger in a cowboy hat. I never seen anything like that before."

I turned first and saw a group of five young white men and three young women. They were maybe a year or two older than us. The guys sported new-looking blue jeans and fancy shirts like the ones Billy wore. The girls had on modern party dresses, slight and short. I was nervous because it was only the two of us against five of them, not counting the girls.

I say "against" because the leader, a tall and skinny white guy with a long and somehow misshapen face, had used the word *nigger*, and that word, in that tone of voice and that situation, meant conflict.

Billy turned and smiled. I had come to associate that expression with sudden violence. This mental connection only added to my fear.

"A peckawood with a problem," Billy said jovially. "That's more common than rattlesnakes down a prairie hole."

"You sound like Texas," the speaker of the group speculated.

"And you sound like horseshit."

"Where you come from, boy?" the white youth asked.

"From a long line a' men."

In any other situation I would have run, but I didn't want Billy to think less of me. So I squared my shoulders and wondered which one of the five I could get at before his friends got to me.

That was what Billy did: he made people happy and proud, brave and courageous—qualities that rarely served a poor black man or boy well.

"You think you man enough take us?" the leader asked.

"At five to two?" Billy asked. "All we got to do is stand our ground and we prove better than some gang a' roughnecks."

The leader smiled. That grin was a close relative of Billy's violent mirth.

I realized that I was holding my breath.

"My name is Nacogdoches," the white youth claimed. "Nacogdoches Early."

"Billy."

"You a cowboy, Billy?"

"I've been in a rodeo or two."

This made me think of Billy taking down that giant on the Hudson. He wasn't afraid because he'd brought down steers with that same hold.

"You got a gun?" Nacogdoches inquired.

Billy shrugged.

"You a gunslinger?" Nacogdoches said to Billy.

"Faster 'n you."

The warped-faced white youth's eyebrows raised, and his smile broadened.

"Is one of these fine ladies your girl?" Billy asked.

A strawberry blonde moved her shoulders in such a way as to indicate that she was the one.

"No bullets," Billy said, as if they had already agreed on the gunfight. "Just a video camera in case it's a close call. If you win, I'll spit-polish your green boots right on that corner. I'll just wear my long johns and hat at high noon on a Saturday. If you lose, that pretty girl will agree to have dinner with me at the place and time of my choosin'."

The girl tried to frown, but instead a smile grazed her lips. She wasn't really that pretty, I thought, but had the kind of face that you'd want to nod to at a party or if you sat near each other on a subway train.

Nacogdoches was biting his lower lip.

"OK," he said at last. "When and where?"

"There's a youth center up on Sixty-Third," I said. "Lazarus House. We do it there in three days at ten at night."

In spite of the offer, my plan was simply to get away.

The principals agreed, and I gave Nacogdoches the address.

"What kinda crazy luck you have to have that you run into another cowboy with a six-shooter somewhere in the middle of a million people?" I asked Billy on the number one train.

"It's the bright lights," the black cowboy opined.

"What?"

"You know a cowboy loves the stars more than anything. He's drawn to the lights like a moth to fire. Times Square is bright like the heavens come down to the ground. And you know two cowboys will see each other. No, no, Felix. It would be a wonder if we didn't meet up sooner or later."

"We don't have to do this thing, Bill," I said. "We just don't show up, and it'll all blow over."

"Maybe so," he said, "but we will be there."

All the youngsters in our neighborhood knew about the showdown, as Billy called it, scheduled for Wednesday night. They gossiped about it and bragged on their black cowboy hero.

In the interim, I saw Billy every day because I was his assigned tutor.

"Hello, Felix," Mrs. Consigas greeted me on that Wednesday afternoon. She was a dark-skinned black woman with a young face. "You're a little early, aren't you?"

"Yes, ma'am."

"What's that you're carryin'?"

"My uncle's video camera."

"What for?"

"My sister's in a dance recital after, and I'm going to video it for my mother. She works nights." It was all lies, but Marion Consigas didn't know my mother or my sister.

"You're a good boy, Felix Grimes."

I spent the next two hours trying to teach Billy about variables in algebra. I was a good student, and as far as school went, Billy was dumb as a post; he said so himself.

"It takes me a long time to get the idea," he said to me at our first tutoring session, "but once I got it, it's there forever."

He didn't talk about the showdown at all. I told six friends where it was happening: five guys and Sheila Grant, a girl I wanted but who only had eyes for the Harlem Cowboy, Billy Consigas.

Billy struggled through the workbook lesson, and somewhere around seven o'clock he said, "Time to go."

*   *   *

We all—Billy, me, Sheila Grant, and five others—arrived early. My brother Terrence, who worked at Lazarus House as a nighttime security guard, was waiting at the side entrance. He told us that Nacogdoches was already inside with his posse.

My brother was nineteen, three years older than I. He was nervous, but Billy ponied up twenty dollars for the use of the gym, and Terrence was always looking for more money.

Nacogdoches was there with the same group of friends. This detail said something about the ugly southerner that I couldn't quite put my finger on.

While I set up the tripod and videocam, Billy and Nacogdoches decided on the rules.

"Best out of three," the white cowboy said.

"And we check to make sure that each other's gun is empty before each duel," added Billy.

"Duel?" Nacogdoches sneered. "What are you some kinda English faggot?"

"I am what I am," Billy said, "and that's more than enough for you."

Nacogdoches frowned and balled his fists. Billy wasn't school-trained, but he once told me that all true cowboys could sing and were poets. The white gunslinger couldn't match him with words, and so he said, "Thalia will count. On three we draw."

Billy nodded, no longer smiling.

The duelists checked each other's guns and then took their places six steps apart. The white guy had a mean look on his face. Billy was as peaceful as moonlight on the Hudson. He wasn't actually a handsome youth, but Billy had a look that made you feel like there was something good somewhere, something you could depend on.

Thalia, that was Nacogdoches's girl, counted out loud. When she got to three, Nacogdoches slapped his brown leather holster, coming up with his black iron gun at incredible speed. But when we looked at the replay it was obvious, even to Nacogdoches's friends, that easygoing Billy had his piece out first. The black cowboy's movements were fluid, seamless.

Nacogdoches was slower on the second draw. We didn't even have to look at the replay.

After that Billy started undoing the leather string that laced the bottom of the black and silver holster to his right thigh.

"What you doin'?" the white cowboy complained.

"Two outta three," Billy said.

"I want the last draw."

"Why?"

"You scared?" Nacogdoches asked in a taunting tone.

Billy smiled and shook his head. He tied the lace again, and I turned on the camera.

"One," Thalia said, and a sense of doom descended upon me.

"Two," she pronounced. It struck me that this last contest meant far more than two young men proving themselves.

"Three."

Nacogdoches was faster this time. He grabbed his piece and had it out like a real gunslinger in a fight for his life.

But Billy was faster still. On the video replay he had the silver gun out and had played like he was fanning the hammer with his left hand before Nacogdoches had his barrel level.

"We could have hot dogs on that corner where I said I'd shine your boyfriend's shoes," Billy suggested to Thalia.

"No, you won't," Nacogdoches said.

"That was the bet," Billy countered, the ass-kicking smile back on his lips.

"You didn't pull the trigger," his rival argued.

"Why I wanna pull on a trigger when I know the gun is empty?"

"You could draw faster if you didn't move your finger. Any fool could pull a gun out by its butt."

Billy squinted as if he was on his beloved prairie trying to make out a shadow on the horizon. He shook his head ever so slightly and then shrugged, moving his shoulders no more than an inch.

"Thank you, Terrence," Billy said, waving to my brother, who was standing next to the exit door. "We finished here."

"You didn't pull the trigger," Nacogdoches said again.

"I won," Billy replied.

Terrence herded us out the door and onto Sixty-Third.

Thalia, who was wearing black jeans and a calico blouse, walked up to Billy and shook his hand. He gave her a quizzical stare, but she lowered her head and turned away.

"I won!" Nacogdoches said, as he and his friends walked toward Central Park.

When we were walking to the train, Billy asked me to come with him while Sheila and the rest took a more direct route to the subway. He said that he wanted to talk about something as we strolled north on Broadway.

But before he had the chance someone said, "Stop right there."

I was already nervous. Most of my life I had spent at my home, at church, or in school, where I had been an honor student every year, every semester. I wasn't used to running the street with armed friends and watching duels.

Two uniformed policemen were getting out of their black and white cruiser. Billy had his six-shooter in a battered brown leather satchel, and the police had the right of stop-and-frisk.

Once again I had the urge to run, but I knew that wouldn't end well.

One cop was pink colored and the other dark brown.

"What are you doing here so late at night, boys?" the black cop asked.

"Good evening, Officer O'Brien," Billy said to the white policeman.

"Consigas?" he replied.

"You get that parade trot down yet?"

"This is the kid I was telling you about, Frank," the white cop said to his partner. "He can do anything on a horse. Honest-to-God cowboy from Texas."

"I was just playin' basketball with my friend Felix here down at Lazarus House," Billy said.

O'Brien asked Billy a few things about riding and then shook my friend's hand.

"I thought the Cowboy Code said you shouldn't lie," I said when we were installed on the train.

"She gave me her phone number," Billy replied.

"What?"

"That Thalia gave me her phone number on a little piece of paper when she shook my hand."

"Damn."

"What do you think I should do?"

I am, as I said, a good student and the kind of citizen that stays out of trouble. I prefer reading to TV and ideas in opposition to actions, sweat, or violence. I was always considered by my parents, teachers, and, later on, by my employers, a good person. My only serious fault, as my father was always happy to say, was that I often spoke without considering what it was that I said. This was most often a minor flaw, but in certain cases it could be a fatal one.

"You should call her and have lunch at that barbecue place with me and Sheila Grant. That way it'll be friendly."

Billy called Thalia the next day. He told her what I had said, and by now regretted, and she agreed to the date.

"She said," Billy told me, "that Nacogdoches had obviously lost, and she felt that it was her obligation to go on a date with the winning cowboy."

The lunch was set for Saturday.

"What you mean he's goin' out with that white girl?" Sheila said when I asked her to come along.

"It's the bet," I explained lamely. "He kind of has to go."

"I bet he wouldn't think so if she was black."

"You know better than that, girl. Billy's doing it because he won and she knows it."

"Sounds stupid to me."

"That mean you're not comin'?"

We ordered hot links, brisket, fried chicken, and pork ribs, with cornbread, collard greens, fried pickles, and a whole platter full of french fries.

"So where all you southerners come from?" Sheila asked Thalia after we'd ordered.

"Only Nacky and one of the others, Braughm, are from the South. They're both out of Nashville. We all go to this private school called Reese on Staten Island. Most of the kids there are rich and have what they call 'social behavior problems.'"

"But all his friends dress like cowboys," I said.

"They just wanna be like him," Thalia said with a twist to her lips. I remember thinking that if she were Caribbean she would have sucked a tooth.

"So you're rich?" Sheila asked Thalia, as if it was some kind of indictment.

"No. My mother teaches there, and she didn't like the kind of friends I had in public school. I like your hair. I wish I could do something like that with mine."

Sheila had thick corded braids that flowed down her back. She was a beautiful girl. She lost her angry attitude when Thalia complimented her.

"So Nacogdoches is like some kind of juvenile delinquent?" Billy asked.

"He got in trouble down south stealing. I think his parents just wanted to get rid of him. Anyway, he's graduating this June. Says he's going out to California."

That's when the food came. We spent the rest of the lunch talking and joking. Thalia was a painter who wanted to specialize in horses. That's what drew her to Nacogdoches. He kept a horse at a stable in Connecticut and promised to bring her up there some day.

"But now I think he was just sayin' that to get in good with me," the white girl added.

Billy said he'd take her to the police stables the next morning. He invited me and Sheila too.

"It's not a date unless you two kiss," Sheila said when we were out in front of the Iron Spur Barbecue House.

Thalia kissed Billy on the cheek, and Sheila snapped the picture with her cell-phone camera.

Billy left with Thalia, and Sheila gave me a few friendly kisses before I walked her home.

The next morning Thalia and Billy met us at the gate of the police stables. They were both wearing the same clothes from the day before.

I had the most trouble keeping up with my horse. I was just bouncing, bouncing—up and down, to the side, and almost to the ground once or twice. But we had a good time. The girls became friends, and Billy was glad that we were there together.

"You know, Felix," he said to me, when we were returning the big animals to their stalls, "I realized yesterday that there are good people everywhere—not only in the place you come from."

Like every other citizen of the world with a cell phone, Sheila was an amateur photographer. She took pictures of us on our horses, out in the park, and of me, Billy, and Thalia walking side by side. Thalia's arm was linked with Billy's.

Things returned to normal after that, more or less. I went back to my secretary post on the student council and helped Billy write a paper for his remedial English class. It was an essay about a book of cowboy poetry his grandfather had given him. Sheila and Thalia became Facebook friends. They shared pictures and started telling each other about their experiences in different boroughs and at different schools.

I asked Sheila to go out with me six times in the next two weeks, but she always had some reason to say no.

Then one afternoon, Sheila was waiting outside my German class, clutching her beloved smartphone.

"Hey, Sheil," I said, trying to sound nonchalant.

"Look at this," she said, thrusting the phone into my hand.

On the screen was a photograph of Thalia. She had a black eye and a bloody lip, and she seemed to be in the middle of a scream or cry.

"Flip it," Sheila said.

There were seven pictures of the white girl. It became obvious after the second shot that she was being beaten while someone took pictures. In two shots someone was pulling her hair and slapping her. In another photo she was hunched over, clutching her stomach with both hands as if someone had kicked her.

"Who sent you these?" I asked Sheila.

"It came from her phone. There was a text too."

The text read, *This is what happens to whores and race traitors.*

As his tutor, I went to Billy's house almost every afternoon. That day we were making the finishing touches on his poetry paper. Billy wrote on an old Royal typewriter.

"I don't really care for computers," he said. But I think he was just afraid of them.

The night before, he'd finished the fifth rewrite of the essay. He really did have deep insights into poetry and its uses by people living the actual lives that they turned into verse. We did a word-by-word examination of his spelling and grammar before I dared to broach the thing that was foremost in my mind.

"I need to show you something, Billy."

"What's that, Felix? You don't think that the paper's good enough?"

I located the forwarded files from Sheila's phone and showed him the pictures. Billy flipped through them saying not a word. His eyes seemed to get smaller, but he wasn't squinting. If he drew a breath, I couldn't tell.

After some minutes and close perusal of the photos, Billy said, "Can you send this motherfucker a note?"

Playground above 150 on the Hudson. Midnight tonight. Come ready. Come heavy.

Billy strapped on the pistol in his bedroom. It was exactly as he had done at Lazarus House, but this time he tied the holster to his left leg.

"I thought you were right-handed?" I said.

"Two-handed," Billy said, showing the first smile since he had seen the pictures. "But I'm a little better with my left."

At 11:35 he donned an off-white trench coat, and we left the house.

"Where you goin'?" Billy's mother called from the kitchen.

"Over to Felix's," said my friend. "He's gonna help me type my paper into his computer so then I can send the file-thing to Miss Andrews."

Outside we hailed a green cab and had the driver take us to the park.

Nacogdoches Early and his posse were waiting for us. Thalia was with them, but as soon as we appeared she ran to me. Her face was all swollen from the punishment she'd received.

"That's right," Nacogdoches said. "Go on over to them. That's where you belong."

A few moments later Sheila Grant, Tom Tellerman, and Teriq Strickland walked into the empty children's playground. I had called Sheila, and she'd notified our other friends.

Nacogdoches was wearing a bright-colored Mexican poncho, which he flung off. Underneath he was wearing his brown holster and black gun. He was hatless, and his pale skin shone in the shadowy light.

Billy took off his trench coat and draped it around Thalia's shoulders. Sheila was holding the scared white girl by then.

There was no need for words. Billy and Nacogdoches squared off with about ten paces between them.

"Thalia?" Billy called.

"Yeah?" she said.

"You strong enough to count to three, honey?"

Thalia walked to the river side of the present-day cowboys. The rest of us, white and black, moved out of the line of fire.

"One," Thalia said, and I was reminded of the sense of fate I'd experienced at Lazarus House.

"Two," she announced, and I wanted to scream.

Before she was able to utter the last number, Nacogdoches reached for his pistol. He pulled out the gun and fired. But before that, with snake-like fluidity, Billy drew and shot. Nacogdoches's bullet went wild, landing, I believe, somewhere out on the Hudson. The young white man was dead before he hit the concrete. I remember that he fell on a chalk-drawn hopscotch design.

There was another shot, and I looked to see Braughm, the other white southerner, aiming a pistol at Billy—who was now down on one knee. Billy shot one time, hitting his assailant in the upper thigh. Two others of Nacogdoches's posse had guns, but Billy shot both of them before they could fire—one in the shins and the other in the shoulder.

After that we all ran.

At a coffee shop on 125th Street, Billy was once again wearing his trench coat, and he was drinking from a bowl of chicken noodle soup. Sheila and Thalia were there with us.

"You think he's dead?" Billy asked me.

"You hit him in the head," I said.

Billy nodded and grimaced.

"It ain't no fun when somebody dies," he said.

After a few minutes of silence I noticed a red spot at the right shoulder of his off-white coat.

"You're bleeding."

"I think I need to get out of town," he said.

"I'll go with you," Thalia offered.

"That'd be nice," Billy said kindly, "but with all them bruises we'd be stopped before the train made it out from Penn Station."

Sheila's aunt and uncle were out of town, and so we cleaned and dressed Billy's wound there. The bullet had come in through the front and gone out the back of Billy's shoulder.

"Lucky that Braughm had steel-jacketed slugs," Billy said. "A soft bullet woulda tore me up."

I went with my friend to Penn Station and waited with him for a train headed to Atlanta. I was worried that there was some kind of internal bleeding, but Billy said that he felt good and strong.

"I never wanted to live up here anyway," he said.

"What do you want me to tell your mom?"

"I'll write her, don't you worry about that. If she calls, tell her I left your place sometime after two and you don't know where I went."

He boarded the 5:11 morning train, and that was the last I ever saw of him.

The police found Nacogdoches Early and followed the bloody trail back to his friends. All they knew was that there was some black kid named Billy who killed Nacogdoches in a gunfight. They got to my brother, but he said that he'd made the deal with some kid named Billy and he never knew where he'd come from.

Thalia told about the beating, but she'd tossed her phone, and the cops were never able to follow the electronic trail.

The three major newspapers loved the romance of a shootout on the Hudson.

In the weeks that followed there were seventeen Western-style gunfights all over the city. Black, white, and brown would-be gunslingers had duels. No one was killed, but the mayor and chief of police ratcheted up the stop-and-frisk program until even rich people started to complain.

Six months later it had all died down. Billy's mother left Harlem, and I graduated a year ahead of time. I was in my fourth year at Harvard, majoring in English literature with an emphasis on Yeats, when I received an unopened letter forwarded to me by my sister, Latrice.

Dear Felix,

Over the past four years I have meant to write to you but I was always on the move and even when I started to write the words didn't add up to much. I am very sorry for what I did when you knew me back then. There was no excuse for what Nacogdoches Early did to Thalia but that didn't give me the right to take his life. Maybe if it had been a fair fight, maybe if I didn't know I could beat him, it would have been all right. But I knew I was the better gunman and so what I did was murder.

I have spent my time since then in the country from Montana to Northern California riding horses and taking work as I find it. I see my mother from time to time. She moved back to Texas because Henry Ryder died and she didn't have to be afraid of him anymore.

You were a good friend, Felix, and I appreciate you sticking by me even though you could have got in trouble too.

Maybe you should burn this letter after you read it. Whatever you do I'll be writing again. Maybe one day we'll even see each other in Times Square or maybe on the Hudson.

Your friend, Billy

I haven't burned Billy's confession—not yet. I keep meaning to.

Over the years I have received eleven letters from the Harlem Cowboy. In the last few he's written some very nice poetry about nature and manhood. His words mean a lot to me. His convictions about right and wrong give me the strength not to see myself as a victim.

I got my PhD from Harvard and now teach American literature at the University of Texas in Houston. In Billy's most recent letter, he said that a girlfriend googled me online and found out that I was there. In that letter he wrote,

. . . Don't be too surprised if I drop by your classroom one day, professor. In a long life you only got a few friends, that's a fact . . .

BREATH

I remember waking up, trying to catch my breath. If someone had asked my name or address, or even what room I was sleeping in, I wouldn't have been able to say. All I had on my mind was that elusive inhalation, that solitary lungful of air that had to be somewhere; it had to be or I was going to die.

The apartment was empty—stripped down to the dust-swirled wood floors. The air conditioner was on, and I wasted precious seconds looking around for my pants. I found the phone, but it was dead. Somebody was crying somewhere nearby, but I couldn't call to them. As I went through the door to the hallway, it came to me that the sobbing was actually the whine of my lungs trying to throw off the congestion.

"Can't bre—," I wheezed.

I must have walked out of my building and across the private road to the unit concierge across the way. I never knew his name, even though he'd been working as a nighttime guard in that complex of university housing longer than I had been a professor at New York College.

He was younger than I by fifteen years at least—not a day over sixty. His eyes were both frightened and suspicious. Maybe I had been shot or stabbed. Maybe the assailant was still lurking somewhere in the dark hours of an early Manhattan morning.

As he helped me into a seat, a flood of thoughts entered my mind, each fighting for the place of my last mortal thought. There was my son, Eric, who had changed his name to Simba, calling on the phone. Simba never called, and even though I could hear him, I still couldn't speak or breathe.

"Dad? Dad, are you there?"

Sarah, my wife, who had passed away in '96, was talking to somebody other than me.

"I know it seems strange," she was saying, in a matter-of-fact tone, "but we've just grown apart."

I tried to speak up, to interrupt, to tell her to shut up and come on back home—to life. But then I was standing on a golden Caribbean beach where a new home was waiting for somebody.

Gravity shifted and I was no longer in my seat. There were voices thundering and lights and darkness. I was blind as well as breathless, thinking about my daughter and wishing that she was with me. My girl, Anetta, would not let her father die. At least, I remember thinking, at least my memory would not be lost as long as she was alive and little Olive, her baby girl, was there in the world beyond the darkness that enveloped me.

"You bettah git away from me, niggah," a man declared in a jagged tone that was steely and thin as a dagger.

The angry words dissipated in the air, and everything was dark and silent again. Breath flowed cold and rich through my nostrils. My head was stuffed with cotton wadding, and there were no independent thoughts rising from my mind.

I drifted.

I was in a coffin, under the ocean, watched over by fishes that did not know or care to know my name or species. They flitted, fornicated, and fled in fear when shadows fell upon them. Water leaked in slowly, excruciatingly so. One drop every thirty seconds or so, that's how I figured it. But what did I know? And what did it matter now that I was dead and interred and forgotten, buffeted by the currents of the deep?

"Hey, brothah. Brothah," a man was saying. He shook my shoulder, disturbing my eternal rest. "Hey, wake up."

I made a noise. It was nowhere near a word, but it seemed to be enough for the grave robber. He was a dark shadow upon a screen of slightly lighter darkness, hovering to my right.

"Somebody in that bed across from you?" he asked.

What bed? What cross?

"Somebody in there?"

"Where?" I managed to say. It hurt my throat, way down past the Adam's apple, to speak.

"I need a bed," the man said. "Is they anyone in it?"

"Mothahfuckah," the bodiless knife of a voice from before warned. It came from somewhere farther off to the right. The shadow moved away.

I tried to raise my head but failed. I tried to imagine myself in the world. That didn't work either. Then I remembered an old trick. I evoked an image of Earth, allowing it to turn slowly. I watched, as I imagined God sometimes did, the passing of terrain, paying no attention to false national borders of fiefdoms. When a place I'd known moved by it would lighten, as if there were a powerful light below the surrounding soil and mountains. Ouagadougou, Cairo, and Accra flashed into my mind. I remembered a sandwich and a young Senegalese woman, an offer and a refusal, and afterward, for years, regret. There was Paris and London and, faintly, Amsterdam . . . New York.

New York. That's where I was on the globe. The light was strongest there.

The cold, dry oxygen was too much. I started coughing and couldn't stop. It was a rolling, hacking, wet and yet dry retching from my diaphragm all the way to my eyes. I was old Mr. Hawkins, dying in the apartment across the hall in 1946. I was the car alarm that wouldn't stop in the middle of the night. I was Cecil Roberts Bentway, PhD, historian and cultural critic. And I would rather have been dead than go through one more minute of coughing.

Hands took hold of my head and jaw. I struggled against them, but most of my strength had been drained by the involuntary exertions. Something thick and wet was forced into my left nostril and down into my throat and then farther, into my lungs.

There was a vibration, a throbbing sensation, and I knew that someone was using a vacuum to suck the mucous from my flooded lung.

The coughing stopped.

For a while I relaxed on the hardtack sheets, sweating and sighing. I realized that the mattress was thin, that I could feel the whorls of the metal springs under my body. I lifted my rump up, let go, and felt the hint of a rebound—proving my surmise. This made me smile. I could still ply my dubious trade even while being but a hair's breadth away from finality.

"Where'd this one come from?" a woman's voice asked.

"I don't know," a young man said. "That bed's s'posed to be empty."

I raised my head enough to see that they were standing next to the bed across the way from me.

"He got an admittance form?"

"Nuthin'. Not even a clipboard."

"Let's go down to the front desk and ask them."

"Nurse," Steel Voice said.

"What?" the woman replied.

"My sheets is torn."

"OK," she said.

"When you gonna gimme new ones?"

"I'll make a note at the nurses' station."

The young man and the woman that was a nurse talked more. Their voices receded as they left the room and moved down the hallway.

"Bastids," Steel Voice said after they were gone.

The room slowly did a backward fade into daylight. For a long time I lay there on my back allowing names to flow through my mind, or maybe they were going that way without my consent. C. L. R. James and W. E. B. Du Bois, the poet and activist Jayne Cortez, and Amiri Baraka, who, under the name LeRoi Jones, wrote the play *Dutchman*. I considered their works and many others. Over the years I'd been a tough and, hopefully, loving critic. I'd taught young people of all backgrounds and races about people and ways of thinking that the university rarely emphasized. At seventy-five I'd bought a beach condo on a small island where I could finally finish my life's work—*Pagans in Pinstripes*.

My throat, instead of hurting, was numb. I thought about my shoulders and elbows between the esoteric texts, and finally, after quite a while, I managed to rise up on one arm.

The room was larger than I expected. There were four beds with a good deal of space between them; one situated in each corner. The bed to my right, where the steely voice had originated, was being worried over by a thin black man in pale blue pajamas who had stripped the blankets and sheets and was remaking the bed. For some reason this task seemed Sisyphean. He worked methodically and with great care. There was something institutional about his movements.

Across the way, past my feet, a smallish but not thin black man was coiled under the blanket, staring suspiciously around himself. He clutched his woolen cover as if he were afraid that someone might come and yank it away.

At the diagonally opposite corner from me was yet another dark-colored brother. Sitting in a wooden chair next to the bed, he was also clad in pale blue pajamas. This silent sentry brought to mind a lost soul who had returned to the last place where he'd been alive. His morose expression and posture added to this impression. The man appeared to me like the only mourner at his own funeral, seated in the pews and at the same time lying in the coffin. He too looked to be past sixty.

I tried to think of the odds that four black men near or past retirement age might end up in the same hospital room together in Lower Manhattan. Weren't there any white or yellow, olive-toned or brown-skinned men in their twenties or forties, any young black men who got sick and needed a bed?

"Hey, brothah," called the paranoid man beyond my feet. I knew then he was the shadow who had first awakened me.

I looked at him but could not speak.

"If they ask you, tell 'em that I was brought in on a stretcher last night. Tell 'em that I was brought in on a stretcher."

I glanced over at the man making and remaking his bed. He paid no attention to what our undocumented roommate was saying. I let my head fall back on the small pillow and felt the little bounces of jubilant springs. It was as if I were lying upon a huge lily pad; a bloated frog waiting for a passing fly. I closed my eyes and tried to remember getting to that place—seventy-five and hospitalized in a room occupied only by old black men. Had I really been a professor at a prestigious university? Had I once been present at Nelson Mandela's eighty-second birthday celebration?

"You OK, man?" someone asked.

I opened my eyes and saw the rail-thin bed-maker. I would have bet that the frown on his face was the closest he ever came to expressing compassion.

"They don't give a fuck about a niggah 'round here, man," he said. "Most the time they late bringin' you your food. An' forget the bedclothes. It don't even look like they wash 'em more times than not."

I wanted to say something, I wanted to echo the roommate's knowledge, but didn't have the strength.

"That's all right, brothah," he said. "Get you some rest. If you need me to get you sumpin', just say it or just raise your hand. You know I always got one eye open."

It felt as if I had only blinked, but the man was gone. I knew then that I had to get out of there. I had to get away before I was swallowed up by that alien room with its condemned souls, devil nurses, and infiltrators.

I tried to remember what I had been wearing before the asthma attack. Most nights I fell asleep wearing a golden, scarlet, and royal blue Ghanaian robe. The first time I'd get up to urinate I'd take it off. Did my attack come before my first trip to the toilet?

"Mr. Holder," someone said. She was addressing the bed-maker.

There was low light suspended in the air like an illuminated fog.

"What?"

"Have you used needles in the past five years?" the woman asked. There was a lilt to her voice. Nigerian.

"I ain't nevah used no needles."

"It says in your file that you were in prison for drugs," she countered.

"Yes, I was. Heroin. But I ain't nevah used no needles. The people I sold to used 'em, but I was always a Johnnie Walker Blue Label man."

I dozed while the doctor and her assistants wheeled some heavy equipment to the side of the bed-maker, Mr. Holder.

I woke up again when a man all in white rolled an IV unit up next to me and lifted my right arm. As he looked for a vein I tried to pull away. But I was so weak that he didn't seem to notice. I thought he should at least tell me what he was doing; that he should ask if I wanted the procedure or whether I was allergic to the yellowy fluid in the IV bag.

Seconds after the needle was pressed into the vein, my body passed out. I say it this way because I was in darkness and without physical sensation, but my consciousness seemed to rise above the bed and the body it held. I could hear everything. It wasn't like normal hearing either. My ears were hypersensitive, like those of an ancient proto-dog at the edge of the Gobi Desert listening for sounds of beloved but feared humanity.

"She, she kicked me out," the sad man who sat beside his bed whined. "Twenty-eight years, and she just kicked me out like a, like a stray dog. And I ain't got nuthin'."

" . . . brought me in last night," the man in the bed across from me was saying to somebody. "Last thing I remembah I was walkin' down One Thirty-Seven and I got dizzy. I grabbed for this lady to keep upright, but she hollered and pushed me away. When I woke up I was in this here bed . . . No. I ain't got no one to call."

"The X-ray reveals a dark spot, Mr. Holder," the Nigerian doctor was saying. "It might be malignant."

"Dark spot where?" the fastidious bed-maker jabbed, in his hopelessly harsh tone.

"The left side of your chest. Over your lung."

"That ain't no tumor. That's where I got shot one time."

"So you think that it's a bullet?"

"Yes, ma'am."

"Why didn't the doctor take it out?"

"What doctor? You think I'm gonna go to some doctor when all they gonna do is call the cops? Shit."

"When I went back to beg her she was gone," the sad man next to his bed said, and then he let out a low moan that didn't sound human. "Carol next door told me that she had gone back down to North Carolina to her people. She had everything a' mines. My Social Security card. My birth certificate. Only shoes I had left was on my feet . . . Yeah, my blood pressure's high. Wouldn't yours be?"

"Sugar diabetes, asthma, arthritis, glaucoma, thyroid condition, herpes, shingles, allergies to milk and shellfish . . . " The man across from me listed what seemed like every disease and condition in the doctor's medical handbook. "No, I haven't been takin' my medicine. I ain't got the money. So sick that I couldn't work. No work, no rent. No home, and sooner or later you get dizzy and fall down in the street."

"Ow!" Mr. Holder, to my right, shouted. "What you doin'?"

"Cutting out the bullet. It's embedded in fairly shallow scar tissue."

"Ain't you gonna knock me out or nuttin'? Shit!"

"That would be more dangerous than the procedure, and a local anesthetic is contraindicated due to the bullet being so close to the heart."

Mr. Holder moaned, and I could imagine the scalpel slicing into his chest while the male nurses held him down.

The IV forced on me was a powerful narcotic. I heard everything, it seemed. I can't remember now if they were all speaking at once or if these conversations and other sounds happened over time. In my memory they all flow together. There was a singular endpoint though.

"There it is," the Nigerian doctor said, and I heard the *plink* of metal on metal; the corroded bullet, I imagined, hitting a shiny chromium tray. This hard, metallic sound ended my free-floating awareness. I settled back down into the darkness that I feared and craved more than anything.

"Do you have a medical-insurance card, Mr. Bentway?" Dr. Ifadapo asked, her sculpted sub-Saharan features glistening black.

It was the afternoon of that same day, though it felt as if weeks had passed.

"It's Professor Bentway," I said, "and I already told your nurse that I'm insured by New York College."

"We need the card."

"Call the school."

"They tell us that Professor Bentway has retired."

"What do you want from me, then?"

"Is there someone we can call?"

"I don't have my book with me. I got my one friend, but his phone is off. All I got to do is go home, and I could get the card for you. My apartment is only mine for a few more days. I'm supposed to leave for Saint Lucia. I got my tickets in the apartment too."

"We can't release you, Mr. . . . . Professor Bentway. You can't go on your own, and there's no one to take you."

"Just get me down to a cab."

"The law won't allow us do that, sir." Her beautiful smile was maddening.

"You can't keep me here."

"We believe that you had a heart attack along with the emphysema episode. We will treat that, and then, if there is no other option, we'll be forced to release you to a state-run nursing facility."

"A nursing home?"

Smiling, the doctor got up and moved away to the charlatan across from me. The ex-con, Holder, was stripping his bed for the fourth time that day, and Bret Lagnan, the man who had been abandoned by his wife, sat there next to his bed suffering the ailment of a broken heart.

All my phone numbers were keyed into the cell phone that was on the dusty floor in university housing. It was midsummer, so no one was around anyway. And I was weak from the emphysema attack that, I was told by Dr. Ifadapo, was brought on by the air-conditioning, which circulated the dust kicked up by the movers. I could barely sit upright.

At times I was aware of the charlatan, Todd Brightwood, hovering around my bed looking for jewelry or pocket change. Holder told him to get away whenever he drifted to our side of the room. Lovesick Lagnan didn't seem to know that anyone else was there.

The TV was on all during the day. I watched shows that I'd never heard of before, game shows and sporting events, the shopping channel and daytime soap operas. I didn't have much concentration. I didn't know how long I had been in that bed or how long it would be before they committed me to the nursing home.

When I tried to get up, the male nurses would push me back down. Anetta might not call for weeks, and I did not call her number often enough to remember it. Simba had moved to Tanzania and refused to talk to me for reasons that he kept to himself.

Days had passed. The beautiful Nigerian doctor dropped by in the afternoons. She was friendly but would not let me go.

Todd Brightwood had been signed in as a patient suffering from various ailments that led to his attack of illness. Gil Holder kept making and remaking his bed, complaining about the hospital staff. Bret Lagnan suffered in silence the abandonment by his wife (whose name I never got.) I marked the time, slowly garnering my strength for the moment when I could escape that wing of Saint Jude's Hospital set aside for the poor, hopeless, and black.

None of the men in my room had visitors, but I met a man across the hall who agreed to have his son bring me some pants and a T-shirt. The son wasn't coming back until Friday though, and Dr. Ifadapo hadn't yet decided which day to have me committed to the nursing home. The attack had exacerbated my emphysema, and so I couldn't walk very far without resting. It was going to be a strenuous escape, if I could even make it.

On Tuesday the doctor told me that I'd be leaving on Thursday. I argued with her, but she just smiled and nodded. I called the college human-resources office, but they told me that all medical insurance for retired employees was handled in Albany and that I had to send them a letter if I'd lost my insurance card.

"I haven't lost my damn card."

"Then show it to the people at the hospital."

It seemed impossible that I could have lost control of my life so easily. From full professor with tenure to a homeless ward of the state. I was on the eighth floor of a building that took up two city blocks. I figured that it was nearly a quarter of a mile between me and freedom. But I had to try—blue pajamas and all. I'd carry a weapon with me. And if anyone tried to stop me, I'd throw down on them.

The only weapon I could find was a serrated plastic knife, but that would have to do.

At two o'clock on that Wednesday I closed my eyes to rest fifteen minutes more, and then I was going to run, regardless of what they did to me.

"Cecil," came a voice with a West African inflection to it.

"Adegoke?" I said, without opening my eyes.

"I finally found you," he said.

I mustered enough courage to open one eye, and there he was. Blacker than my doctor and tall and handsome in that gaunt way only Ghanaian men can manage: Adegoke Arapmoi, professor of film and culture, stood there beside my bed. Behind him was Jack Fine, a light brown and beefy teacher of archaeology who hailed from Baltimore.

"Why didn't you call me?" Adegoke asked.

"I did. Your phone went straight to voice mail."

"What happened?"

"Get me outta here, man. They wanna put me in a nursing home."

Adegoke wore a lavender jacket, black trousers, and a bright, bright yellow shirt. All this topped off with a Panama hat. His white teeth glistened against black skin.

"I was in Ghana," he said, "at the ten-year anniversary of the death of my father. When I got back you weren't home. I had to wait until the night guard was on duty. He told me about your attack, but he didn't know where the ambulance had taken you. Jack and I have been going from hospital to hospital."

"Hey, Cecil," Jack said. He was grinning, and so was I. "You look like shit."

"You brought me new sheets, but they got stains on 'em," Gil Holder was telling his nurse.

"Excuse me, ma'am," Jack Fine, who was at least six five, said to the woman.

"Yes?"

"Tell the doctor, and whoever, that we're takin' Professor Bentway home."

"He has to be released by a doctor," the young, pink-skinned woman explained.

"That's OK," Jack said. "Just as long as that release coincides with our egress from your institution."

Jack was thirty-three years old and not that far away from his student days. He still slung big words around as if they made him sound smart. I usually felt embarrassed by the way he spoke, but that day I was filled with glee.

Gil Holder was actually smiling at my big friend.

"I brought you some of my son's clothes, Cecil," Adegoke said as the nurse fled the room.

He placed a large brown-paper bag on my bed.

Many years before, Addy had been my student at San Francisco State. He and my son, Eric/Simba, were the same age, forty-eight, but it was Adegoke who searched all the emergency rooms in Manhattan until he'd found me.

With my friends' help, I got up and dressed. Jack even tied my shoes.

"What's going on here?" Dr. Ifadapo asked as she came into the room flanked by two black men in security-guard uniforms.

Jack moved toward the little group. Addy got in front of him.

"I am Dr. Arapmoi from New York College," he said. "Dr. Bentway is one of our professors. We have come to bring him home."

"I have already signed the papers to release him to Morningside Nursing Home. You can apply for his release there."

"He's coming with me to my home now," Addy said with certainty.

"The forms are filled out."

Jack Fine snorted. The guards took notice of him. Gil Holder picked up some kind of bludgeon from under his pillow. Brightwood pulled the blanket up to his chin, and lovelorn Lagnan didn't notice a thing.

The beautiful Nigerian stared into the handsome Ghanaian's eyes for half a minute at least.

"Are you his guardian?" Ifadapo asked.

"I'm his nephew," Addy lied. "And he's coming home with me."

For the next two hours they filled out forms and made recommendations. We walked down three long halls, took an elevator, and went to the checkout desk to retrieve whatever it was that I had in my pockets when I was brought in.

"This is a blue form," the big bald brown man said from behind his marble desk. "You need a yellow form to get what we have. A blue form will get your clothes from the emergency room closet."

Back to the elevator, down the halls, we returned to the nurses' desk near my room.

"Oh," the pink-skinned nurse (whose name tag read "Laura") said. "I'm sorry. I should have given you the yellow form. Give me that one, and I'll fill out another."

"But he needs the blue paper to get his clothes," big Jack Fine bellowed.

"Oh, right," the nurse said. "You know we're very understaffed. I'm lucky if I remember to make my rounds."

* * *

The man wanting the yellow form had my wallet, in which I found my medical-insurance card.

"You go through that door on your left," he said, now quite friendly, "and down the hall until you get to the emergency room. You pass through there and come to a desk behind a Plexiglas barrier. The woman there will help you find your clothes."

There were dozens of people sitting in the disheveled maze of blue vinyl-and-chrome chairs that furnished the emergency-room waiting area. A sleeping, or maybe unconscious, child in his mother's arms, a man with blood seeping from his face and both arms, an old man (my age) staring out a window with his lower eyelids drooping away from the orbs—open and red. One man sat silently crying, his hand swollen to the size of a football. A young woman with haunted eyes had such severe flatulence that no one could sit near her. You could see the pain from her belly in the twist of her mouth and the humiliation of her eyes.

"Where's the doctor?" an old woman in a wheelchair asked me.

"I don't know."

"This is terrible," Jack Fine said to Addy.

"At least they have a place to go," the Ghanian said.

Behind the Plexiglas window on the other side of suffering sat an ocher-skinned, almond-eyed woman. I thought she might be Cambodian or Vietnamese.

"Put the form in the slot in front of you," she said without looking up.

I placed the blue form where she asked, and she picked it up. When she noticed what it was, she frowned, then sighed.

"We're very busy," she complained.

"It's my clothes," I replied, realizing that my breath was coming short again.

"You came in DP-twenty-seven," the woman replied.

"What's that supposed to mean?" Jack asked.

The hospital sentry hesitated. She said, "DP. Deceased Person. The first doctor who saw you declared you dead."

Ana, the young nurse/receptionist, led us to a door behind her kiosk. It was small and green and opened into a dark room. A light came on automatically when we entered. We realized with awe that we had entered a vast chamber lined with deep bins that were filled with hundreds of bundles of clothes bound in brown paper and secured with tan masking tape.

I could hear the breath singing in my windpipe.

"You OK, Cecil?" Addy asked.

I didn't answer. While Ana searched through certain piles of bundles I looked around. Most of the brown-paper packages had the name and date of death scrawled on the tape. One read: REYNARD, MILTON 10/11/07; DECEASED. Some of the slips had fallen from their bundles. There was Julia Slatkin, Harris Montoya, and Po Li. The dust and lint gathered in my throat and lungs, and I felt the beginnings of another respiratory attack. I should have run out of there, but running for me was a thing of the past.

That one room led to another, where there were no bins and even more bundles of clothes, piled all the way to the eighteen-foot ceiling. I thought about the concentration-camp films that came out when I was a young man just out of the air force, right after the war. The Nazis took everything that their victims owned: hair and teeth, shoes and clothes. I felt that I was in the presence of some great crime that I would never be able to prove.

"Here it is, Cecil," Addy said. "Here's that robe I brought you from Accra."

In the taxi I opened the window and let my head loll out, the wind forcing its way into my lungs. All I had to do was open my mouth.

Adegoke's wife is spending the summer with her family in Nice. His daughter has gone to Singapore, and his son is on a film shoot in southern Mexico. My old student gave me a room with a window on the twenty-seventh floor of university housing. Here I've been sitting for the past three weeks waiting for breath to return, so that I might escape to a Caribbean island; there I hope to forget what I learned among the bundles of death.

REPLY TO A DEAD MAN

When the doorbell rang, I had no inkling of who was there or what his or her business might have been. I was sitting at the dining table in a room that had never been used for entertaining. Books and notepads, two weeks' worth of newspapers, and a few stacks of dirty dishes were piled here and there around the dark-stained hickory plank. I had been perched there writing a letter to my sister about the death of our brother in the fall.

It was now spring, and this was the first time I'd reached out to Angeline. I had missed the funeral. Our brother had been buried in Cincinnati by Dearby, his fourth wife. She, Dearby, told me that if she was going to pay for the burial, then he'd be interred in the same cemetery as her and the rest of her family.

I was having a hard time, financially, when Seth passed. I'd just lost my job as a regional manager for Lampley Car Insurance, and my unemployment checks hadn't been enough to pay the rent. I couldn't take time off from my temp position at Lenny's

Auto Parts, and the funeral was on a Wednesday, a workday. My boss, Alan René Bertrand, didn't particularly like me, and so I couldn't even take the chance of asking him for the time off. Lenny's paid $22.50 an hour, the best temp rate in town, and so I sent a dozen white lilies and a note thanking Dearby for honoring my brother.

You see, I knew that Dearby and Seth were on the outs when he died. My sister told me that Seth had been seeing his second ex-wife, Althea, again, and Dearby was threatening to kick him out of the house.

She, Dearby, called to tell me about Seth.

"He had a heart attack," she said. "I warned him about the high blood pressure and his weight. He wouldn't listen. He never listened."

I was thinking that Dearby was pretty big herself.

As if she could read my thoughts across the two thousand–plus miles that separated us, she said, "I know that I'm big, but my heft is fruit fat, weight from fresh fruit with fiber and natural sugars. My doctors tell me that I'm OK the way I am."

"I know you are," I said, to fill the empty space in our conversation, an emptiness that loomed like the blank line at the bottom of a boilerplate contract.

"What do you want me to do with him?" she asked.

"Um . . ."

"The body, Roger. What do you want me to do with the body?"

"I don't understand what you mean," I said. "He's dead."

"I know that," Dearby said. "He's gone, and somebody has to bury him."

"Oh . . . Oh, yeah. Right. Um . . ."

* * *

I got up from the table, remembering that awkward moment, half a year ago, when I had to tell Dearby that I didn't have the money to help pay for a funeral.

The walk from my worktable to the front door wasn't long. No distance in my 634-square-foot half-home in the Wilshire district was that great. The other side of the subdivided house was inhabited by a woman named Rose Henley. I had seen Rose only once, a few days after I'd moved in seven years and ten months earlier. She'd rung my bell and introduced herself as my neighbor.

Rose Henley was old, maybe sixty, and she had one gold tooth. She was fairly short, even for a woman, and her black hair was sliding into white. She was a white woman, broad-faced and stout.

"Mr. Vaness?" she had said, all those years ago.

"Yes?"

"I'm Rose Henley, your neighbor."

"Oh. Hello."

"I don't mean to interrupt, just wanted you to see my face. And I wanted to see yours."

"Would you like to come in?" I asked, not putting much heart into it.

"No, no, no," she said. "I just wanted to greet you. I don't get out very much."

This was no exaggeration. I had not seen nor had I heard from my neighbor since.

But that day, when I was writing to my sister, Angeline, about our brother Seth's death, I was sure that Rose was at my door. I didn't get much company since losing my job. The friends I had liked to party, and I couldn't afford the gas money, much less my part of the bill at our favorite bars and restaurants.

After I was fired, I had asked my girlfriend, Terri, if she would move in so we could share the rent.

Terri broke it off with me three days later.

No one ever knocked at my door, and Rose was the only person I was acquainted with in the neighborhood. It had to be her, I thought; that was just cold, hard logic.

So I opened the door looking down, expecting to see my diminutive neighbor's wide face under a thatch of black hair turning white.

Instead I was looking at the red and blue vest of a white man even taller than I. He had a bald head and not much facial hair. His skin was the color of yellowing ivory, and his eyes were a luminous gray—like a mist-filled valley at dawn.

"Mr. Vaness?" the stranger asked, in a magnificent tenor voice.

"Yes?"

"My name is Harding, Lance Harding. I am here representing the last wish of Seth Vaness."

"What?"

"I work for a small firm called Final Request Co. We execute the last wishes of clients who have passed on."

"You're a lawyer?"

I looked the slender tenor up and down. He had on a nice suit, but it was reddish brown, not a lawyer's color in my estimation.

"No, Mr. Vaness. We at FRC don't execute wills. Our job is to deliver messages from the dead." He smiled after the last word, giving me a slight chill.

"Uh-huh. You use a Ouija board or somethin'?"

"We are engaged by the deceased before their demise."

"My brother hired you to give me a message after he was dead?"

Harding smiled and nodded.

"He died six and a half months ago," I said. "What took you so long?"

"His wish was for us to execute his desire not less than half a year after his demise."

"Is this some kinda legal thing?"

"It is a simple agreement between FRC and your brother," Lance Harding said, maintaining an aura of imperturbable patience. "Often individuals wish to pass on knowledge outside of the rubric of wills and other legal formats. Some leave a spoken message, others might wish to pass along a note or a small package."

"Seth didn't have much," I said. "He couldn't have anything to hide."

"We all have something to hide, Mr. Vaness. Either that or something is hidden from us."

"So you're—"

"May I come in?" Harding asked, cutting off my question.

"Oh," I said.

"Is this a bad time?"

"No, no it's OK, I just . . ."

"I came by on Wednesday, but you weren't here," Harding said. "Your neighbor, Mrs. Henley, told me that you were at work."

"You talked to Rose?"

"May I come in?"

My house was untidy, to say the least. When I have a girlfriend, I usually pick up and air out my little place at least once a week, but I lose the drive when I'm unattached. As a rule, the mess doesn't bother me unless I have unexpected guests.

Harding didn't seem put off by the clutter. I moved a small stack of old comic books from a chair next to the one I had been sitting in and gestured for him to take it.

"The Fantastic Four," he said, looking at the topmost magazine as I set the stack on the table next to him.

"They were my father's," I said. "I have one through twelve. Know anybody who might want to buy them?"

"Your blood father?" he asked. "Patrick Hand?"

I nodded, wondering how he knew my real father's name.

He flipped through the issues, smiling slightly. Harding was maybe ten years older than I. That would have made him about fifty.

"Not in mint or near-mint condition," he said. "That makes them nearly worthless. At any rate, these books call up your father from across the pale. That's a connection that money can't buy."

"How do you know my father's dead?"

"Both of your fathers," he said. "Patrick, who sired you, and Norland, who married your mother and adopted her three children."

"How do you know all that?"

"They were Seth's fathers too."

"Oh . . . yeah. That's why you're here."

"Shall we begin?"

"It's funny that you came here just now," I said. "I mean, not funny, but . . . I was just writing to my sister—"

"Angeline Vaness-Brownley," Lance Harding of the FRC interjected. "She lives in Cambridge with her husband, Ivan Brownley, the union organizer."

"Wha'? Oh, right, Seth's sister too. How much do you know about us?"

"About you, particularly, we know that you have never been charged with, much less convicted of, a crime and that most of your adult life you were either employed or at college. You have three years matriculation at Cal State. Your concentration was in history, but you dropped out and began to work for various businesses. You've never been married, but you were once engaged to a woman named Irene Littleton."

"Seth told you all that?"

"No."

"Then where'd you get it?"

Harding's face was oblong and a little larger than even his tall frame might predict. For the most part his expression was tranquil, but my question teased out a mild frown.

"I am here at your brother's request," he said.

"But you know all this shit about me, and he didn't tell you. So I'd like to know where you got it."

"Nora Dunbar," he replied, his face once again at peace.

"Who?"

"She is the statistical and research analyst at our firm. When a client engages our services, Miss Dunbar does a background check on the client and the recipient of the message or package."

"Why?"

Harding sighed and then said, "Suppose the message that someone wished to pass on was a name and an address. If the recipient was a known killer, or maybe someone who had a grudge against a person with the name we were being asked to deliver, we would refuse the job. We are not bound by fealty to the state, but we are a moral corporation."

"So you wanted to make sure that I wasn't a hit man or a stalker or somethin'?"

"Quite right."

"But you figured that I was a good bet and that you could deliver your message without messin' anything up."

The great sculpted face smiled and bobbed.

"You got a sliding scale you charge?" I asked. I realized that I wasn't eager to obtain information passed on to me across the border of death.

"We charge five thousand dollars, plus expenses, for every message a client wishes to charge us with."

"Expenses?"

Lance Harding smiled and seemed to relax a bit. He gave the impression of having surrendered to my fear of his charge.

"Once we were engaged by a woman to deliver an apple pie she'd baked to the man she loved but never married," he said. "In order to keep the pie in fair condition we had to freeze it. The accommodations were made, and she was charged accordingly."

"So, Seth paid five thousand dollars for you to deliver this message to me?"

"That is the fee all clients are charged," he said, "plus expenses."

"That doesn't make any sense."

"Why do you say that?"

"Three reasons. First, I can't see Seth payin' that kinda money, when he coulda sent a letter to my sister or our mother to give me after he died. Secondly, I can't see Seth spendin' that kinda money on me—period. And third, traveling all over the country and the world makin' these kinda visits would cost a lot more than five thousand dollars."

I would have talked all day long to keep this man, the most official man I had ever met, from discharging his message.

"As to your first two arguments—we question our clients, but never their money, once they've passed our qualification test. Your third dispute would make sense if the FRC didn't have regions of responsibility divided among its various agents. My area is California. You asked why I'm late delivering this message. That is because I was in central and northern California for the last two weeks. We would like to have delivered this communication exactly at the six-month mark, but the wording of your brother's last request allowed me some leeway: 'not less than six months after my demise.'"

I had nothing left to ask, but still I was not ready for any information from the dead.

"Are all the people who work for the FCR white?" The question was one my stepfather would have had me ask.

"FRC," Lance corrected. "Most of the employees of the company are Caucasian but not all. Now, may I deliver my charge?"

I took in a deep breath, exhaled, and then nodded.

Lance Harding reached into the left side of his red-brown jacket with his right hand.

I leaped up from my chair, sure that he was going to take out a gun or a knife—my fear was that great.

But the FRC agent merely brought out an ivory envelope, almost exactly the same color as his skin.

"This is the letter that your brother charged us to deliver," he said. "As I hand it to you, our duty in this matter is fulfilled."

He extended the hand, offering me the rectangle of paper. I hesitated before taking it.

The mood was so ceremonial that I expected some kind of devastation or revelation to follow. But nothing happened.

The FRC agent stood abruptly.

"I will leave you to do with the letter as you will," he said.

"Don't you want me to sign something?" I asked. "To prove that you actually gave me this?"

"The client didn't ask for corroboration," he said, smiling. "That usually means that the delivery contains nothing of material value. I can see myself out."

*　*　*

I sat there at the messy table, holding the still-sealed envelope, for long minutes after Lance Harding was gone. Something about the white man's demeanor—coupled with the fact that I had been writing a letter concerning Seth when the strange note from him arrived—was, to say the least, eerie. Something having to do with me not attending his funeral, I thought, and now he was reaching out to me . . .

I put the letter down and picked up my smartphone. I entered A-N-G, and Angeline's number appeared.

She answered on the fourth ring.

"Where are you?" she said, instead of hello.

"At home."

"But you're on your cell."

"I had the landline disconnected, figured I didn't need two numbers. People hardly ever call one."

"You're not a kid anymore, Roger. Having your phone disconnected makes you seem transient."

"How's Boston, Sis?"

"Cold. They're predicting snow for tomorrow."

"Snow? It's not even Thanksgiving yet."

"How are you, Rog?"

"All right. Have you heard from Seth?"

"What?"

"A letter, package, or somethin'?"

"Seth is dead."

"I know," I said. "I know, but a guy just dropped by and hand-delivered a letter to me that Seth had set up before he died."

Angeline didn't say a word for at least a minute. This told me more than any confession or lie: whatever it was that Seth was telling me, Angeline knew before I did.

"Did you read it?" she asked at last.

"No. Not yet. I was wondering if he'd sent the same note to you and Mom."

"You should burn it, Roger," she said. "Nothing good can come from a dead man's hand."

"The guy brought it to me was very much alive."

"Burn it, shred it, or just throw it away, Roger," she said, in her best big-sister voice. "You know how Seth was always trying to mess with you."

"What does it say, Angeline?"

"How do you expect me to know?"

"Don't *you* mess with me, Sis."

"I haven't heard anything from Seth, and neither has Mom, for all I know. I talked to her last Monday, and she didn't say anything about any letters."

"How is Mom?"

"Fine. She said that she hasn't heard from you in over six months. You know you could go to her house. She's just a few miles from your place. It's a shame I see her more often than you do, and here I live three thousand miles away."

All the anger that I had at my mother and sister and deceased stepfather, Norland Reese, came up in my breast.

"I gotta go, Angeline," I said.

"Wait, Roger. What about that letter . . . ?"

I pressed the red icon on my smartphone, and the connection was broken. Putting the little device down, I picked up the sealed envelope again.

Seth had terrorized me when we were children. He would lock me in closets and trunks just for a laugh. I learned the value of silence from him. Because if he put me in the big trunk in the attic of our house, I learned that he would never let me out as long as I yelled. But if I was quiet, he worried that maybe I had suffocated or something. He was the kind of torturer who fed off the screams of his victims.

I might have hated my brother, but his brand of torment wasn't nearly as bad as that of my parents—I should say my mother and her husband Norland. My blood father was a white man named Patrick Hand. The story goes that he abandoned our family when I was two, Angeline was four, and Seth five.

"He just ran off and left me with three children and a dollar seventy-five," my mother would say. Then she'd spit on the ground, cursing him.

Seth never believed that our father abandoned us. Patrick Hand was a known gambler, and Seth was convinced that he had been slaughtered over a bad debt, and that our mother, instead of cursing him, should have gone out looking for his killers.

Norland wouldn't let Seth tell that tale. He was of my mother's opinion and ruled over us with an iron fist.

In my mind I managed to believe both Seth and my mother. Sometimes I hated my father; at others I prayed for his murdered soul.

Dear Roger,

I know that we haven't talked in a long time. We might not ever talk again if what the doctors say about my heart is true. They're telling me that I better settle up my business because I could die any minute. That's why I'm writing you this letter. It hurts to admit the truth and so I'm using the Final Request Company to deliver it after I die. I'm not proud of what I did but at least this much is right.

I guess you remember back when you were seventeen and going with that white girl—Timberly Alexander. You broke up with her because Mama and Norland leaned on you so hard. I was mad that you didn't even tell Timmy why you stopped talking to her and so one day I went over to her house out there in West Covina. I told her how much Mama and Norland thought that interracial relationships only ended in heartbreak. I tried to explain how much you needed Mama and that her rules were too much for you to deny.

That's when Timberly told me that she was pregnant. She was so broken up because her parents were mad and you wouldn't even talk to her on the phone.

She was so upset that I told her she could always talk to me. And she did.

For the last twenty years I've been giving Timmy a couple hundred dollars a month, and her little girl, Sovie (named after Sojourner Truth), has called me Uncle Seth from the day she could talk.

Timmy didn't want me to tell you about your daughter because she was mad and hurt that you left her without a word. I probably should have told you but I guess I got a little possessive. I kind of thought of Timmy and Sovie as my little family.

At the bottom of the page is Sovie's full name and address in Los Angeles. Yes, she lives in L.A. just like you.

Timmy died a year ago from breast cancer and so, when I'm gone, Sovie's going to be alone in the world.

I'm sorry for keeping this from you, Little Brother. I know it's worse than anything else I ever did. I hope you can forgive me.

Seth

My heart started beating rapidly a minute or two after the third time I'd read the letter. I could have sat there and guessed for a hundred years and never come up with what Seth had to say. I had a child in the world and hadn't known it. I was a father with none of the responsibilities, fears, or joys of parenthood.

I went out to the liquor store and bought two quarts of Jack Daniels and three packs of filterless Camels.

* * *

For a day and a half all I did was drink and smoke. I had given up both habits when I was twenty-three years old. I realized one day that I was trying to kill myself with the legal drugs of my culture.

And every day for seventeen years I had wanted to end my smokeless sobriety.

I crashed around the house, cursing my brother, mother, and sister —all of whom seemed to have known but never told me the truth. At one point, near the end of my private orgy, I raised a hickory chair up above my head and smashed it on the hardwood floor. Then, melodramatically, I crumpled to my knees and cried over the broken furniture.

Maybe five minutes after my outburst, a rapping came at the door. A few seconds later I heard another, bolder knock.

I climbed to my feet, suppressed a gag reflex, and stumbled to the door.

Standing there on our common porch was Rose Henley; she was as short as ever, but her hair had not yet turned completely white.

"Are you all right, Mr. Vaness?"

"No, ma'am, I am not."

"What's wrong?"

"Nothing I can point at but everything else."

"I don't understand. I heard a crash and I wanted to make sure you weren't hurt."

"You're a brave woman," I said, barely aware of the words I mouthed. "Somebody could have been killing me over here."

"Does it have to do with that man who came here a few days ago? The tall one in the nice suit?"

"Yes. But he was only the bearer of the bad news. The messenger."

"Why don't you come over to my house and have a cup of coffee?" she suggested. "Sober up a little bit."

Rose Henley's home was everything that my apartment was not. The floor was carpeted, and not a hair was out of place. A painting on the living room wall was of a reclining nude woman who looked somewhat like a younger version of my neighbor.

She had me sit on a tan sofa and served me a weak cup of percolated coffee.

"Now," she said, when we were both settled. "What's the problem?"

Her face was broad, but her black eyes were set close together. The concern in that face was something I didn't remember ever having been shown me before.

I told her everything, all about how Seth tortured me and how my sister probably knew about the child I'd fathered, about my mother and father and stepfather, and about my failure to surpass the image that everyone seemed to hold of me.

"I don't even know why I dropped out of college," I said at one point. "I don't know when I gave up on myself."

"You haven't been to work this week, have you?" she asked.

"I'm sure they fired me. The temp agency called, but I didn't answer."

"You need to take a cold shower, get a good night's sleep, and then go to see your daughter," Rose said.

"I have to get a job first," I replied. "You know Mr. Poplar wants his rent."

"Poplar works for the landlord," she said. "I don't think the owner would kick you out under these circumstances."

"Oh? Why not?"

"Because I own this house, Mr. Vaness. And I like you."

The address for Sojourner "Sovie" Alexander was on Cushdon, just south of a Pico Boulevard. It was the smallest house on the block and in need of a paint job. But the lawn was green and manicured, and there were healthy rose bushes under the front windows of the home.

The door was open, and the screen closed. I saw a doorbell but knocked anyway. After a few moments, a tallish, honey-colored girl in her early twenties appeared.

"Miss Alexander?" I said. I'd practiced calling her "Miss."

"No," she replied, pursing her lips, as if she were going to whistle or maybe kiss someone. "Who are you?"

"I'm here to see Miss Alexander," I said. "Is she home?"

Staring quizzically at me, the honey-colored young woman shouted, "Sovie! It's for you!"

The young woman went away, and before I could count to ten, a young white girl, more or less the same age as her roommate, walked up. She had light blond hair and looked at me with a furrowed brow. All at once she realized something and took in a sharp breath.

"Roger Vaness?" she said.

"Um, yes."

"You look a lot like Uncle Seth. Three days ago I got a letter from him," she said. "This tall bald guy brought it. The man told me that Uncle Seth had died. He gave me the letter that said, Uncle Seth said, in the letter, that my real father was . . . was you."

"I got a letter from Seth too. I never knew. Nobody . . . not your mother or Seth or anybody ever told me that I had a little girl."

We stared at each other through the gray haze of the screen, both of us unsure of what to do.

"Can I take you out for coffee?" I asked.

"I'll get my sweater."

We commandeered a small round table at the window of a coffee-house on Westwood near Pico. There we talked for hours.

Timmy had told her daughter that she didn't know who her father was, that she had been wild as a child but had sobered up when Sovie came. Seth was an old friend who dropped by regularly. Sovie had often wished that Seth was her father or at least her real uncle.

"I guess he was my uncle," she said at one point, realizing for the first time the blood relation.

"But Timmy never told you that I, I mean that your blood father was black?" I asked.

"Never."

"Does that bother you?"

"It bothers me that she lied about you."

"I mean, it doesn't bother you that you're black?"

"Oh," she said, looking very much like me and not. "I didn't even think about that. Wow."

"I don't know what to say to you, Sojourner. I'm sittin' here with a stranger, but I feel so much love that has been lost."

"Me too. When I read Seth's letter I, I felt like . . . I don't know . . . I felt like an old-time explorer on the verge of discovering a new continent."

"Did he give you my address?"

"Yes," she said meekly. "I drove by, but I couldn't make myself stop. I was just so nervous."

"That's OK. It's better that I came to you. A father should be there for his daughter."

I could see in Sojourner's eyes that she had been waiting an entire lifetime to call a man *Father*. I put my big brown hand on her clenched white fists. She relaxed, and I thought that this was how I would have wanted it to be with my own father.

I called Absolute Temps and talked to the receptionist, Tanya Reed. I explained to Tanya exactly what had happened, and she hooked me up with a six-week gig at Leonine Records on Sunset. It was only $16.75 an hour, but that covered the rent and gas.

For the next month Sovie and I saw or talked to each other every day.

She's a history major, like I was, and has a boyfriend, Chad, whom I met and liked very much. I gave her my blood father's stack of Fantastic Four comics, saying that it was the only thing of value I owned. She didn't like comic books but took them anyway. I don't know why, but giving her those magazines felt like taking a two-ton weight off my skull.

A month later, on a Saturday, I was cleaning my apartment to prepare for her and her roommate, Ashanti Bowles, to come over for dinner the next day.

When the knock came, I didn't think before opening the door.

Lance Harding was wearing a pink suit with a red shirt and no tie. I wondered then if agents of the FRC had a dress code.

"Mr. Vaness," he said.

"I'm so glad to see you," I said, opening the door wide and ushering him in to my clean house. "Come in, come in."

Sitting in the same chairs as before, we faced each other. Harding crossed his left leg over the right one and nodded.

"I wanted to call you, but I couldn't find a number for the FRC in the Yellow Pages," I said. "I planned to get on somebody's computer and look it up soon."

"Why were you looking for us?"

"You," I said. "I wanted to ask you something that I didn't think of the last time we met."

"And what was that?"

"You mentioned my real father when we talked before. Do you know when he died?"

When Harding reached into his breast pocket, I was reminded of the fear I had of him the first time he sat at my table.

He came out with a small notepad and flipped through the pages. He stopped for a moment, reading something, and then turned a leaf.

"Nineteen seventy-four," he said, "when you were two years old. He was found murdered in the home of a young prostitute named Pearl Watson."

"Do you know if anybody claimed the body?"

"Have you gone to see your daughter?" the FRC agent asked.

"How do you even know to ask that?"

"I'm here with another final request."

"Another five thousand dollars?"

"Have you visited your daughter?"

"Yes. Yes, I have."

"Do you love her?"

"I do. But what does that have to do with you?"

Instead of answering, Harding took another ivory envelope from his pocket.

Again he handed me the letter.

Again I hesitated.

When at last I accepted the final request, I expected Harding to leap up and leave, like he did the first time. But he remained seated, staring at me.

"I am supposed to wait for a reply," he said.

"A reply to a dead man?"

Harding hunched his shoulders, and I tore open the envelope.

Dear Roger,

By now you've probably met Sovie and I know because you're reading this letter you at least say that you love her. I've been telling Dearby that I've been visiting with Althea because she has cancer and is dying. Althea does have cancer and she is dying but I've also been doing my old thing in her house on her phone. Seems like bookies are back in style. I couldn't tell Dearby because she'd want the money I'm making and I needed that money for Sovie. I also needed to tell you about your daughter and to make sure that you cared for her.

The FRC agent sitting in front of you has a third letter. This one has a legal document saying that the bearer of this letter should be allowed access to my safe deposit box at Concordia Bank in downtown Cincinnati. There's $137,941.00 in that box.

I saved that money for Sovie but I owe you something too. And so you can either accept the document and help the child with her bills or you can turn the whole thing over to her and let her decide how to handle it.

It's up to you, Little Brother.

Seth

I folded the note and put it in my pocket.

"I got another question for you, Mr. Harding."

"Yes?"

"Do you take in trainee agents now and then?"

246

"Yes."

"Could I apply for that job?"

"I can make the proper connections. I happen to need an assistant, and your background fits our major criteria."

"Then you give that letter you got in your pocket to Sojourner Alexander and send me the application form."

THE LETTER

My wife, Corrine, and I had the same financial advisors—Walton, Barth, and Wright. The firm uses oversize light blue envelopes with its return address printed in red in the upper left-hand corner. The partners' names are writ large in block lettering, while the address, in italic print a quarter the size, sits on a single line just below. We had separate accounts with the firm, but I took care of most of the correspondence. Corrine doesn't have much patience with finances and had been more than happy to let me take care of our accounts, taxes, and monthly bills.

"Just show me where to sign," she'd say when I tried to explain the forms and requests.

So on that Wednesday morning, when I saw that Corrine had laid two of the WBW blue envelopes on the dinette table in the nook, I picked them up and put them in my briefcase to read at lunchtime.

"Do you have time for breakfast?" I called down the slender hallway.

Corrine stuck her head out from the bathroom while rubbing a tan towel against her head vigorously. Her coppery skin glistened slightly from the moisture of the shower. Dark gold freckles tempered the serious cast of her face.

"I thought you said you were late."

I could see her right breast. The nipple was a dark rose, a kind of in-between color from her mixed parentage.

"I am, but I thought we could sit together for a bit. We haven't really talked in a week."

"I don't have time to cook," she said and then ducked back into the bathroom.

"We could have cereal," I suggested, raising my voice to be sure I was heard.

"I'm watching my carbs."

"You're not fat."

"You don't have to be fat to be careful about what you're eating." She came out from the bathroom with the towel wrapped around her, then went the other way down the hall toward our bedroom.

I wondered what she would do if I ran after her and pushed her down on the bed. Would she resist? Push me away? There was no desire in this idle musing. I didn't want to have sex with her. We'd been together for nearly twenty years, since she was twenty-one and I thirty-five. We didn't have sex much anymore, and when we did there was usually some red wine and a little blue pill involved.

I hadn't needed chemical help the three times that I'd had affairs. When I was with a new woman in a secret place, I could do things the way I did when I was in my twenties . . . or at least my thirties.

My last affair had been with a Korean woman, Donella Kim, who had temped in my office for a month or so. I didn't call her until after she'd left Korn/Wills. After that we rutted like rabbits for almost six weeks.

During that time I fell behind in my work, came home late every night, and never had sex once with Corrine. She noticed, but I blamed a muscle strain, and she seemed to accept the excuse.

In the end it was Donella who broke off the relationship.

"I don't want to do this anymore, Frank," she said, when I called her from my office, also on a Wednesday.

"But I love you," I said. My tongue had gone dry, and a dying rodent was keening in my chest.

She hesitated.

I didn't love her, but I didn't want to lose her either. She made me feel alive, and life was, to my mind, better than love. Life was a sweet thing no matter how old you got.

Don't get me wrong, I love Corrine. I didn't think so on the morning Donella broke up with me—but I was wrong. As bad as I felt about the abrupt break from Donella, Corrine had the power to devastate my heart and not even know it.

"No, you don't," Donella said over the phone, three months past. "You just want the sex and the excitement."

"How can you break up with me and not even talk about it?" I asked. "Don't you care for me?"

She canceled the call and turned off her cell phone. She must have gotten a new number, because she didn't answer any of my messages for the next two weeks. And I called her at least a dozen times a day.

"You look like you're losing weight, Frank," Corrine said, nine days after Donella dropped me.

"They're changing over to a new system at work and . . . it's hard. I keep fucking it up. You know how when I get worried I don't eat right."

Corrine looked at me then. It was her suspicious look. I think I must do something noticeable when trying to hide despair with a lie.

251

"Why would a new system cause you to be that upset?"

"I lost a forty-thousand-dollar sale because I didn't see a flag that one of the reports put out. Miss Francie blames me."

This was true. We did have a new system, and I had missed a flag—because I'd spent the afternoon and evening with Donella and then gotten up early in the morning to see her again. I was late for work and missed the deadline indicated by a systems flag that had shown up the afternoon before. On top of the money, we had almost lost the client, Medidine, a medical-equipment distributer based in Kansas City, Kansas. Adeline Francie had given me an official warning comprising a lecture and a pink slip of paper embossed with the red time stamp of the HR office.

I had a bachelor's degree in political science but worked for Korn/Wills selling orthopedic devices to specialized stores, hospitals, and distributers—all online. KW sells other medical devices, but somehow I ended up running the orthopedic line.

"All you have to do is come in in the morning and log on," straw-haired Francie told me in her office. "Just look at the left side of the screen and make sure there are no red checks. That's all. A teenager could do it."

My supervisor was twenty years my junior. At one time, I suppose I could have argued that she had the job because she was white and I am a black man or, at least, a half-black man. But it was impossible to make that argument, because Ira Flint, Miss Francie's boss, was black. Ira was also an unapologetic Republican and greatly loved at Korn/Wills. Both of his parents had dark skin, and he had a southern accent too.

"I'm sorry, Miss Francie," I said.

I didn't care. I was distraught over losing Donella. It felt like I was dead.

*　　*　　*

By the morning Corrine left the two blue envelopes on the dinette table I was pretty much over Donella. I had once seen her walking down the street arm in arm with a tall Asian guy; that cost me two nights sleep. I missed another red check and got a second official reprimand, but after that things evened out. I'd been coming in early for nearly three months and had broadened our orthopedic presence on the web by calling second-tier distribution houses and giving them our preferred rates.

I stayed late most nights and kept my lunches down to forty-five minutes, usually at my desk.

I'd lost thirty pounds pining over Donella, and that felt good, so I tried not to eat much lunch. I took care of personal business over a cup of coffee and a Gala apple.

The financial advisors' envelopes were the same size, but the one addressed to me was very thick. That was our year-end tax statement. Forty-five minutes wouldn't be nearly enough time to review it, so I decided to read the forms in Corrine's letter.

I remember glancing out the window as I tore off the top of the large envelope. I was thinking, idly, about dying. Often when I gazed out over Midtown at midday I wondered what impact my death might have. Certainly most of the people who knew me wouldn't have given it more than five minutes' thought. The thousands walking up and down the streets would never know, would not want to know, and if they somehow found out, they wouldn't care.

My father had hung himself in our backyard in Baldwin Hills, Los Angeles, when I was fourteen. Winslow, my older brother, had found him hanging from a low branch of a fruitless apple tree planted by the previous owners.

"His face was black," Winslow had told me that night, after the police were gone, along with the coroner's white station wagon and my father's corpse. "Much blacker than he was. And his tongue was sticking out. At first I thought it was a joke he was playing on me. I said to stop foolin' around."

My brother started crying then, and I ran from the room out the front door and into the street. I needed to get away from that house and my brother and my mother, who never really recovered from the shock.

Standing at the window, thinking about my death and my father's, I looked at the envelope in my hand and saw that there was a smaller white envelope in the bottom of the blue fold. This letter, also with the return address of Walton, Barth, and Wright, had been sent to Corrine's studio. But that didn't matter because they had gotten Corrine's studio address wrong. That was on Adams Street in Park Slope, but the sender wrote down Adams Avenue. It was a valid address, just not hers. Somewhere in the computer system of WBW they had the wrong address for her office rather than the right one for our home in Brooklyn Heights. Whenever somebody got it wrong, a very nice woman in their mailroom named Dixie would resend the mail.

This was a personal letter. The address was written by hand. It was a stubby little envelope, the kind that someone might use for an invitation to a wedding or bar mitzvah.

I shoved the letter into my pocket, intending to give it to Corrine when I saw her.

At four in the afternoon she called me on my cell. She always used my cell number.

"Hi, honey," she said and went on, not waiting for me to reply. "Merc called and said that he needs money for a book in his lit class. It costs sixty dollars. I said that you'd transfer the funds over. You might as well send him a hundred."

"I thought we said we'd talk about these things," I said.

"Take it out of my account then."

"It's not the money."

"I'm busy, Frank. I don't have time to discuss the obvious."

"But we said that we'd talk before sending Mercury any more money."

Corrine's parents wanted her to name our son Todd, after her father, who represented the white half of her family. I hated that name. I really hated it. But what could I say, except that he was my son and should be named after my father, Mercury Brown.

It turned out that my dad had killed a man named Simons in a fight that happened over a woman in Houston's Third Ward. Simons had beaten my father pretty badly, but when he turned away, my father took out a knife and killed his rival. That day he took a bus to LA, and, I guess, he thought he'd gotten away with it. But the police had come around asking for Bernard Lavallier; that was my father's real name when he killed Simons. After the murder my father went by the alias Mercury Brown.

Regardless of all that, I named my son Mercury.

"OK," Corrine said, in her reserved and yet exasperated tone. "Call him and tell him that we're teaching him how to go to school without the books he needs."

She hung up. It was that one action upon which I hang the dissolution and the inverted-salvation of my life.

In anger, I transferred $1,757, all the money in my checking account, over to our son. I worked until late in the evening sending e-mails to potential clients, offering them the lowest possible preferential rates.

It wasn't until after nine, when I was on the A train heading back to Brooklyn, that I remembered the little letter that Corrine had gotten from WBW.

Even just thinking about the money managers made me angry. They only kept me on as a client because of Corrine's growing income.

After finishing college, Corrine went to work for a fashion designer. She'd always wanted to study fashion, but her parents wouldn't pay for her to go to FIT. I was expecting to go back to college for my master's so that I could teach at university, but then Mercury was born, and we needed a steady paycheck. Corrine could do her work for the designer at home.

Her career took off. Within four years she was making more than three times my salary, including the sporadic bonuses, and was welcomed into the minor circles of New York fashion society. She had her own bank account and spoiled our son, whose middle name was Todd.

I tore open the letter. I shouldn't have. At any other time I wouldn't have. But I was upset, and the size of the envelope was suspicious. I mean, why would anyone from our money managers' office be sending a personal note to Corrine's studio?

Dearest Corrine,

I'm sending you this letter because I can't think of anything else to do. I know that those lunches we had probably didn't mean anything to you. I know you just wanted to get a leg up on your finances. I wish I could have found something wrong with the way Frank is handling your money but really he's following your advisor's plan perfectly. The market is volatile but he's kept to the program and has done better than many.

I'm glad you came to me because I treasure those lunches we had. It has been a long time since I've had such deep and truly meaningful talks with anyone, man or woman. When you told me about the cancer scare, and how brave you had been not telling anyone, I was moved. And when I found out that you read Márquez I was in heaven. He has always been my favorite author. So I guess this is a kind of selfish note. Corrine, I want to get to know you better. I need to have someone in my life that I can talk to. I'm not asking you for anything except a few hours now and then——to talk and listen.

I know how lonely and yet how committed you are. I'm in the same place in my life and I'd just like to be able to get together now and then.

I'm sending this snail mail to your studio so as not to cause trouble. If you don't write back I'll understand. I want you to know that I would never want to upset your life. I only think that maybe we have something we could share that would make our lives, certainly mine, better.

Yours, TB

I missed my stop. The train was twelve stations past High Street when I looked up at a homeless woman staggering into the car.

I had read the letter at least twenty times. I had no idea who TB was, but then again, neither had I known about a cancer scare or that Corrine questioned how I took care of our money. I knew that she loved *One Hundred Years of Solitude*, but we had never talked about it because I couldn't get past the first page.

She'd met with this guy more than once for lunch, and now he was, in a sly way, trying to build on their . . . intimacies. There was no mistaking his intentions, but I couldn't blame him. Corrine had obviously sought him out and opened her heart to him.

There's a small bar a few blocks from our upper-floor brownstone apartment. I stopped there and ordered a cognac. Somewhere after the seventh drink I found myself walking down the street with the same gait as the homeless woman who had made me aware of having missed my stop. She'd worn soiled tan pants, with a thick, dark green skirt over them, had a calico blanket draped around her shoulders, and was carrying at least a dozen plastic bags. She smelled of dust, I remember. That was what brought me out of my stunned reverie.

"Frank, where have you been?" Corrine asked as soon as I was in the door.

She was wrapped in the chiffon pink robe that she loved. It was sheer, and she was naked underneath. Corrine did Pilates and yoga and had a very nice figure at thirty-nine, thank you very much.

Even though I'd lost thirty pounds, I was still another forty overweight.

"Was it that you didn't want me eating cereal?" I asked her. "You think I'm too fat?"

"Have you been drinking?"

"I never go to that bar on Montague," I said. "I was walking by tonight, and I thought, hey, why not?"

"What's wrong, Frank?" she asked. Placing her fingertips on both my shoulders, she stared into my eyes with real concern.

"I was thinking on the way here that men must fall in love with you all the time. You're beautiful and very well known. And here I am a slouch who works in an office where most of the people don't even know my name."

"Come sit down, honey," she said.

She led me to the jade-colored sofa in our den. It was a small room that we rarely used now that Mercury was grown up and off to college.

"Merc said that you wired him over seventeen hundred dollars," she said, floundering for a way to keep my attention.

"Why don't you call him Todd?"

"Because his name is Mercury. What's wrong, Frank?"

"You know, Corr," I said. "I was thinking that we hardly ever talk. I mean there's people I see once a week at work who I know more about than I do about you. You work late. I leave early. Sometimes we don't even eat together for weeks."

"You're exaggerating."

"No," I said. "Not at all. Like, for instance, when was the last time you went to see a doctor?"

"My last checkup."

"Did your cholesterol rise or maybe your blood pressure? Is that why you're cutting down on carbs?"

"I'm fine." She was looking at me as if I were a stranger, a potentially dangerous man she'd just met and had to tread cautiously around until she understood the territory—a man like my father, who might jump up and stab you in the back.

"You see?" I said. "I didn't know that. You could have had any kind of thing wrong, and I wouldn't know. And I didn't ask because we hardly ever talk. I mean, how can you live with a man who doesn't even ask about your health?"

"Why did you send all that money to Mercury?"

"He's a good kid. I bet he was glad to get it."

"I told him to give it back, all but the sixty he asked for."

I looked right past her words and blinked once or twice.

"I feel kinda sick," I said. "I think I'll go to bed."

In the morning I couldn't sit up without the room spinning. Getting out of the bed was a comedy of wobbling knees and stiff ankles.

At the kitchen table I was trying to see straight, and Corrine was talking to me, though I missed most of what she said. I did understand that she would call work for me and that she had an appointment in the city. She seemed to be worried about me.

For some reason I resented the nicety.

*   *   *

I got to work at about three in the afternoon. I don't know why I went in; nowhere else to go, I guess.

On the Walton, Barth, and Wright website, I searched for names that had the initials of a degenerative disease. I found Timothy Bell. Timothy was the vice president in charge of all personal investors. Bell was at least three rungs above our agent, Mark Delaney, the man who told us that Corrine's income kept us *above the cut* at WBW. Timothy Bell was a smiling white face on an electronic résumé sheet that each of the vice presidents had. He was thirty-eight and had an MBA from Harvard. He was athletic too, the former captain of a rugby squad—rugby, not Ping-Pong.

I wondered if Corrine was somewhere fucking him right then. The letter had been traveling back and forth for over a month. I could tell that from the postmark. Maybe he called when she didn't reply, or maybe she broke down and called him. I wasn't worried about that though. Whether or not Corrine had fallen into Bell's muscular arms wasn't the problem.

The problem was that his letter was very convincing. He wanted to talk to her and read what she read. In their meetings, he must have looked into her dark brown eyes and seemed like he really wanted to know what was going on with her. She opened up to him, while we hadn't really talked in years.

It was obvious from the letter that he wanted to be her lover but was willing to settle for less. That was more than I had to offer, much more.

After reading Bell's letter, I wondered whether I had the right to hold Corrine back from the kind of life that she might have.

"Brown," a man's voice said.

I didn't have to look up to know that it was Ira Flint, my boss's boss.

"Mr. Flint."

I kept my eyes on the screen as he lowered into the chair beside my desk, a shadow looming in my peripheral vision. Flint was a tall man. Even sitting down he seemed to tower. He was heavy too, but his weight bore witness to strength, whereas mine was soft and getting softer. And the blackness of his skin made me feel rather pale.

Flint stared at me. I knew this even though I was pretending to be paying attention to something on the screen.

"What can I do for you?" I asked.

A glimpse at the bottom line of the computer screen told me that it was 7:17. We were the only ones on the floor.

"I have a problem, Frank," Ira Flint said.

I looked up then. "Does it have something to do with me?"

The big boss nodded his heavy head.

"I got three complaints on you in three months. The economy is down, and they're on my ass to adjust the bottom line."

"It's only two pink slips I got, Mr. Flint."

"The third is you giving out discounts like they were Christmas cards."

"Oh."

I knew that we had to get permission to give out lower rates. I knew it, though somehow I'd convinced myself that it was more important to bring in the business than to waste time making rate requisitions. But sitting there in front of Flint I knew how wrong I had been.

"Well, Frank?"

"I don't know, Ira."

He waited a moment or two. His expression was one of mild confusion.

"Is that all?" he asked.

I shrugged.

"I need something, Frank. Adeline wants to let you go. She's already got somebody lined up to cover your accounts."

Ira was warning me, trying to save me. He was reaching out, and all I wanted was to ask him why. Why help me? Why would he care?

"Frank."

"Let it go, man," I said and then turned back to my screen.

After a while the heavy presence of the big boss rose like a morning fog, and I was alone in my cubicle.

Corrine tried to talk to me that night, but I said I had a virus and went to bed early.

The next day I was given my notice.

"I'm sorry about this, Frank," Adeline Francie told me in her office down at the far end of the hall.

"Uh-huh."

"I mean, you just haven't been carrying your weight."

"Listen," I said, in a stern voice that I hadn't meant to use. "You got me down here with my hat in my hand. You're letting me go. Don't you try and make me feel worse."

I looked into the young manager's eyes, and we both experienced an animal moment. It was a confrontation. She was invading my territory, and I intended to protect it.

"You have two weeks' notice," she said.

"Fine," I said. Seven minutes later I left the office for good. I didn't even collect the belongings from my cubicle desk.

From the following day on, I fell into a new routine. In the mornings I'd get up before Corrine and go off to Midtown libraries and museums. I dressed well and ate in good restaurants. I carried Timothy Bell's letter to Corrine in my wallet. Every few hours I'd take it out and read it.

When the two weeks were up, I applied for unemployment benefits, using a rented mailbox to collect my checks. I went out on job interviews, but no one wanted to hire a fifty-four-year-old man with no real experience in anything but orthopedic online sales.

I didn't tell Corrine what was going on, and she didn't notice any difference. I hoped that she would see that there was something very different happening, but she didn't.

I read *One Hundred Years of Solitude*. It was beautiful. The sadness and melancholy resonated with my feelings. Sometimes I'd sit across the dinner table from Corrine, wishing that she'd bring up the book, that she'd want to talk about anything that would lead me to show her how much that I and my life had changed. But it didn't happen. And so for four months I wandered the streets of Manhattan and came home to my wife, one stranger to another.

One day I was walking down Fifth Avenue, and someone called my name. I turned, wondering who among all those thousands would know me. She ran up and kissed my cheek.

"How are you?" the woman asked.

It took me a few seconds to realize that I knew the smiling face. She was slight of build, with olive skin and heavy but quite beautiful features.

"Donella."

"I almost didn't recognize you," she said. "You're so skinny."

I'd lost my appetite months before.

"Went on a diet," I said, struggling with each word.

"You need a new suit."

"How are you, Donella?"

"Do you have time?" she asked. "Can we get coffee?"

*   *   *

We took a window table at Dingus and Bob's Coffee Emporium on Forty-Eighth Street. She held the seats while I bought us lattes.

When I got back to the table she told me a story about her boyfriend, a young Korean man named John Park. They had broken up the day before I had first called her, and that's why she'd thrown herself so madly into our affair.

". . . but then he came back and asked me to marry him," she was saying, the middle finger of her right hand barely touching my wrist on the tabletop. This hint of a connection felt like a faraway memory in another man's life. "I said yes, and that's why I broke up with you. But after a few months I realized that I don't want to be married. I left John and called you to apologize, but your cell phone was disconnected, and they said you didn't work at Korn/Wills anymore."

"I'm taking some time off to reevaluate my life," I said, realizing that in a way this was the truth.

"What's wrong?" Donella asked. "Is it because of what I did?"

"No," I said, "not at all. I hated that job, and I was no good at it either. I needed to get away."

"What are you going to do now?"

"Using the time to think."

"Would you, would you like us to see each other again?"

The question gave me the feeling of coming to a precipice, the edge of a vast and deep vale. The other side was so far away that it was shrouded in mist.

"No," I said.

"You hate me."

"I just can't do it, Donella. I have enough trouble taking one step after the next. I really have to go."

"Will you call me?" she asked, as I rose from the wooden chair.

"Yes," I lied.

* * *

That evening I called Corrine on my new pay-as-you-go cell phone. I told her that I was working late. I came home in the early morning and got into the bed so quietly that my wife didn't even shift in her sleep.

I had not seen my father, Mercury, after his suicide. The police were already there when I got home from baseball practice. My mother had a closed-casket service. I suppose they all thought they were protecting me. But I had in my mind the image of a naked man with a brown body and a black face—his tongue sticking out as if he were taunting the people after him.

My brother hadn't said he was naked, but that's the image I had. That night I dreamed of him. It was a sad reunion.

When Corrine tried to wake me the next morning, I told her that I was taking a personal day, after having worked so hard for so long.

At ten I sat down at the dinette table in the breakfast nook and took TB's letter from my wallet. On the other side I wrote this note:

Corrine,

I've been holding this letter for months now. The most important thing it meant to me was that I didn't get angry about it. I was just sad that we had drifted so far apart. I don't know if you care for this man or if his feelings for you make any difference. But I do know that you didn't trust me with our money and that you couldn't share your fears or joys with me, that you gave these feelings to a stranger because I left you no other choice. I know that whatever feeling we once had packed up and moved out with Mercury. So I'm going to leave. I'm breaking it off in one quick movement because I know that that's the only good thing I could do for you.

Frank Brown

I spent three days and two nights in Central Park. The weather was temperate, and I slept on a bench. One guy tried to rob me, and I went crazy. I actually picked up a trash can and hit him with it. After that I went to a homeless shelter on the Bowery. My joints were sore, and I realized that my clothes smelled like dust. I had put all my financial papers and important documents into a safe-deposit box at My Bank on Madison. I figured that I could live a life just off the streets for years with what I had. I'd get jobs washing dishes or maybe as a box boy in a local market in Queens. I could read *Love in the Time of Cholera* and learn to play chess competitively in Washington Square Park. I had been pretty good at chess in high school and later at college.

I dreamed one night that Corrine and I lived in a room. We were on a bed separated by an unbreakable glass wall. We couldn't hear each other through the thick barrier and so could only communicate through gesture. She pointed with both hands at her eyes and then at her stomach. I didn't understand. Then she touched her right foot with her right hand and looked beseechingly at me. I hunched my shoulders.

This dream played over and over, like an experimental film on a continuous loop. At one point I realized that the dream wouldn't stop. I wondered how long I had been asleep. My joints ached. I wanted to wake up but couldn't.

Finally I was conscious, but I couldn't open my eyes because they were glued shut by secretions. I tried to lift my hand to open them, but I was too weak, so I concentrated on forcing my eyelids open. After a while they came apart, scraping the sand of sleep across my corneas.

I was in a long hall tenanted by at least a dozen patients on slender hospital beds. A middle-aged Indian woman in a white smock was standing over me.

"What is your name?" she asked. It seemed as if she had asked me that question before.

"Frank Brown."

"Do you have family?"

I shook my head and the room also shook.

"Health insurance?"

"No."

"You're very sick, Mr. Brown," the doctor said. "You're suffering from malnutrition and probably walking pneumonia that has given way to full-blown pulmonary disease. Your lungs are a mess, and antibiotics don't seem to be working."

"How long have I been here?" I asked.

"They brought you from the shelter four days ago."

"Am I going to die?" I whispered.

"That's why we want to know if you're insured or if there's someone who can help."

When I wasn't moving or blinking too fast, I felt very warm and secure.

"Can I stay here?" I asked.

"For a week," she said. "After that we have to move you to a state facility."

I closed my eyes, and when I opened them again the Indian doctor was gone.

I felt warm and swaddled. In that bed there were no desires, not even much discomfort. There were beds around me, but I didn't know who was in them. I didn't have to eat or get up to go to the bathroom. All I had to do was sleep and awaken now and again. Each period of sleep seemed to have a longer arc. It was as if my consciousness was a skipping stone over placid water that built up speed and power as it went. I was completely satisfied knowing that

I'd sleep, open my eyes, and sleep again, until finally one day the sleep would go on, leaving me behind.

"Dad?"

I'd heard the word before in my death-sleep. It was a single note but also a word, a class of men . . . me.

Mercury was sitting in a pine folding chair next to my bed. His butter-brown face was drawn.

"Hey," I said. "What are you doing here?"

I looked around and noticed that I was no longer in the crowded infirmary. It was a single room—just for me.

"How do you feel?" my son asked.

I took in a long, deep breath, realizing how shallow my breathing had been.

"Good," I said. "Better. Where's your mother?"

"I want you to come home, Dad."

"Why aren't you in school?"

"I took a leave to come back and find you. I've been going all over the city to hospitals and shelters, the police and city social workers."

"Where's your mother?" I asked again.

"She thought, she thought you might not want to see her."

There was a lot of information in that stuttered sentence. But it didn't matter. Mercury my son had done for me what I was unable to do for Mercury my father.

"If I live," I said.

"What, Dad?"

"If I live, I'll come home."

HAUNTED

I was sitting at the dining room table surrounded by stacks of books and old newspapers, dirty dishes, bills, and first, second, and third drafts of handwritten letters to editors of various literary reviews. My laptop computer screen was open to a staff-page photograph from the *Black Rook Review*'s website. The *BRR* was a small literary quarterly out of the Lower East Side of Manhattan. I was looking at the picture of young, milk-soppy Clark Heinemann, holding in my hand his rejection of my one-thousandth story, "Shootout on the Wild Westside." Mira, my girlfriend of the last sixteen years, was leaving to sleep at her mother's house in Hoboken because, she said, and I quote, "your continual vituperation is too much for me to bear."

"Call me when you're human again, Paul," she said, before rolling her black-and-pink-polka-dotted roller bag out the door of our fifth-floor walk-up apartment.

I remember it all so clearly: Heinemann's rejection letter was in my hand, and his smug, slack face was on the screen; I could hear the thump and slide, thump and slide, thump and slide of Mira's bag as she lowered it step-by-step.

. . . while the concept is interesting the execution leaves me with more questions than answers. I think you might have greater success sending this story to a genre magazine where the readers have more sympathy for the ambiance and tone . . .

Heinemann's words were in my head while his doughy face smirked at me. Mira's bag's bump and slide down the stairs was fading when my hand, seemingly of its own volition, crushed the letter. This minor act of anger was exacerbated by a pain in my middle finger. It felt as if a bone had broken. Before I could react, the sharp ache jumped from my hand to my shoulder, and my breath got short. I was convinced that these were psychosomatic manifestations of the rage I felt about Heinemann and his condescending, typewritten, type-signed letter.

Here he used a typewriter on watermarked paper not as a sign of respect but because of his supercilious conceit.

There was no personal intention to that letter; I was sure of this even as I tumbled from the dining room chair to the bare oak floor. My left ankle got tangled in the power cord, and the laptop fell with me. It didn't break. Lying there sideways on the floor, Clark Heinemann sneered at my diminution, my impotence.

I hated him so much.

As I reached over to pick up the computer, intent on smashing his image, I realized that it was not my spiritual heart but the physical one that was causing the numbness in my left forearm and the fire in my chest.

I managed to take in half the breath I needed, exhaled with a very audible wheeze, and then inhaled with half the capacity of the breath before.

Clark Heinemann sneered. My breathing became mere puffs. Mira was right about me, but Mira was gone. I had stormed around the apartment for three days cursing the editor and drinking expensive red wine that we could not afford.

My thousandth story, and I was dying, and Clark Heinemann would probably make some snide remark when he heard I was gone.

Just like they used to say in the old movies, everything was going dark. I was dying, and the only witness, the only light left to me, was Clark Heinemann and his sidelong smug indifference.

After a short while that nevertheless felt interminable, darkness overwhelmed the light. I had died hating a man twenty years my junior, a man I had never met or spoken to. I was, for all intents and purposes, dead and gone, but somehow my hatred cohered. The details of my final humiliation floated on a deep well of spite that did not, would not drain away.

Even as my body rotted and festered under the unblinking eyes of Clark Heinemann, the thoughts I had at death survived. One thousand unpublished stories, 26,473 rejection letters, and all those editorial twits that never gave me a break. The only thing left of me was a raging emotion at every publisher of every insignificant quarterly—but most of all, Clark Heinemann.

"Paul Henry is dead," a young woman's voice said from somewhere in the void.

I was suddenly back in proximity to the living; aware, seeing the world from a set of eyes that were a bit stronger than mine had been.

"Who?" The man's voice seemed to reverberate.

"That guy who has sent us a story every six weeks for the past twenty years."

"You mean Mr. Again and Again?"

"That's him."

"What happened? Did some editor finally shoot him?"

"Sixty-eight and overweight. He only lived three blocks from here. He had this younger girlfriend who left him, and so they didn't find his body for five weeks."

I was floating over the head of a man in his late forties who looked somewhat like Clark Heinemann. He wore a herringbone jacket, a dark blue shirt, and a yellow and blue bow tie.

"The poor fuck," Clark said. "I must have rejected hundreds of his bad stories."

A thousand, I thought.

"What did you say, Carrie-Anne?"

"What?"

"Did you say something?"

"No."

"Oh well," said the human stalk to which my hateful consciousness clung. "He wrote all that genre stuff and tried to pretend it was literary. At least I won't have to make our interns read any more of his ghastly prose."

You didn't even read it yourself?

"What?" Clark said.

"Are you hearing things?" the copper-haired young woman asked. She wore horn-rimmed glasses and grass-green lipstick.

"Too much to drink at the PEN Gala last night, I guess," he said. "Did I tell you? I sat three tables away from Rushdie and Paul Auster. My head's been buzzing all morning."

After that Carrie-Anne left the small office. Clark gazed at her posterior as she went, and so I did too. Clark had a desk and a bookshelf, an old IBM Selectric typewriter, and an almost as old Apple Macintosh computer. His windows were open, and there was a breeze; you could see it wafting in the partially drawn window shade.

Alone Clark Heinemann studied the computer screen, perusing a story submission to the magazine. I tried to read the words, but they didn't make sense. The world was fading again as it had when I died weeks before.

Finally I was once more merely the memory of hatred for anyone having to do with publishing.

The acrid smell of urine, dead skin, and sour breath assailed a nose close to me. I came to consciousness, again attached to Clark Heinemann. This time we were in an old folks' home sitting before an ancient woman in a wheelchair. She was listing to the side, and her eyes darted around aimlessly, as if searching for something worth seeing. Looking at her, I perceived a memory that must have belonged to Heinemann. It was his mother when she was younger and he was a child. She'd been a handsome woman. Now her once fair skin had darkened and was creased with a thousand wrinkles. Her white hair stood away from her tiny head like dead grass rising up from the weight of the first snow at the onset of winter. The only glimmer of life, even beauty, was in her blue eyes, which looked out from under a creased brow. She peered closely at the space above Clark's head.

"How are you, Mom?" he asked, and I wondered what I was doing there.

"Who are you?" she asked.

"I'm Clark, Ma, your son."

"Who's that on your head?"

"My . . . my head?"

"Yeah. That fat Negro on top a' your head. Isn't he heavy?"

Heinemann waved his hand over his head; it passed right through me.

"Nothing there, Mom. See?"

"I see a Negro on top a' your head."

Clark turned away from his mother and looked into a mirror above a sink anchored into the wall of the nursing-home cell. I saw what he saw—him, as pasty-faced and weak-jawed as ever, and my dark countenance hovering just above for only a second and then fading. I was still there, but Clark soon lost sight of me.

"What was that?" he said.

"He's gone," Mrs. Heinemann said. "Now, who are you?"

For the next hour or so, Clark sat with his mother, fed her, and told her over and over again that he was her son and that he loved her.

"Will you take me with you to your house?" she asked, emotional craft combined with the eternal despair of an orphaned child.

"You're happier here," he said.

"I hate it here. They don't feed me."

"I'll talk to the nursing staff."

"Will the Negro take me home with him?"

The smell was horrible; the feeling of mortality unbearable. I could sense death descending all around. This reminded me of my own expiration, and I moaned.

"Did you hear something, Mom?"

"It was him," she said, gesturing at me with an arthritic claw.

It was then that I understood what was happening. I existed only through my hatred of Clark, and then I was called into existence through my name being mentioned or when someone like that old dying woman could see me.

I wanted to get away from Clark and his mother and that building full of people whose souls were crying out as mine was.

Six or seven times during the torture, Clark turned to look in the mirror, but I wasn't there—or at least he could no longer see me.

When he left the nursing home, I faded again, hoping that this would be the last conjuring, that I would pass over into oblivion.

For a long time I floated in hateful darkness. My feelings about Clark Heinemann had become a physical thing, or maybe metaphysical; they, those angry emotions, had turned into instincts that I could not eschew.

"Miss Stern to see you, Mr. Heinemann," a voice through an intercom announced.

"Send her in."

I was aware again, sharing the eyes, ears, and nostrils of Clark Heinemann.

He looked up, and I did too. Mira walked in, wearing her job-hunting medium-gray dress suit.

She was thirty years younger than I. We met when I was teaching a class on fiction at the uptown Y. She still had a great figure. And that outfit really showed it off.

Clark noticed what I did, and I wondered if somehow my awareness informed his.

He stood up and said, "Nice to meet you, Miss Stern. I was so sorry to hear about your husband."

"We weren't married. Paul didn't believe in marriage." It sounded like an indictment.

"Oh, I see," he said. "Um, please have a seat."

Mira took the chair and crossed her legs, showing her lovely knees.

"How can I help?" Clark asked, looking at her legs with me.

"I wanted to ask you if there was some way that you might publish something of Paul's. He left me the stories in his will. And it's the only thing I can imagine that would be a fitting remembrance. His body was cremated. He was an only child, and his parents are both dead. The only things he left in the world were one thousand stories and seven suitcases filled with rejection letters."

I caught a whiff of rose oil, the perfume I preferred on her.

"You don't have children?" Clark asked.

"I was with Paul most of my adult life," she said. "But he didn't want kids. He said he needed the time to write."

Clark gazed at Mira's café au lait complexion. Her father was Jewish of Russian descent and her mother a rare Christian from Mali. She was a beautiful woman. I couldn't remember the last time I'd told her so.

I'm so sorry, honey, I said reflexively.

"Did you hear something?" Clark asked.

"Just the traffic from the street," she said.

She uncrossed her legs and then recrossed them in the opposite direction. Then she tilted forward in a movement both innocent and suggestive.

I was happy that she was trying so hard to get me into that magazine.

"You know, Miss Stern, Paul's work was not the kind of fiction we publish. The writing was passable, but he always threw in some genre aspect that made the work, um, what can I say . . . neither here nor there."

"But," she said. "I don't know . . . I was thinking that maybe you could publish it with an introduction. You know, an article saying that the story was an example of how Paul took his own path in spite of expectations."

That's my girl, I said.

"I like that," Clark agreed.

"I know Paul was stubborn, but he worked so hard at it that it would be a shame if he was never published."

Mira stared directly into my nemesis's eyes, and I was aware of a quickening in his pulse.

"I'll tell you what," he said. "Why don't we have dinner tonight, and you can tell me what stories best fit your idea. I mean, I can't make any promises but . . . I don't know; we'll see."

"Thank you so much," she said, with real happiness in her voice.

They made plans to meet at an Italian restaurant that night. He gave her the name, D'Oro. She said that she knew the place.

She stood, and he did too. He walked her to the door and then kissed her cheek. I could smell the rose attar rising from her breast and feel the touch of her fingers on the back of Clark Heinemann's hand.

After she left, Clark sat there for a while looking at the door she'd gone through. Then he picked up a manuscript, and my mind slipped back into the brackish bile pond where it festered and throve.

In that vile darkness my mind was only partially aware. I realized that even though I was a ghost, I was the one being haunted by the animosity I'd worn like a badge through my life. I never made anything of myself, and I held Mira back. I wrote stories that I knew would never be published, and I hated freely.

I was my own private hell.

Knowing this, I tried to let go of my feelings, hoping that this release would let me find oblivion, if not actual peace.

There in the darkness I strained to let my hatred of the arrogant editor fade. For a moment there I felt that I had succeeded, and then . . .

"To Paul Henry," Clark Heinemann saluted.

He and Mira clinked wine goblets over two plates of half-eaten pasta. They drained their glasses, and a waiter came up to refill them.

"The wine is kind of going to my head," she said.

He reached over and took her hand.

"Come home with me," he said, and I tried to remember the last time Mira and I had made love.

*   *   *

The sex went on and on, all night long. Riding on Clark's undulating body, I cried out in the pain of loss and betrayal. He experienced my cries as some kind of inner ecstasy, while Mira urged him on, whispering that she had not felt this much and this good in many years. She told him how beautiful he was and how caring and gentle.

In the early morning they went into the hallway outside of his apartment after a series of half-drunken dares. There they giggled and fucked until someone opened a door down the hall, forcing them to laugh and run for the refuge of his apartment again.

After that they fell asleep, and I eased back into my grotto of spite. But before I could sink into blissful unconsciousness . . .

"What are you thinking?" Clark asked my girlfriend of sixteen years. He was nuzzling her nipple with his pudgy nose.

"About Paul," she said wistfully.

"Are you feeling bad?"

"No," she said, and I felt like I was a balloon filled past capacity, about to burst with rage instead of helium. "The reason he was left in the apartment for so long was because I had decided never to come back. I couldn't. I'm thirty-seven, and nothing had changed between us since the day we met. We were in the same apartment, sleeping on the same mattress on the floor. He made scrambled eggs with lox and onions in the same skillet five thousand mornings in a row. And he kept writing stories that I knew would never be published. I think he knew it too."

"I'm sorry," Clark said. "I guess sometimes we just find ourselves in a rut."

And as if the word had poetic power, they began rutting all over again.

*   *   *

I was hoping that Mira had seduced Clark so that he would publish my work. But the following morning I was stirred back to reality by a phone call.

"Hello?" Mira said.

"Hi, Mira, it's Clark . . . Heinemann."

"Hi," she said, with an élan I'd never heard in her voice before.

"I've decided to go ahead with our plan and publish an original Paul Henry story."

"Oh my God, that's so wonderful. It's perfect."

They discussed the details for a while, and then he said, "I had a great time last night."

"We should get together again soon," she agreed.

"How about tonight?" he asked.

"I'm supposed to see my mother," Mira said.

Yes! I thought. *Lead him on until I'm published and then tell him you did it all for me.*

"OK," Clark said rather sadly. I could feel his disappointment through our connection.

"But I could call her," Mira offered. "I could change it to some-time next week."

"I'll get the wine, and we can eat in my apartment."

"We don't even have to eat," Mira promised, and I cried out.

"Is there some interference on the line?" Clark asked.

"Not on my end."

Every night for the next three months Mira was at Paul's apartment doing things we had never done.

When she told him that she was pregnant, I hoped that the smug editor would see his error and kick her out. But instead he kissed her and asked her to marry him. He didn't think about it for one moment. What kind of fool does something like that?

But I was relieved anyway. They would have a life where my name would never be mentioned. I would slowly fade from consciousness and then finally follow my body into death.

I hadn't considered what would happen with the publication of my story "Shootout on the Wild Westside" in the fall edition of *Black Rook Review*. Clark wrote a moving testimonial to me, " . . . a writer who never gave up; who died working on his next story."

I was dragged through a series of interviews, to a dozen public readings, and finally to a publishing house that wanted to put out a collection of my multi-genre tales.

Clark and Mira didn't stop having sex until the seventh month of her pregnancy, and then, and then . . . they decided to name their son Paul Henry Heinemann.

Clark became an expert on my work and often gave talks about me.

. . . Paul Henry was a complex man who was ahead of his time. He wrote fiction that was destined to outlive him. He selfishly used his time for the one thousand stories he crafted over thirty years.

He wasn't a happy man. He wasn't nice or good or caring or even very friendly. He hated editors like me because we couldn't see his value . . .

And after talks in Cincinnati, Seattle, Boston, LA, and twenty other towns and cities, he'd meet some young woman writer and make love to her the way he would to Mira when he got home.

I hated him then, because I had never cheated on her. Maybe I didn't treat her as well as she deserved, but at least I was faithful in my mediocrity.

When Clark came home I never rested, because he'd made a career out of me and so talked about me and my work almost every day.

And when he wasn't dealing with me directly he was calling out to his son, "Paul Henry," and I was forced into the life I never had, paying for my small-minded, selfish ways.

And then one day Mira found a letter in a pocket of the brown corduroy jacket that Clark wore when on the road. It was some love letter that a young woman secreted for him to find, so he would think of her when he was far away.

The fight went on for hours. Mira cried, and Clark tried to explain, then to apologize, and then to say he had no excuse. She told him to get out, and instead of being happy about his misery, I felt, for the first time since the heart attack, real pain. Their pain was mine. I couldn't escape it. My consciousness was melding with their emotions.

At one point Clark and I saw Paul Henry standing in a doorway that led down a hall to the boy's bedroom.

Clark told his son to go to bed.

"What's that man doing on your head, Daddy?" the four-year-old asked.

After putting his son to bed, Clark returned to the living room, and Mira kissed him.

"What's that for?" he asked.

"Seeing you with our son," she said. "I'm still mad but I forgive you."

Later that night, Mira and Clark came in to say good night to my namesake, kissing him and promising strawberry pancakes in the morning to make up for all that yelling.

I wasn't looking forward to what was going to happen next. When they had even the tiniest spat they made up for it with marathon sex sessions. I was going to experience Clark's rolling doughy body making Mira cry out for him as she'd never done for me.

But that didn't happen. Clark and Mira turned on Paul Henry's night-light and departed, somehow leaving me in the room with their son.

Alone, the boy dutifully picked his teddy bear off the short chest of drawers next to his bed and squeezed it tightly.

He had golden skin and similarly colored curly hair.

He seemed to be thinking about something when he said, "You look so sad."

He seemed to be talking to me.

This was a surprise. Even those people who rarely saw me, usually senile and near death themselves, never addressed me directly. They would ask Clark who I was and why I was there.

"You," Paul Henry said.

"Me?"

He nodded. "Why you look so sad?"

"I do?"

"Uh-huh. Why?"

"Because your mother used to be my girlfriend, but then I, I died, and now she loves your father." I didn't want to say all that, but somehow his questions demanded answers.

"And so you're sad because you love my mommy?"

"No."

"You don't love her?"

"No, I don't," I said, surprised at my own answer.

"Then why are you so mad at my daddy?"

"Why do you say I'm mad?"

"Because when I see you and you say things, it makes him upset. I don't think he can see you, but he knows you're there. He knows it, and he gets mixed up."

I felt something give, like a tether pulling out of the soil.

"I guess I was mad at your father because he never published my stories when I was alive."

"Oh," my young namesake said, and I felt another tether give. "Maybe you could forgive him if I said I was sorry he didn't do that. I could tell my daddy that you were mad, and then he would be sorry too."

There was a breeze suddenly blowing through the room, and another tether pulled out of the firmament of my hatred. There was a light shining somewhere, and I realized that most of my existence after death had been swathed in darkness.

Everything was becoming light.

Paul Henry was talking, and I might have responded, but I was only aware of the light shining and the darkness that was dissipating, the strong breeze, and the weightlessness I felt from the tethers loosening.

"Will you come back?" Paul Henry asked. It was part of a longer conversation that another part of my mind had been having with him.

Before I could answer, the wind picked up, drowning out all other sound, and the light became excruciatingly bright. I was still there in the room with Paul Henry, as the world turned and Mira called out Clark's name in ecstasy.

I would, I realized, always be there, and that was a relief so profound that time ceased and my antipathies turned into silver-scaled fish that darted away somewhere, leaving me once again breathless.

THE SIN
OF DREAMS

July 27, 2015

"So, who's paying for all this?" Carly Matthews asked.

"There are a few investors," Morgan Morgan replied. "A man who owns the largest cable and satellite provider in China, a so-called sheikh, the owner of two pro teams in the US, and a certain, undefined fund that comes to us via the auspices of the White House."

Morgan gestured broadly. Behind the milk-chocolate-brown entrepreneur, through the huge blue-tinted window, Carly could see center city LA, thirty-two stories down. The San Bernardino Mountains stood under a haze in the distance. The summer sun shone brightly but still failed to warm the air-conditioned office.

"Government money?" she asked.

"Not exactly," the director of New Lease Enterprises replied, looking somewhere over the young scientist's head.

"What does that mean?"

"Someone close to the president has called together a small group of billionaires and shared with them the potential of our research. He has also, unofficially, given NLE's holding company, BioChem International, access to the Justice Department and three constitutional experts."

"What does the Justice Department have to do with neuronal data analysis?"

Morgan Morgan, executive vice president and principal director of NLE, gazed at the twenty-three-year-old postdoctoral student. Her pleasant features and youthful expression belied the razor-sharp mind that, his advisors assured him, her published articles so clearly exhibited.

"What business does a black hip-hop promoter from the Motor City have running a subsidiary of a biological research company?" Morgan asked.

All the fair-skinned blond scientist could do was raise her eyebrows and shrug.

"The only reason I'm here," she said, "is because my former professor Dr. Lawson asked me, as a favor to him, to meet with you. I'm in the middle of three very important experiments, and I have to be back by no later than nine o'clock tonight."

"What reason did Rinehart give you?" Morgan asked.

"Dr. Lawson told me that I would be amazed by what you had to say. It is for that reason alone I left Stanford to come down here."

"I paid Rinehart three hundred and seventy thousand dollars to say that to you. One hundred thousand for his second family in West Virginia, two hundred to cover gambling debts in Atlantic City, and seventy to end the annoyance of a blackmailer who has been collecting money from him for twelve years. I don't know how he plans to spend that seventy, but I doubt he'll use it for payment."

Young Dr. Matthews tilted her head and peered blankly at the ex-hip-hop manager and impresario. For a full minute she couldn't think of anything to say.

"Well?" Morgan asked, managing not to smile. "Are you amazed?"

"Yes. But I don't see why Dr. Lawson would want me to come down here to learn about his, his indiscretions."

"He didn't." Morgan allowed. "I've already told you that the work we're doing has to do with the transmigration of the human soul. Our work in that field is truly astonishing."

"What's astonishing is so much money being spent on this rubbish," she said.

"Two years at Oxford, right?" Morgan pointed at her and smiled, knowingly.

"Yes, but why do you ask?"

"*Rubbish*," he said, with an almost boyish grin. "Americans don't really use that word, even though it's a very good one."

"I didn't come here to dig up dirt on my mentor or to listen to your opinions on the nationality of language."

"No," Morgan said. "You are here because I paid your mentor good money to make sure you came."

"And the question is, why?"

"The same reason the board of directors of BioChem International opted to give me a free hand in this soul business—sales."

"Sales?"

"We have, as I've already told you, all the theoretical and technical knowledge to read and therefore copy the contents of a human brain into electronic data storage and from storage back into that mind or another. But because of the complexity and mathematical nuances of this process, there isn't enough memory in our facility to contain even a fraction of a normal adult's experience and intelligence, learned and inherited instincts, and conscious and unconscious memory—at least that's what the experts tell me. The amount of data attached even to a simple phrase in a human's mind could take up trillions of bytes in memory. The experience of a single day would fill up every storage device the Defense Department has."

"Oh," Carly said, the light dawning behind her eyes.

"Yes," Morgan agreed, nodding. "I realized your macromolecular studies trying to simulate DNA development would give us a way to store information that is only a thousand times the capacity size of the human brain and naturally compatible with human physiology. If we could harness your bio-storage methodology with our neuronal I/O systems, we could combine them with the cloning process to transfer the human soul from one body to another."

"But Mr. Morgan, what you have to understand is that I do not believe in a soul."

"No," the director agreed. "You don't. But you're an American citizen aren't you?"

"Of course."

"You believe in the freedom of religion, do you not?"

"Certainly."

"And all religions believe in the human soul."

"So what?"

"So if I offer to sell a customer a new, younger version of himself, then he has to believe that it is not only his consciousness but his actual soul that will inhabit the new body."

"But it isn't," Dr. Matthews argued. "Even if the new body contained his memories when the old body dies, the origin, the sense organs that recorded and experienced those memories will die with it."

"Not the originals," Morgan Morgan noted. "My scientists tell me that our physical body is completely replaced by new materials every seven years; our memories, if material, are therefore not original."

"That's just sophistry."

"But what if we copied Mr. X's memories into the macromolecular computer your research postulates, talk to Mr. X in that form, and then copy those memories back into his old body?"

"His brain will remember the experiences his mind had as a machine."

"Yes," Morgan said happily. "We copy him back and forth a few times like that and then, with no warning, move these memories into the new body. His mind, his experiences, and his thoughts will be indistinguishable from the three storage units he's experienced. Therefore the new man and the old man will be the same—exactly."

"It's kind of like three-card monte," Carly said.

"Kind of," Morgan agreed, pursing his lips and shrugging slightly.

December 3, 2019

Dr. Carly Matthews was remembering this first meeting with Morgan Morgan as she sat in the witness box in a pine and cherrywood California state courtroom, seven blocks east of the ex-impresario's former office.

"You believed that Mr. Morgan was a huckster," Ralph Lacosta, the prosecuting attorney, said. He was a short man in a black suit that seemed to call attention to his small stature. He wore glasses, as Carly did. At their last meeting, in preparation for her testimony, he had asked her out for dinner.

"Objection," Melanie Post, the defense attorney, said. "Leading the witness."

Melanie was buxom, around forty, and Carly found her intimidating, though she didn't know why. The defense lawyer never raised her voice or bullied a witness. It was something about the way she looked at and listened to people—with unrelenting intensity.

"Reword, counselor," a seemingly bored John Cho, the presiding judge, advised.

The judge was sixty-nine, Carly knew from Wikipedia's newly instituted public official bio-repository. He had presided over some of the most important murder cases in recent years and had survived three bouts with liver cancer.

"How did Mr. Morgan impress you when you first met?" Lacosta asked Carly.

"He told me that he planned to migrate souls. I thought he was joking."

"You didn't believe him?"

"He was a music producer who was all of a sudden at the head of the subsidiary of a major medical corporation. That alone was ridiculous."

"But you went to work for him the day you met," Lacosta claimed. "Why is that?"

"Five million dollars."

"Say again?"

"He paid me five million dollars and promised over a hundred million in capital to design and build a macromolecular computer for New Lease Enterprises. He also offered to let me retain copyrights and patents on the theory and the physical device."

"And you accepted?"

"I didn't believe in the existence of a soul, but to have the funds to build a new bio-based computer system was too good to pass up."

"And did you accomplish this goal?"

"Yes."

"And did NLE's other researchers manage to copy the contents of a man's mind, completely, from a human brain into an analogous synthetic construct?"

At the defense table, over Lacosta's left shoulder, Carly could see the codefendants, Morgan Morgan and a young man named Tyler Edgington Barnes IV. Morgan reminded her of her father. Not her biological dad, but Horace Granger, the black man that married her mother after Thomas Matthews had abandoned them.

"Miss Matthews," Judge Cho said.

"I cannot say that the data transfer was complete," Carly said. "But the responses from the various I/O devices on Micromime Six were exactly the same as the subjects gave with their own bodies and minds."

A woman in the courtroom began to cry. That, Carly knew, was Melinda Greaves-Barnes, the seventy-six-year-old self-proclaimed widow of Morgan Morgan's codefendant.

"So you communicated with these synthetic memories?" Prosecutor Lacosta asked.

"Yes. For many months, in over a hundred test cases."

"And where were the original patients while you conducted your experiments with the synthetic device?"

"Each was placed in a medically induced coma. That was the only way we could assure an even transfer of information, by lowering the metabolism to a catatonic state."

"Like death," Lacosta suggested.

"Objection."

"Withdrawn. Those are all the questions I have for this witness, your honor."

"OK," John Cho said. "Let's break for lunch and reconvene at two P.M."

"It's all so crazy," Adonis Balsam was saying at the Hot Dog Shoppe across the street from the courthouse. He was demolishing a chili-cheese dog with onions. Carly ordered a soy dog on whole wheat. "I mean, they're trying Tyler Barnes for murdering himself. That's insane."

"But the man in the defendant's chair," Carly said, "is just a clone, a copy of the original man."

"An exact copy, with all of the original guy's feelings and memories," Adonis said. He was black-haired and rather stupid, Carly thought, but he was a good lover, and he seemed devoted to her. She didn't mind that he was probably after her money. After she started her own line of Macromime computers and computer systems, everybody was after her money—everybody but Morgan Morgan.

"No," she said. "To be exactly the same, you have to be the original thing, the thing itself. Morgan and Tyler murdered the original Tyler Barnes."

"OK, baby," Adonis said. "You're the scientist, not me."

He took her hand and kissed her cheek. She always smiled when he called her baby and kissed her. She didn't love Adonis and didn't care if he loved her or not. All she wanted was a word and a kiss.

"What defines a human being?" was Melanie Post's first question when Carly sat down in the cherrywood witness box that afternoon.

"Objection," Prosecutor Lacosta chimed. "The witness is not an expert in philosophy, medicine, or psychology."

"Ms. Post?" Judge Cho asked, a friendly and expectant smile on his lips.

"Your honor," the defense said. "Ms. Matthews has designed a memory device that is almost indistinguishable from the structure, capacity, and even the thinking capability of the human brain. I would argue that there is not a human being on the face of this Earth more qualified than she."

The judge's smile turned into a grin. Carly wondered how well the two knew each other.

"I'll allow the question," Cho said, "as long as the answer remains within the bounds of the witness's expertise."

"Ms. Matthews?" Melanie Post said.

"It's, it's mostly the brain I suppose," Carly said. In all their pretrial sessions, the prosecutor's team had not prepared her for this question. "But there are other factors."

"The soul?"

"I don't believe in a soul."

"Man is soulless?"

"The brain is an intricate machine that functions at such a high level that it feels as if there is something transcendent in the sphere of human perception."

"But really human beings are just complex calculators," Melanie Post offered.

"Objection."

"Overruled."

"I don't know," Carly admitted. "Emotions are real. Dreams are not real, but they arise from biological functions. So even dreams are physical entities; they exist as one thing but are perceived as something else. It is a very difficult question to answer."

"Are the defendants men?" Melanie asked.

"Yes."

"No more questions. You may step down, Ms. Matthews."

August 15, 2020

Carly Matthews sat in the back row of the courtroom. She'd attended the trial every day it convened for more than half a year, having left the running of Macromime Enterprises to her stepfather. The day after Carly's testimony, Melanie Post presented John Cho with a request from Tyler Edgington Barnes to separate his trial from Morgan Morgan's. Barnes was now claiming that he had been brainwashed by the NLE director and was not responsible for any criminal act he might be blamed for.

Ralph Lacosta, after meeting with Tyler and his former body's wife, Melinda, had decided there was merit in the billionaire's claim and withdrew her accusations; she now admitted that the young Tyler was truly innocent of the murder of his earlier iteration. The crime was, in the state prosecutor's opinion, solely the responsibility of Morgan Morgan.

For his part Morgan did not protest the decision, but in the transition it turned out that he was broke. BioChem International, which had been paying Melanie Post's steep fee, withdrew their support for their former VP, saying that they too had been convinced of his perfidy. That's when Carly stepped in and hired Fred Friendly to represent Morgan.

Carly didn't feel any guilt for what had happened at NLE, but neither did she think that Morgan alone should shoulder the burden.

Ralph Lacosta approached Morgan after he was seated in the witness box.

"Mr. Morgan," the prosecutor said, as a kind of greeting.

The ex-VP, ex–music mogul nodded.

Morgan wasn't a particularly handsome man, Carly thought. He was only five seven, at least twenty pounds overweight, and his features were blunt, with no hint of sensuality. But despite these shortcomings, his smile was infectious.

"What is your education, Mr. Morgan?" the prosecutor asked.

"Degree in general studies from Martin Luther King High School in Detroit, Michigan."

"That's all?"

"Yes."

"But still you were at the helm of the most advanced biological research company in the world."

"Only the sales arm of the NLE branch of that company," Morgan corrected.

"Excuse me?"

"They made the science," Morgan said. "I provided the marketing context."

"In other words, you're a huckster," Lacosta said.

"Objection," Fred Friendly cried.

"Overruled," Robert Vale, the new presiding judge, intoned.

"What do you sell, Mr. Morgan?" Ralph Lacosta asked.

"Dreams."

"What kind of dreams?"

"That depends on the marketplace," Morgan replied easily. "When I worked in music, I repped a rapper named Johnny Floss. He'd been a paid escort who dreamed about being a star. I facilitated that dream."

"And he fired you."

"Yes."

"What were the circumstances of your dismissal?"

"Johnny let me go when he'd gotten what he wanted. It hit me pretty hard. He was my only client. I went into social media, found out that there were all kinds of kid geniuses out there who designed platforms to get the word out on anything from toothpaste to fortune telling. With that I took a skinny pop singer and made him the highest-paid musical act of 2016. That's when Bio-Chem reached out and asked me to help them merchandise their work in cloning and soul transmigration."

"Soul transmigration?" Lacosta said.

"Moving the human soul from an old body to a new one."

"Do you believe in the soul?"

"I'm from Detroit, Mr. Lacosta, that's the home of soul."

Laughter came from a few quarters of the courtroom. Carly found herself smiling.

"Answer my question," Ralph Lacosta said.

"I believe in my soul."

"How about Tyler Barnes? Did he believe in a soul?"

"He must have. He paid BioChem International one-point-one-three billion dollars to take his soul out of a cancer-ridden dying body and put it in a new model."

"Move to strike, your honor," Lacosta said to the judge. "Mr. Edgington's dealings with BioChem have been sealed by the court."

"Just so," the lanky, bald judge agreed.

He instructed the jury to disregard any statements about Barnes's dealings with BioChem.

The questioning of Morgan went on for six days.

"Did you kill the elder version of Tyler Barnes?" Fred Friendly asked Morgan on day five.

"No, sir, I did not. I left Tyler the younger alone in the room with himself. I told him how to turn off the life-support machine, but I gave no advice on what he should do. Why would I?"

296

"He claims that you brainwashed him."

"My company copied his brain, but there was no cleanup involved."

September 3, 2020

"I had no idea who I was or where," Tyler Barnes said to the prosecutor's associate, Lani Bartholomew. He'd been on the witness stand for the previous two days. "Sometimes I'd wake up in my mind, but I had no body. Questions came at me as images or sometimes words but not spoken. It was like remembering a question that was just asked a moment ago. Other times I was in my older body, but I was drugged and disoriented. Finally I came awake in a younger, healthy form—the way I had been as a young man. It was exhilarating. I was young again. I believed that my soul had been removed from my older self and placed inside the new man.

"Mr. Morgan brought me to the room where the old me was lying on a bed, attached to a dozen different machines. He, he told me that they had taken my entire being from the ailing husk on the bed before me and made the man I was now."

"You're sure that's what he said?" Lani Bartholomew asked. She was young and raven-haired; a beauty dressed in a conservative dress suit, Carly thought. "That they took the soul from the body before you and placed it in your new body."

"Objection."

"Overruled."

"Yes," Tyler Barnes said. "I was given the definite impression that there was only one soul and that it was moved between bodies and the Macromime computer. I turned off the life support certain that what was lying before me was a soulless husk."

"That's what Morgan Morgan led you to believe."

"Yes. Yes, it was. If I had known the truth, I would have never turned off the life-support system. Never. Mr. Morgan indicated that the man lying in that bed was already brain-dead."

April 9, 2029

When the trial was finally over, the jury took only three hours to return a verdict: guilty of first-degree murder with extenuating circumstances. Fred Friendly managed to get the rider attached so that Morgan wouldn't face the death penalty.

There had been two appeals that had failed to produce a retrial, but Friendly and Carly kept trying.

By 2027 legislation allowing suicide had passed in thirty-one states, and BioChem International was the richest entity that had ever existed; Macromime was the second wealthiest.

It was speculated that the cost of cloning and soul migration would come down to a million dollars per transfer by the year 2031, and banks had started advising their customers how to prepare for this expense. The phrase *life insurance* took on a whole new meaning, and religious zealots around the world were stalking BCI facilities.

Catholic terrorists especially targeted doctors and medical schools that worked in cloning and bio-based computer systems.

The world's largest amusement park corporation bought a small island off the coast of Cuba to create a resort that would specialize in New Lease soul-transfer technology.

A movement of a different sort had begun in Europe. People there claimed that since the Macromime memory systems were eighty-five percent biological, the copies of individual personalities that dwelled inside them—for no matter how brief a time—were sentient beings, and so when the memories were erased it was the same thing as murder.

While all this was happening, Morgan Milton Morgan III made his residence at one of the oldest California state prisons. He'd lost two teeth in brawls, had been slashed from the left temple down to his right cheek by a razor-sharp blade fashioned from a tomato can, and he'd shed twenty-seven pounds.

Morgan refused every request to be visited or interviewed, until one day when Carly Matthews asked, for the twelfth time, to be granted a meeting.

Morgan was awakened at six on the morning of the meeting. He was taken to the assistant warden's personal quarters, where he was allowed to shave, shower, and dress in street clothes that no longer fit. He had to ask his guard to poke a new hole in his leather belt and opted to wear his bright orange prison T rather than the white collared shirt that made him look like a child wearing his father's collar.

After his morning toilet, Morgan was served a breakfast of steak and eggs, orange juice, and French roast coffee, along with sourdough toast with strawberry jam.

By 11:00 A.M., the appointed hour, Morgan felt like a new man in an old man's body.

Morgan was brought to the warden's office and ushered in. Carly stood up from the chair behind the warden's desk. The warden, a copper-skinned black man, was already standing by the door.

"Mr. Morgan," Warden Jamal said.

"Warden."

"At Ms. Matthews's request, we're going to leave you two alone in here. I don't want any trouble."

"Then tell her not to hurt me, Jeff, because you know trouble is a runaway truck on a one-way street headed right at my nose."

When Morgan said this and smiled, Carly got a clear look at his battered visage.

"If you want to smart off we can end this session here and now," Warden Jeffry Theodore Jamal said.

"Please," Carly interrupted. "Warden, Mr. Morgan and I are old friends. He won't do anything to hurt me or jeopardize your possessions, will you, Mr. Morgan?"

"That's what I said."

When they were alone, Carly Matthews returned to the warden's oak swivel chair, and Morgan sat in the leftmost of the three visitor seats. For a full two minutes the two sat appraising each other.

"You growin' up, Carly," Morgan said at last. "I hear you and that Adonis guy had twins."

"We've separated.

"Heard that too."

"That's what I get for letting him hire the nanny, I guess. You look . . . well."

"My face looks like a raw steak been pounded for fryin'," he replied.

She smiled. "You shouldn't be in here."

"Somebody had to be. You cain't do what we did and not have somebody got to pay for the shock alone."

"But the rest of us are rich," she said. "I've been to the White House six times this year, and I didn't even vote for her."

"That's the blues, Mama."

"You're talking differently," she said.

"The way I always spoke when I was on my side of town with my people. I hope you don't think that a hip-hop promoter started out erudite and loquacious."

"I guess not." She was wearing a simple yellow shift that hid her figure somewhat.

"That lipstick you got on, girl?"

"I'm dating."

"Damn, must be hard for the richest woman in the world to be datin'. You'd have to have fifteen phones and forty-five operators just to field the invitations."

"You lost weight."

"Fightin' trim. As you could see, I usually lose, but I give back some too."

"I'm so sorry, Morgan."

"No need. I knew this was bound to happen the first time I made ten thousand dollars in cash. I was seventeen years old. Even way back then I knew that money came and went, came and went."

"Your name will go down as one of the most important men in science and world history."

"Or maybe I'll be forgotten. Maybe they'll say that the board of directors of BCI was the movers and shakers. I'm just another hustler or, or, or—what did that Lacosta call me? Yeah, a huckster."

"Even now the youngsters are saying that it was you who discovered the human soul."

"And here I'm just like you," Morgan said. "Never thought one way or t'other 'bout if there's a soul or not."

"But you were the one who articulated the upload-download process," Matthews said. "You were the one who convinced Tyler Barnes that his soul had been placed in a new form."

"And that's why I'm here. I did the devil's work, and now they got me on the chain gang."

For a time the old colleagues sat in silence.

Carly felt powerless to help a man who she'd come to recognize for his greatness, and he was just happy with a full stomach and the sun flooding in from the window at her back.

"Why you here, girl?"

"I was told by an ex-employee of BCI that they abandoned you because you didn't tie up my patents and copyrights with them."

"I never thought a' that. Damn. I bet your source is right though. Them mothahfuckahs in corporations actually think they can own everything from the ants crawlin' on the wall to the ideas in our heads. Shit. The blues tell ya that you come in cryin' and alone and you go out the same way."

Morgan started moving his head as if he was moving to the beat of a song unsung.

"How can I help you, Morgan?"

"You know what's gonna happen, right?"

"With what?"

"Macromime."

"I don't understand."

"Here these corporations and shit think they found an untapped commodity, but one day that machine is gonna do like them people in Europe say and think itself an entity. That's why they should have us all in here."

"That will never happen," Carly Matthews said with absolute certainty.

"Well," Morgan replied, giving her a shrug, "here I am in prison, and there you are free in the sunlight. So I guess I must be wrong."

The Fourteenth Day of
the Month of Morgan, 3042

"Where am I?" Morgan Milton Morgan III thought.

A flood of information poured into the fragile consciousness contained in a small corner of a memory system the size of Earth's moon. This download contained his history: he was downloaded and lost, stored in a Macromime mini-system, and buried with his body by Carly Matthews in a final gesture of fealty. The world was growing, and humanity had been mostly replaced by biologically based synth-systems. There was a war being waged, but Morgan wasn't clear on the nature of the enemy.

"Is this like heaven?" he asked with thought alone.

"And you, Morgan Morgan," a deep and disembodied voice rejoined, "are our God."

AN UNLIKELY SERIES OF CONVERSATIONS

1.

Laertes Jackson showed up at the human-resources office of Martin, Martin, and Moll at 10:37 on a Tuesday in March. The midsize investment firm was located on Maiden Lane in the Wall Street area of Lower Manhattan. There was no ostentatious sign outside, and only the initials MMM appeared on the legend next to the elevator. Even there just one floor, the fourteenth, was identified as housing MMM, when the firm actually occupied seven floors.

In the past two years MMM had been sued by various individuals and government agencies for multiple civil rights and sexual harassment violations. The CEO and several VPs had been relieved of their positions, and the corporation itself had been fined millions of dollars in restitution and reparations.

The new CEO, Miss Winsome Millerton-Pomerantz, had made a public statement vowing that the investment firm, which

oversaw more than a dozen multibillion-dollar retirement funds
that, either fully or in part, served public-employee unions, would
make *a supreme effort to right the listing ship of our intentions.*

Taking this intelligence to heart, Laertes decided to apply for
an entry-level job at MMM.

Arriving at the fourteenth floor, Laertes encountered B. Chang, a
young Asian woman sitting within a semiopaque, azure circular
desk.

"HR is on the twentieth floor, Mr. Jackson," she said with a
lovely red-stained smile. "Take the elevator to the right."

On the twentieth floor Clarissa Watson, a woman whose skin was
even darker than Laertes's, gave him a confused, turquoise-tinted
grin, saying, "But your appointment isn't until one forty, Mr.
Jackson."

"I'm usually early," Laertes said, cocking his head and smiling
softly. "My father always told me to get there before your competi-
tor, because you can never tell what will be left over later on."

Young Miss Watson smiled and nodded. She said, "We have
magazines and bottled water. You can sit in the waiting area, and
I'll try to get you in early. Ms. Rodriguez is interviewing applicants
for the trainee broker position all day, but sometimes the interviews
take less time."

Laertes picked up the *Wall Street Journal,* turning pages until his eyes
fell upon the phrase *trying to define the first stock transaction.* It seemed that
there was a great deal of disagreement among economic scholars
about the age of the idea of stocks, investments, and interest.

* * *

"Mr. Jackson?" a woman said, so softly that Laertes wondered if indeed he had actually heard the utterance.

He looked up and saw a roundish woman with pale skin, dark locks, and eyes that seemed to see past him into some other realm beyond his comprehension—and maybe hers.

"I'm Jackson," he said.

"My name is Rahlina Rodriguez. I'm supposed to interview you."

"OK," Laertes said. "I took the day off from work, so I have as much time as you need."

"Where do you work?" Rahlina Rodriguez asked as Laertes rose to his feet, clutching a pint-size plastic bottle of water in his left hand.

"Maritime Merchants Bank over on Twenty-Third."

"Savings and loan," she stated.

"It's pretty much mom and pop," he said. "Mostly residential mortgages. I've been a teller there for more than twenty years."

"Have you worked with investments?"

"Not really."

"What does that mean?" The expression on Rodriguez's wary face was a leftover from childhood, when she was too cute for her parents to punish; at least that's what Laertes surmised.

"I'm supposed to ask new clients opening savings and checking accounts if they want to connect their money to an investment account, and if they do, I check that box on their online form. But whatever it is, I don't understand it or have anything to do with where the money goes."

Something about what Laertes said seemed to bother Rahlina.

"We should go to my office," the bank officer suggested.

"OK," Laertes replied, with a forced smile. He followed her down a gray-tiled hallway toward a bright yellow door. Rahlina moved through the doorway like a dancer, swaying from side to side, creating an aesthetic out of mere walking. Laertes followed her the only way he knew, with a dogged, straight-ahead gait.

The yellow door led to a room that was drained of any hue. The white floor, walls, and ceiling contained an ivory-colored desk and a whitewashed pine chair where the candidate who was to be interrogated had to sit.

"Have a seat, Mr. Jackson."

He knew where to go. In his mind, because he didn't need to ask where, he'd answered the first question correctly.

Rahlina Rodriguez settled in the seat behind the smallish pale desk. She placed the fingers of both hands on the ledge before her, giving him a wan smile.

"Before we begin," she said, "do you have any questions?"

"Are you Mexican?"

"Um," Rodriguez said, maybe as a criticism.

"I said, are you Mexican?" Laertes repeated.

"We don't ask questions like that here at Triple-M."

"If not, then how do you plan to right the listing ship of your intentions?"

"That is a corporate-wide initiative unattached to any individual's nationality, race, age, or gender."

"But still you have a black man named Laertes meeting a maybe Hispanic woman named Rodriguez during a hiring period where the cultural tendencies of the company in question are not serving the makeup of the unions that that company represents."

Rahlina Rodriguez was not happy with the direction of the interview. Laertes's little paragraph sat his interlocutor up straight in her chair.

"The facts that you are African-American," she countered, "and that my name has roots in the Spanish language have no direct bearing on your application for the entry position of trainee investment advisor."

"The letter I got from human resources said that this interview might be recorded," Laertes said. "Is it?"

"It might be."

"Is that the answer you're supposed to give me if the cameras and tape recorders are turned on?"

The flesh around Rahlina's dark eyes darkened. The locks of her raven hair took on the appearance of razor wire.

"I don't know," she said. "We have both signed away our right to privacy in this conversation, and so we may or may not be recorded."

They gazed across the white expanse of the desk, under the pallid ceiling.

"That's the other thing," Laertes said, after a minute of this white-walled silence.

"What is?"

"You called me African-American, and I don't answer to that description. People who come from another country to this one use the hyphenate name. You know, Italians who came over a generation or two back calling themselves Italian-Americans. Maybe they kept up contact with home or followed cultural norms that are particularly Italian. But a man like me, a man whose ancestors were kidnapped, chained, and dragged over here centuries ago is not, cannot be, a hyphenate. At least not the kind of hyphenate that you say. You might call me an Abductee-American, an originally Unwilling-American. You might say that I'm a partly Disenfranchised American. But African-American? I mean, even if my mama was from Guinea, you'd do better to call me a Guinean rather than an African-American. Africa is a continent, not a country, not even one race. You don't use the term *White-American* because that has no cultural basis; even saying *Euro-Americans* makes very little sense."

"We say *African-American* because that is the parlance," Rahlina interjected.

"Used to be the parlance was *colored, Negro, Afro, nigger, coon, jigaboo.* Parlance don't make a word right. And I refuse to be called after a continent that no one in my line remembers."

"Well, Mr. Jackson, if you say that you are not African-American, I suppose this interview is over."

"Why is that?"

"The commitment of this firm is to hire and promote peoples from various ethnic backgrounds, including African-Americans." With that Rahlina Rodriguez stood up and waited.

After a moment or two Laertes realized that he was being asked to leave.

He stood also, raised his eyes to the ceiling, and said, "If this conversation has been recorded, I want a copy of it delivered either to the address on my application form or to the e-mail address thereupon."

After that he exited the white room on the twentieth floor of the offices of Martin, Martin, and Moll.

2.

Three Thursday afternoons after Laertes's failed interview, he was offered what turned out to be $112.37 in change from Madeline Chan—a seven-year-old child. Her mother, Angelique, had presented the child's canvas bag of coins while little Maddie pulled her head up over the ledge where the money was being passed from mother to teller.

"You know, Ms. Chan," Laertes said. "We aren't supposed to take loose change in these amounts."

"But that's my money," little Maddie called over the banker's counter.

"I know your rules, Mr. Jackson," Maddie's mom said. "But you and I both know that one day, when she has money of her own, Maddie will remember the bank that made an exception for her Christmas savings."

Laertes noticed a short man in a black suit standing at the front of the line for the next free teller. The window belonging to Ms. Becky Blondell opened up, and the short man offered his place to the bulbous woman behind him. She smiled and moved ahead.

"So will you take my money?" Little Maddie asked, hoisting herself up once more.

"Of course," Laertes told the medium-brown child. "Leave it here, and we'll count it in the machine overnight."

"Yaaaaaa!" Maddie cried.

"Thank you," said her mother.

"You're from Jamaica, Ms. Chan?" the teller asked.

"Yes, I am. How did you know?"

"Your *r*'s."

The next visitor to his window was the short man in the black suit who had let the woman behind him go to Becky Blondell's window.

"How can I help you, sir?" Laertes asked.

"Howard Sansome," he replied. "I started a regular checking account at your Fort Greene branch a short while ago, but now I wish to upgrade it to investment-plus."

The man calling himself Sansome handed Laertes a plastic card designed in metallic gold, red, and blue colors. His name was superimposed in lowercase black lettering across the middle of the card.

"I'll need to see some ID," Laertes told him.

"Of course."

Laertes checked the New York State driver's license and entered the bank number on his computer.

"Changing your account would be easy enough," the fifty-something teller advised. "But the order has to be OK'd by the manager of the branch where you started the account."

"I moved from Brooklyn to Manhattan since then," Howard Sansome said, with something approximating an apology on his wide face. "Can't you just make a note on my file or something like that? It would be inconvenient for me to try to get out to Fort Greene at the hours the branch is open."

"You could make the change by mail," Laertes suggested.

"I don't trust the post." Sansome's eyes were searching the teller's face.

"I'd be happy to make the update . . ." Laertes said.

A canny look came over the bank customer's face.

". . . if you just talk to the manager here and have her call your branch," the cashier continued.

"Can't *you* call him?"

"No phones at the windows."

"I could let you use mine," the customer offered. There was the hint of a smile on his face.

"Also against the rules." Laertes shrugged to underscore the apology.

"Well," Howard Sansome said with a sigh, "I guess there's a trip to Brooklyn in my future."

With that he turned and walked away.

Friday was much like Thursday. Eighty-six customers with 216 transactions, a zero balance, and a trip to the vault to install his cashbox.

On Saturday Laertes had lunch with his ex-wife, Bonita, and their eleven-year-old daughter, Medea. Bonita and Laertes had met at the Twenty-Third Street branch of Maritime Merchants Bank when they were both tellers. Now she was a senior vice president at National Trust Investments and Loan. They divorced because she claimed, and he agreed, that he had little ambition in his banking career.

"How's history coming?" the father asked his daughter after the first few awkward moments amongst the three at Jammy's Diner on Eighteenth Street.

"It's great," the child said. She was a deep brown color and had big eyes and an infectious smile. "I just read everything three times like you told me to, and then I know it without thinking."

"You always have to think," Bonita corrected.

Fifteen years younger than Laertes, Bonita was slender, tall, and strong. He was still attracted to her, even though she'd married Hero Martin, a German-American from Pittsburgh. He had nothing against Martin except for the fact that Medea called him Daddy.

"There's nature, second nature, and thought," Laertes said, in response to his ex-wife's criticism. "The first is physical, the last of the mind, and the middle is something you know so well that it's just there, like a sleeping fish in calm waters."

Medea's big eyes seemed to be fixed on her father's words. At moments like this he liked to think that she saw something worthy in him.

"Are we going to order?" Bonita asked. "Medea promised her father that they'd go to the Met together this afternoon."

On Sunday, Laertes went to the All Saints Rest Home in Nyack to visit Helena Havelock-Jackson, his mother.

"Pompey!" the ninety-one-year-old matriarch exclaimed. For the past five months or so, Helena had seen Laertes's father's face when looking at him; another kind of fish in a different depth of water, Laertes thought.

"Hi, Mom."

"You look so tired, honey. I'll make us some marrow soup, and we'll go to bed early." She placed four fingers on her son's left hand, and a sigh came unbidden from way down in his throat.

"How are you, Mom?"

"You know nothing's wrong with me," was her rote reply. "Are you having trouble at work?"

"No."

"Are you gonna get that promotion soon?"

"They went with somebody else."

Helena's skin was dark like her son's and similar to long-deceased Pompey's. Her eyes were both assertive and vulnerable.

"What do you mean?" she asked, pain tucked in with the words.

Holding her hands, Laertes explained to her about his hare-brained scheme to get a job at MMM. And though she thought she was talking to her late husband, Laertes knew that she heard and mostly understood his words.

"That's always been your problem," Helena Havelock-Jackson said to her son through the medium of her husband. "You think bigger than the people believe they already big. That's why you called our children by them Greeks and why your daddy named you for a general to freedom."

On Monday afternoon at 4:21 P.M., Laertes Jackson departed Maritime Merchants Bank. He left behind a zero balance and a cashbox containing $6,627.14. He had executed in excess of four hundred transactions that day.

"Excuse me, sir," someone called. "Mr. Jackson."

Laertes turned and saw a short man in a muted maroon suit trundling toward him. There was something familiar about the man, but because he saw people all day long, Laertes had learned to disregard faces, features, and names.

But now he was shaking hands with someone who at least knew his name.

"Uh?" Laertes said.

"Howard Sansome," the small but powerful man said.

"Um?"

"Last Thursday. You told me that I had to go to Fort Greene to update my account."

"Either that," the teller said, "or send it by mail."

"Can I buy you a drink?" the man with the wide face asked.

"Excuse me?"

"I know," Sansome said, with an air of confidentiality. "It seems kind of odd for someone who just knows you from a single encounter through a window of bulletproof glass to act like we're friends."

"Yeah."

"But we have a lot more in common than that."

"And what is it we have in common?" Laertes asked. In spite of himself, he was intrigued by Sansome.

"Martin, Martin, and Moll," the man said, a glimmer of conspiracy in his eye.

"What?" Laertes said. "What do they have to do with you?"

"My title is VP in charge of investigations at Triple-M."

"Investigating what?"

"Right now, you."

"Me, for what?"

"Can we get a drink? There's a bar down the street called The Dutchy. They serve a great Manhattan all afternoon for half price."

*   *   *

Half an hour later, the drinks had been served to the short white man and his much taller black guest.

"This *is* very good," Laertes agreed after his second sip.

"They use bourbon instead of rye, and the vermouth they got isn't nearly as sweet as most."

"So," Laertes said, hoping to prime the explanation of why they were there.

"You know the cards are stacked against just about everybody in America," Sansome said instead of complying.

"You including all of North and South America, or do you just mean the United States?" Laertes couldn't help himself.

"So, is that your thing, Jackson?" the pickup host asked. "You need to argue with every word the bosses or their representatives say?"

"No, not at all."

"You told Ms. Rodriguez that you weren't African-American," Sansome offered.

"Is she Mexican?" Laertes asked. "Either that or any other kind of New World so-called Hispanic?"

Howard Sansome downed his drink and gestured at the bartender, a sallow woman of middle age who had the look of having lived hard. He told her to bring two more.

Then the man turned to Laertes and said, "No."

"No to what?"

"Rodriguez is not any kind of New World anything. Her people are French, but her ex-husband was Puerto Rican."

"So it just happens that she's Triple-M's drive for integration?"
"I doubt it."

The drinks came, and Howard asked the haggard mixologist to keep them coming.

"So it's like a, like a capitalist conspiracy," Laertes said. "They put somebody there who will represent their needs and fuck mine."

Sansome sipped and thought. After a minute or so he almost said something but then decided to drink a little more.

Finally he said, "I believe that the head of HR thinks that Rahlina really is Puerto Rican. The only thing that matters to Mr. Hawthorne is that all the employees dance to the same beat. So it's kind of like a conspiracy, but one that nobody is quite aware of."

Laertes felt as if a light had been turned on in his chest, casting a brilliance that traveled everywhere.

"That's what I mean when I say that I'm not arguing with everything the bosses say," Laertes averred. "If you told me that the sky was blue or that this drink was good, I wouldn't argue. But if you tell me that the word *American* only meant US citizens or that I am in any way the cultural outcome of the continent of Africa, that I'm African-American before I'm Slave-American, well then, I'd have to argue."

Two more drinks came.

"So," Sansome said. "You're on a quest for justice and not a job."

"Not justice," Laertes said, and then he downed the cocktail in one swallow. "Not justice, no. Uh-uh. The expectation of justice would be like waiting for the Second Coming. It would be like thinking I could absolve myself of all the pain that is the true inheritance of my ancestral history."

Laertes could see that his answer was unexpected. Sansome had thought that he understood why Laertes said the things he did. But now he could see that he'd been wrong.

"If not justice then what?" the vice president in charge of trouble asked.

There was yet another Manhattan before Laertes.

"I would just like," the bank teller said, "for the words people say to have some modicum of truth to them. I'd like it for people to see that some folks are named after countries and cultures, whereas others are ill-defined by race and continent. That's all."

Having told his truth about truth, Laertes downed his fifth cocktail.

"Your records say that you only have a high school diploma," Howard Sansome said.

"Education is simply the process of thought being applied to knowledge," the bank teller said. "Thought . . . applied to knowledge. Most people just say things having never thought about what what they say means. You got presidents do that."

Sansome turned on his barstool so that he was facing Laertes.

He said, "So you're saying that you bollixed up your interview because the woman was white with a Spanish name and she called you African-American."

"I'm saying that the words I hear and the words I speak should make sense. You can't live a life in terms that are wrong—not a good life."

"And are you living a good life?" Howard Sansome asked.

Laertes felt the full force of the five cocktails upon hearing that question. He blinked and shook his head, trying to find an answer that he felt should be second nature.

"I'll be in touch, Mr. Jackson," Sansome said.

Watching the short man in the dark red suit walk from the bar, Laertes felt that the room was tilted to the right. This impossibility made him smile.

3.

Weeks later Laertes's life had changed in small ways that promised to be large. *Are you living a good life?* The question resonated at the back of his mind, through every activity, and even in his sleep. There was certainly goodness in his life. Medea was a beautiful child, and she loved him even though she called another man father. Things had been good with Bonita before her ambition cast its gaze on him. He was good at his job, rarely had other than a zero balance. His rent had gone up twelve percent in the last three years, and another hike would necessitate a move. He needed more money but didn't want an officer's position, because he felt that they misrepresented the value of the accounts and loans they pushed on customers.

He hadn't been on a date in six years—since the divorce. So now he bought his first computer and start trawling dating sites for companionship. His explanation of who he was and what he wanted was seventeen pages long, and his photograph was of a dark-skinned man who wasn't smiling and seemed confused by and leery of the camera.

The few responses he had online were tentative but interested.

Agnes327 wrote, "Your profile was so serious, Laertes8, what do you do to have fun?"

"I read the *Times*," Laertes wrote, "and take each story apart, imaging how what they say happened could have happened. Then I write responses when I feel that I've struck upon a contradiction."

Lucy!! asked, if he could change the world he found so problematic, how would that look?

Laertes wrote a sixty-two-page response over a three-day period in which he addressed the economic system, the problems of a *standardized education*, medical care, the environment, the misconceptions of race and gender, and the waste of human potential on distractions created to keep human passion limited.

Laertes got only sixteen responses to his dating-site profile. After answering all of them he got only one second response. This was from Mona_Loa_Love. She had asked him where he'd retire when he could. He replied that the notion of retirement in the animal kingdom was tantamount to exile and not something one should pursue.

"I believe that when we age we lose our physical edge but gain wisdom and patience. I'd like to become an advisor to younger members of our nation; that and maybe I'd like to tend a flock of sheep."

Mona_Loa_Love had written to Laertes in the second week after Howard Sansome had asked his devastating question. He used a facility on the site to allow her to read his answers to the other fifteen conversations. By the fifth week she had crafted an intricate reply.

Dear Laertes8,

It intrigues me that you included a photograph of yourself but refused to identify by gender, race or age. There's something genius in that. I love the long, well thought out answers you gave to the others who responded. And I can understand why they didn't answer. These women are looking for something they've already seen and don't want to be challenged but rather loved—and cared for in various ways.

I am not interested in dating you. As a matter of fact I can see no reason in our meeting. But I am deeply moved by your convictions and your resolute inability to compromise. I hope that we can have an epistolary relationship over this medium, or maybe you'd like to send me your email address. I could use your wisdom and, I believe, you might have some use for my understanding.

Mona_Loa_Love

Laertes was devastated by Mona_Loa_Love's response; *your resolute inability to compromise* was the most painful phrase. She saw something in him that he had not seen himself. As a matter of fact, even though he saw the truth of her words, still he did not understand how to leave, or live with, them.

Laertes did not go on the dating site for a week after this last response. He went to work, visited his mother and estranged family, and read the *Times* but did not perform his usual exegeses on its articles. On that Saturday, around midnight, he felt very much alone in his studio apartment on the third floor, next to a woman whose hound dog howled every evening from six to just about seven. The bank teller felt the urge for a Manhattan cocktail. He took a shower and put on his medium-gray suit. He buttoned the white shirt up to the throat but forwent a tie. He took sixty dollars from a manila envelope in his writing desk, pocketed the house key, and went to the door.

His hand was not yet on the knob when the landline rang. He rubbed his fingers together, and the second volley of sound pealed. He turned to look at the phone he had no intention of answering. This would be the third and last ring. After that the automated answering service would take over.

The fourth ring surprised him, as did the fifth, sixth and seventh. By the eleventh ring Laertes was certain that the world he'd known, and despised, had fallen off its axis.

"Hello?"

"Mr. Jackson? Laertes Jackson?" a woman's soothing voice asked.

"How come my phone didn't send you to voice mail?"

"Our technology sidesteps that process," she said. "Mr. Jackson?"

"Yes. I'm Jackson."

"So pleased to meet you, sir. You have been on my mind for quite a while now."

"And who are you?"

"My name is Winsome Millerton-Pomerantz, CEO of Triple-M."

"It's Saturday night, Ms. Pomerantz. Most people are taking it easy around now."

"Money never sleeps."

"My little bit of change been nappin' my whole life."

"Exactly."

Laertes felt that there was deep meaning in the words they shared, but he still hankered after a well-made, not-too-sweet Manhattan.

"Ma'am, I was just about to go out. So if you want something, just ask, and I will try to answer."

"Monday morning, seven forty-five, seventy-ninth floor," she said. "Number two Broadway."

"What are you talking about?" Laertes asked.

"I wish to discuss your job interview at Triple-M."

"I'll be there."

Laertes didn't remember much about the rest of that Saturday night. There was a bartender and a woman named Briance. He bought quite a few drinks, and someone might have helped him up the stairs. His sixty dollars were gone, but that was all, and in two days, on Monday morning, he had a meeting set with the CEO of Triple-M.

The hangover kept him from seeing his mother the following day. He wondered if Helena Havelock-Jackson would miss her husband's weekly visit.

Laertes arrived at number two Broadway at 6:10 Monday morning. The security guard let him in after verifying his identity and looking his name up on the computerized schedule.

Howard Sansome sat at the receptionist's desk on the seventy-ninth floor.

"Hey there, Laertes," the squat, powerful vice president greeted him.

"This your job too?"

"Ms. Pomerantz wanted to make sure that it would be you who came."

"Who else could it be?" Laertes asked.

"You got any listening or recording devices on you?"

"No, sir," Laertes said.

The VP in charge of trouble grinned, then took a device from his pocket. It looked somewhat like an extra-thick cell phone.

"I'm just gonna run this around you to make sure," Sansome said.

When he was finished, he asked Laertes if he wanted coffee "or something stronger."

"No. I'll just sit here and compose my thoughts."

"Suit yourself."

Sansome gave Laertes a nod and then departed through a doorway that had no door.

Laertes expected the man to return, but he didn't.

Later the bank teller would see that brief space in time, the moments between Sansome's departure and his interview with Millerton-Pomerantz, as the most important span of his life. He wasn't concerned with a future job. What he thought about was Mona_Loa_Love and her, if indeed it was a woman, deep understanding, in simple language, of the thought processes he'd been swaddled in for so many years that he could no longer separate the bondage from the man.

I am my own prison, he thought. *The truths I've wielded have hidden that fact from me. Whatever I do from this moment on will derive from those unassailable facts.*

"Mr. Jackson," a strong and yet melodious voice pronounced.

She had soft red hair and eyes the color of pale blue diamonds. Ms. Winsome Millerton-Pomerantz was tall and Laertes's age but much younger-looking. She was slender like him, and there was a smile on her lips letting him know that she had been anticipating this meeting. She wore a blue and white woman's business suit that might have been made from silk or maybe, Laertes thought, some space-age material.

"Yes," Laertes said.

"So happy to meet you," she replied, holding out both hands.

He rose and took those hands as he had his mother's on Sundays over the past seven years.

"Would you like to go to my office or meet here at the front desk?" Winsome asked. "I gave everyone else but Howard the day off."

"I leave it up to you, ma'am. This is your fief."

The CEO grinned and said, "Follow me."

Laertes remembered walking but not the spaces through which he traveled. His mind was on the topic of his imprisonment and the unlikely meeting with a woman of both beauty and power.

Ultimately they came to an office, the outer wall of which was a single pane of glass. From there one could see the entire panorama of Lower Manhattan and beyond.

"Let's sit on the sofa," Ms. Winsome Millerton-Pomerantz said.

It was a yellow divan upholstered in fabric that reminded Laertes of velvet-like pigskin. It seemed to hug him, to pull him in.

Winsome turned toward her guest and said, "Before we begin, do you have any questions?"

"Rahlina Rodriguez asked me that. Is that a prescribed beginning around here?"

The CEO smiled and shook her head, *no*.

"Then could you tell me how I got here?"

"Would you like me to start with the *Jesus of Lübeck*?"

It was Laertes turn to grin. He knew about the slave ship from 1564.

"No, ma'am," he said. "I'm just interested in why a major firm like yours would have me followed, questioned, and brought to this amazing place. I thought I'd been rejected by Ms. Rodriguez."

"You would have been," Millerton-Pomerantz said simply. "But when you announced to our recording devices that you wanted a copy of what had transpired, our lawyers got nervous."

"Nervous about what?"

"We've spent more than fifty million on suits and settlements, lawyers' fees, and golden parachutes. Our legal team has been trying to stem that flow."

"So I'm here because you're worried that I'll sue?"

"No." Her smile was lovely. "I sent Mr. Sansome to talk to you, and by the time he'd finished, the legal team said that there was nothing we had to worry about."

"Then why am I here?"

"Howard likes to make full reports. He was, in his way, very impressed by your mind. He told me that almost everything you said surprised him and that you might be a valuable asset to our firm."

"I don't know what he means by that. I've been a bank teller for two and a half decades. The only promotion I ever got was from entry teller to senior cashier. Your boy told me how I didn't have but a high school diploma."

"He said that you told him that education was merely the process of applying thought to knowledge."

"He remembered that?" Laertes asked.

"You are a unique individual, Mr. Jackson. You understand a world that most others don't even suspect."

"I can hardly walk a straight line without tripping over my own feet."

"I believe that. Genius, true human genius, has no patience for the mundane."

Laertes was suddenly aware of his heart beating. There was sweat on his hands, and his hands had never perspired before.

"Would you like some water, sir?"

"Are you telling me that you don't think I can be a normal person?" he replied.

"Yes."

"How come you know about the first slave ship?"

"I studied world history at Sarah Lawrence. I met a man from a wealthy family named Jared Pomerantz. We married, he died, and I assumed the mantle that he'd left behind. We are cut from similar cloth, Mr. Jackson. The only difference is that I've been lucky with money."

"Not with love?"

"Jared was a pig. It shamed me that I was happy that he died."

"OK, then," Laertes Jackson said.

"OK what?"

"If you got a job for me I'll consider it."

4.

Dear Mona_Loa_Love,

I got your e-mail and it nearly broke my heart. I always thought that it was my choice not to compromise, but when you said it was my inability I knew it was true. I was never going to reach out to you again but then something happened . . .

Laertes explained about MMM, Howard Sansome the Vice President of Trouble, and the CEO Winsome Millerton-Pomerantz.

. . . they offered me a job, Vice President in Charge of Reeducation. I'd have a desk on the seventy-fifth floor and an inbox that brings in data (knowledge) and an outbox that reflects my thoughts on that knowledge. They just want me to think about what they should do and they promise to take my ideas into consideration. I asked my ex-wife about it and she invited me out to dinner. I told my manager about it and she laughed in my face.

Dear Laertes8,

I am so happy that you finally decided to answer me. Reading your communications I felt for the first time in so long that there was finally a kindred out there for me. Not a lover or a husband, not a sugar daddy or father figure. Not even a mentor, not really. You are, at least potentially, a friend.

And as a friend I feel your fear and confusion. The office of that CEO is the heir to the offices that made your people slaves. Would working for them, no matter how good all intentions were, be a betrayal of your truth? Can you make a difference? Probably not. But should you try? That is a question that only you can answer.

Mona_Loa_Love

All that happened six months ago. Laertes still has his job at Maritime Merchants Bank. He still has the most zero-balance days of any teller ever. His ex-wife asks him on Saturdays if he's taken the new job. His mother has taken to asking him if he's seen his father anywhere. He and Mona_Loa_Love write to each other every other day. Winsome Millerton-Pomerantz calls on Saturday nights to ask whether he has finally made up his mind.

"I figured if I waited long enough that you'd find someone else," Laertes told the CEO.

"There is no one else, Mr. Jackson. It is either you or nothing."

GROVE PRESS

Reading Group Guide

by Keturah Jenkins

THE AWKWARD BLACK MAN

Walter Mosley

ABOUT THIS GUIDE

We hope that these discussion questions will enhance your reading group's exploration of Walter Mosley's *The Awkward Black Man*. They are meant to stimulate discussion, offer new viewpoints, and enrich your enjoyment of the book.

More reading group guides and additional information, including summaries, author tours, and author sites for other fine Grove Atlantic titles may be found on our website, groveatlantic.com.

QUESTIONS FOR DISCUSSION

Why do you think Walter Mosley decided to focus *The Awkward Black Man* on these kinds of characters? What does that say about our expectations of how black men's lives are portrayed or chronicled?

―――――――――

How well do the title, *The Awkward Black Man*, and the titles of the individual stories set the tone for what happens in the book?

―――――――――

Discuss how marriage, identity, and sexuality are used in the collection to provide fresh commentary on the evolving nature of relationships.

―――――――――

How do New York City and California inform the individual character's social and economic struggles?

―――――――――

In "Pet Fly," what is the significance of the fly to Rufus Coombs? How did you read Rufus's actions toward Lana Donelli? Why does Lana say he sexually harassed her? Do you agree? Why or why not?

―――――――――

While the seventeen stories in *The Awkward Black Man* tackle different styles and genres, all are narrated by unique black men. Explain which character you identify with the most.

―――――――――

Analyze the connection "I knew him better than I did my own brother" (pg. 187) at the heart of "Otis." How does Crash's brief encounter with Otis reverberate through their lives?

―――――――――

What is the best order in which to read the stories in the collection? Explain your answer.

The short story format of *The Awkward Black Man* introduces troubled protagonists ranging in age, from early adolescence to late middle age, with rich family histories. Consider what Mosley is sharing with the reader about the complex dynamics of black families.

"Cut, Cut, Cut" is the only story told mainly from the point of view of Marilee, a white woman. Consider why the author uses a woman's perspective to tell this story. Analyze how the revelation of Martin's anticipated secret changes your understanding of the story.

"The Black Woman in the Chinese Hat" revisits the character of Rufus Coombs. Why do you suppose the author chose to tell more of this character's story? Analyze how he has changed since "Pet Fly."

What is Mosley trying to impart to the reader about the aging process, mental health, and addiction depicted in stories like "Breath" and "Almost Alyce"? Are his efforts successful? Explain your answer.

On p. 208, the Harlem Cowboy says in a letter to Felix, "In a long life you only got a few friends, that's a fact. . . ." Consider the other examples of friendships depicted in the novel. What does the author have to say about the power of friendship and how it can transform lives?

In "Haunted," how does the presence of a ghost change the reading experience? What does the ghost of the story represent to the characters? Why does the spirit of failed writer Paul Henry start to untether after speaking to his namesake?

In "The Sin of Dreams," why is Morgan incarcerated? On pg. 303, Morgan asks in confusion, "Is this like heaven?" and a disembodied voice responds, "And you, Morgan Morgan, are our God." Examine what has transpired in the distant future to humanity. Did Morgan's warning to Carly come true? Why or why not?

Which story from the collection would you like to see Mosley expand into a novel? Why do you think this?

The collection opens with a dedication to Toni Morrison, "who raised the dialogue of blackness to the international platform that Malcolm X strove for." Discuss how Mosley also contributes to this conversation.

SUGGESTIONS FOR FURTHER READING

Deacon King Kong by James McBride

Hitting a Straight Lick with a Crooked Stick:
Stories from the Harlem Renaissance by Zora Neale Hurston

The Night Watchman by Louise Erdrich

Black Bottom Saints by Alice Randall

A Rage in Harlem by Chester Himes

The Absurd Man: Poems by Major Jackson

Song of Solomon by Toni Morrison

Drinking Coffee Elsewhere by ZZ Packer

Slapboxing with Jesus by Victor LaValle

Woman Hollering Creek by Sandra Cisneros

Everyday People edited by Jennifer Baker

The Best of Simple by Langston Hughes

Afterparties by Anthony Veasna So